SAFEKEEPING

EVA MACKENZIE

Published by Craven Ink Press

PO Box 3081 Warrenton, VA 20188

ISBN: 978-1-7333939-4-2 (eBook)

ISBN: 978-1-7333939-5-9 (paperback)

Editors: Sandra Haven (Haven4writers),

Lillian Schneider (Murphy Rae)

Cover design: Stu Bache (Bookscovered)

Love is a trap. When it appears, we see only its light, not its shadows.

Paulo Coelho

1

SONIA

I SHOULD HAVE PEED before leaving work was her last thought before a black pickup truck rammed into the passenger side of her vehicle. Metal screeched against metal as her momentum jerked her loose from the road and hurtled her toward the ditch. A crack sounded as the windshield splintered like ice giving way on a bitter wintry day against the sun's glare. Only it was summer, and the air was hot and saturated. Adrenaline sped through her veins at her sudden weightlessness as her car plunged through the air.

Her mind struggled to grasp what was happening as the airbag exploded into her face, snapping her neck back against the headrest. Pain shot down her spine and vibrated into her limbs, energizing every cell of her body.

Smoke mingled with a cloud of dirt from the ditch where her car now rested on its driver's side.

I think I peed myself.

But it wasn't pee she watched spread over her pants: a bright red blood blossomed through her jeans. The Honda's motor had died, and she listened to the hiss and ping of the engine as fluid spit under the rumpled hood. Visions of explosions imploded her mind. *Get out!*

She moved, biting back the pain that wracked her body. It radiated from her right leg. The Honda was pinned in the ditch. She would need to crawl up and out. She fumbled to quickly unbuckle her seat belt and immediately felt her body sag further down. The odor of motor oil mingled with the tang of gasoline.

Clawing her way past the center console, she pulled herself up to the passenger's door and grabbed at the handle. The door would not budge, its center caved inward from the hit. The passenger window was broken, a gaping mouth with brittle bits of glass surrounding the hole like intricate lace. She would need to push off the center console to make it through the window.

Sonia sucked in a deep breath as her right leg protested from the movement. She could almost stand up through the opening but wasn't sure if she could bring out her badly damaged leg without passing out from the pain.

A soft crunch of gravel outside the car alerted her. Was the pickup's driver coming to help? She thought she heard sirens, but a low ringing in her ears grew, making it impossible to determine.

"Help me," she called in a raspy voice. No response. They had run right into her. Didn't the driver see her coming up to the two-way stop? By the time she'd noticed the truck in her peripheral vision, it had been too late for her to react.

She navigated her good leg up onto the console and pushed off. Her head and chest were now out of the car and she could peer around. The black truck lay overturned twenty feet away. Angry black smoke wafted into the clear blue sky. There was a shadow in the driver's seat of the truck, unmoving. Sonia planted her palms on the exterior of her car and began to push off when she remembered her purse with her cell phone inside.

She would need to leave the car and get out of here before the police arrived, but she had to check on the other driver. All kinds of scenarios raced through her head. The police searching her car for clues on the owner. Running her fingerprints, harvesting her DNA. She looked down and spotted her bag hanging from the passenger headrest into the back seat. Careful not to put too much weight on her right leg, she reached over and retrieved it. She hooked the strap over her shoulder and stood back up. Dizzy, she planted her palms on the scarred metal and pushed herself up with all her strength. It took her four tries, but she finally pulled herself out and slowly lowered her feet to the ground. Her body ached, and she was all but certain she'd broken her right leg on impact. She let out a soft whimper as she tried to put weight on it and decided she would be better off crawling. The idea of getting away before the cops arrived faded. She was losing blood. Another wave of dizziness hit her as she dropped onto her knees. She was on the precipice of passing out.

"Are you okay?" she tried to yell, but it sounded like a loud mumble. No reply.

She crawled across the road, wincing as small stones burrowed into her palms and poked at her kneecaps through her jeans.

She didn't have time for this. Someone would soon drive down this road. She looked in all directions, trying to catch sight of the police or ambulance that was sounding in the distance. She looked over the vast landscape of trees; the mid-afternoon sun warmed her skin. How far could she get in the dense Montana forest before they found her? She couldn't even walk.

The shadow hanging down from the driver's side seat swayed, but she couldn't tell if it was her eyesight failing or if it had actually moved. A body cradled in a seat belt hung in the upturned truck.

Two feet away now and she could clearly see the man's face. It was red and angry looking, blood rushing to his head. His eyes were closed, and a slash of bright red blood stained his forehead and dripped down onto the metal roof like the beating of a light rain. He had black hair and a neatly trimmed goatee. Even with his eyes closed, she knew they were a warm brown. Her body shook. She also knew he liked bourbon and playing cards. She knew where he lived and the names of his wife and kids. A host of memories flashed of the casual time she had spent with this man.

Sirens in the distance carried over the still, hot air, moving closer, breaking through the ringing in her ears. Her instinct told her she had no time.

Especially now that she knew this was no accident.

He had found her. Fear crackled through her, leaving a smoldering shadow behind.

She jerked her bag up from her shoulder to search for her phone. This would be risky, but she had to do it. Everything was in place, except she should have sent the pre-planned message, but she couldn't be sure this man was working alone. Someone could already be at her house. She dialed and cursed as her shaking fingers hit the wrong buttons several times. Sirens closed in on her. Their sounds echoed in her mind as pain built against the back of her eyes. She didn't want to think about what she had to do next.

She picked up on the second ring. "Are you almost here?"

"Listen." Sonia's voice was shrill. "You need to get out now. Plan B. Don't call me. Watch your back." She could feel the tears pooling in her eyes as the sun blazed down on her and radiated up from the blacktop where she lay. She couldn't look away from the man's familiar ruddy face. There was no protest from the other end of the line, and the silence sliced through her.

"Just remember: *safekeeping*. I'm sorry."

She ended the call and screamed out toward the clear blue sky. A realization hit her so hard that all the air pushed from her lungs and a hollowness ballooned inside her. An instant taste of her bitter future caused rage to tear through her now broken body, outpacing all the physical pain. She used the tip of her nail to pry the SIM card out of the phone and threw it as far as she could from her awkward position in the road. She screamed out as her arm arched over her head. She threw the phone in the opposite direction.

Flashing lights caught her eyes as she watched a State Trooper approaching rapidly, an ambulance trailing behind. She pulled her hands to her ears, cutting off the piercing sound.

Sonia knew it wouldn't last forever. Her freedom.

A door slammed and rapid footfalls approached her as someone rushed to her in the road. The female trooper was young with soft ginger hair. "Ma'am, where are you hurt? I've got help here." She crouched beside her.

Sonia nodded; the trooper's hat blocked the sun from her eyes. Sheer panic hovered over her and her throat went dry. She forced out a cough and it carried a hollow ring. Voices moved closer as medics drew near. "I don't think he's doing too well," Sonia said, nodding toward the driver in the truck.

"Do you know him?" the trooper asked.

Sonia didn't know how to respond to the question, so she didn't.

"What happened here?" a medic asked as he dropped his bag to the ground.

"Him first," Sonia said. "I'm okay. Just a broken leg, I think."

"Someone else is taking care of him, ma'am," the young medic assured her.

She looked up at the state trooper, her fear colliding with her fate. "My name is Sonia Rossi, and I'm wanted for murder."

2

SONIA

FIVE YEARS later

She heard the muted squeak of their shoes. And then she felt it, a blow to the back of her head, something hard and round. It made contact with a dull thwack, sending a white-hot flash behind her eyes causing her balance to waver. She had to move. Sensing another blow was soon to follow, she quickly rolled away. A raucous crack of something hit the ground so close to her that she felt a puff of air brush past her leg. Whoever it was, they were not alone: a chorus of harsh whispers had erupted as she hit the floor.

"Don't kill her."

A kick to her ribs landed, a whoosh of air pushed from her lungs.

"Shut up. I know what I'm doing."

How many were there?

"We're just supposed to mess her up."

Sonia felt the rough edges of a sheet being folded over her face before she could stand and run away. It smelled like cheap soap, rough and scratchy against her skin. Her hands rushed to her face to yank it away, but they were pulling too hard, keeping the sheet taut in its place.

"A little gift from an old friend." A rasp-kissed voice. "I wonder how many gifts you'll get before you die?" A laugh echoed off the walls of the laundry area. Another hit to the head triggered floaters to dance behind her closed eyelids. A sloppy kick landed on her right hip and caused it to buckle. She involuntarily yelled out into the sheet, her hot breath warming her face.

"Shut up, or it's going to get real bad."

What's really bad, if this isn't it? Sonia's impulse to run or fight kicked in. *Run, fight* kept repeating in her mind as her muscles twitched with the instinct.

Fists and open palms from every direction landed several more blows.

She sensed the rabid group's fatigue as she tried to lift her arms away to fend them off. Suddenly the sheet fell away and the echo of footsteps receded out the doorway and down the hall. Sonia groaned as she reached up and pulled the sheet away. Blood rushed into her mouth and she spit it into the white material. A loose tooth threatened to pull away from her gums as she slowly rolled up to a sitting position. She couldn't hear where the other inmates had gone over the rushing of blood in her ears.

She flinched as voices moved toward her, and soon she wasn't alone in the room. Two guards approached her pooled body. Each time she tried to move, a searing pain radiated from her chest. It took her several long moments to realize they were speaking to her.

"What happened?" asked the guard. Sonia looked up to see Tahara Roberts, who everyone called Remmy, hovering above her. Sonia had felt in her bones that Remmy would come. It was always during Remmy's shifts that she got the worse beatings.

Sonia shook her head before she spoke. "I slipped." Her tongue was swollen, causing the words to slur as blood and spittle leaked over her lips. Voices seemed too far away, and the room tilted in her blurry vision.

A look passed between the gathering guards; Sonia's lying was evident, but no one challenged her. Sonia never snitched; they knew that.

"Might as well start the slip and fall report," Sonia said. She ground down on her teeth as a bitter laugh formed in her throat.

Remmy's beat-mate, a guy named Nicolas, got on the radio. "I need medics down in the laundry. Bring a bed."

"I can walk," Sonia said, but did not move. She needed air in her lungs, but with each new breath came a splinter of pain. "Just give me a minute."

"You're gonna wait for the medics," Remmy said, annoyed, her eyes never settling on Sonia's. A byproduct of her guilt, perhaps. How many times had Remmy been missing from her post when Sonia got attacked?

Sonia reached up to touch the ridge of her nose and immediately felt tenderness and the slickness of blood.

A few minutes later, a team moved down the hall, pulling a stretcher along with them. Sonia didn't want them to touch her, but she couldn't stand unassisted. She just wanted to continue to lie on the floor for a while, but soon the other inmates would begin their duties in the laundry room, just as she had been doing. The quiet rumble of the dryers soothed her, in the same way the monotony of folding laundry reminded her of Joey's starched pants and soft polo shirts sparking with static against her fingers whenever she forgot the dryer sheets.

"Do you think you can stand up?" a nurse asked.

Without answering, Sonia pushed off the floor and stood through the pain long enough to be ushered onto the movable bed.

"We're going to get you all checked out back in the infirmary."

Sonia thought of her attackers as the stretcher moved noisily over the floor. Its wheels, shaking back and forth, caused her nerves to jolt. She was sure she knew at least a few of the women who did this. There had been several, but Ginger was always leading the group. She had attacked Sonia before. There must be some reason they'd covered her face this time. Maybe an unknown girl in the crew Ginger didn't want Sonia to see. There were cameras everywhere in the Flint Hill State Corrections Facility, Sonia's home for the last four years. But she'd quickly learned that most of the guards here didn't care if an inmate was beat up or even killed. There was never any follow-up after she was attacked, and Sonia never asked.

The staff moved wordlessly through the halls until they finally got to the infirmary.

"So, what happened this time?" Dr. Cho asked. She was small in stature, but her tone was commanding, her black hair cut in an angular bob, her brown eyes sharp and appraising.

The infirmary ward was sterile, with muted gray and brown tones. Only two personal items caught Sonia's eye. These were new. One, a photo booth strip. In the photos, a smiling Dr. Cho pressed next to a pretty pale woman, her hair a shock of blond and her blue eyes somehow warm in their coolness. Both women smiled or playfully displayed silly faces to the camera. Sonia couldn't picture the woman who was tending to her now acting in such a way. Carefree. It made her smile.

The second item hung from the edge of the picture on two delicate cords.

The first time Sonia had seen an omamori, she was walking in Tokyo under Joey's heavy arm. The hot air smelled of clean laundry and dirty pavement as they moved past a shrine where booths loaded with touristy treasures held thousands of these small, silk-bagged amulet keepsakes, each bringing the owner a different blessing or special kind of luck. People were bustling down the street, and the sound of scooters revved past. Puddles of dirty water shot up to the curb. Joey had tugged her toward the colorful talismans that resembled beautiful tea bags. He'd picked one up and paid the woman, who smiled warmly and bowed. Its latched bag was black and white, with meticulously stitched letters.

"What does it mean?"

"It's a love amulet," Joey whispered in her ear and kissed her temple while slipping it into her pocket. Her head fell to his shoulder as they continued walking. Could they grow old like this, just the two of them? Joey hadn't said it, but she knew he'd planned this trip after she had lost the baby, only three weeks after announcing her pregnancy. As it turned out, a cloud had always seemed to hover over them, just waiting for the right time to rain.

"Lucky in love," Sonia whispered, watching the doctor don her latex gloves.

A blush kissed Dr. Cho's cheeks as she realized Sonia was referring to the pictures. "Let me guess," she said. "You fell?"

"That's right. You got my M.O.," Sonia retorted, a bitter laugh escaping her lips. Unrelenting pain settled in her chest like her lungs were in a vice. The banter between the two was easy, even in her pain. She was seeing Dr. Cho too often lately.

Dr. Cho moved toward her. "You know they're going to kill you one of these days."

"Yup," Sonia agreed, all traces of humor gone. "And there is nothing anyone can do about it." She shifted onto the bed in the infirmary with the nurses help.

"That's not true," Dr. Cho said.

The doctor's small, cold hands palpated her ribs. Sonia winced but ground her teeth to stifle a cry. Her head sunk into the pillow and she closed her eyes. She felt her shirt being lifted away to reveal the recently healed scars, rimmed with lip-like pink scar tissue, that marred her stomach. Bruises, red now, would soon darken to blue and yellow. She wouldn't be able to walk for a few days. It was too bad; she was just getting into a nice prison cell workout routine. Some good it had done her. No matter how strong she got, she was powerless to defend herself against the group attacks. Ginger and her gang were up eleven to nothing by Sonia's count.

She knew she shouldn't be too upset over the numbers; for four years, that wasn't bad. Her first year was spent in protective custody while on trial in jail. Then she was moved to an all-women's prison in central Virginia. After her confession, Sonia had known she was in for a rough road. But she had no idea what it would do to her psyche. She'd expected to get jumped, but never feeling safe, always looking over her shoulder...it was exhausting. She was wondering if death was the best option.

"I'm going to have to set your nose," the doctor said.

Sonia felt her eyes pinch shut, and she groaned. "I would rather get beat again." This was always the worst part.

"Maybe if you let us help you."

"Who's us?" Bitterness weaved into her tone. "What are you going to do?" Sonia's eyes found the small rectangular window near the top of the wall. Beyond it she could see vibrant blue sky dotted with fat white clouds. Was the sky always this blue?

The room was silent except for the doctor's muted movements as she cleaned up Sonia's wounds with antiseptics. The cold liquid rushed over her injuries and reminded her of Emma D'Luca, the woman she'd thought about every day for the last six years, ever since Sonia had seen her lying on the floor, cradled in her own blood, her beautiful features frozen in lifelessness. The day Sonia's entire life changed. It should have gone differently, but she'd panicked.

"Well, this isn't a surprise." Sonia heard a voice come from the doorway. "Sonia Rossi in the infirmary again."

Warden Gibson moved closer to her. His balding head was tanned from the sun, his thin nose too angular for his round face. She tried to ignore the emotional response from her body, but it wasn't easy. It felt like a betrayal to let him see her squirm under his haughty stare. She wanted to disregard his smugness. *You don't affect me.* But he did.

Sonia forced herself not to roll her eyes at the sight of him. She'd known he would show up—he always did. But the taunting was...unexpected.

"What happened this time? Get into a fight with the washer?"

"I fell."

"At least your stories are consistent," he said, moving alongside her. "I'm putting you back in P.C."

Sonia tried to sit up, but pain shot through her midline, and she felt Dr. Cho's fingers press gently on her arm. She didn't like the disadvantage she felt while he hovered over her prone body.

"I think it's a good idea," Dr. Cho agreed as she continued to work. "This is the second incident in two weeks."

Warden Gibson's nose crinkled. "I'm not going to have a dead inmate on my watch."

His statement was ludicrous. Sonia knew of at least two deaths since she'd arrived here, but the prison had deemed them accidents, rather than murders. As if it was normal for someone to fall on their fork in the cafeteria.

She noticed that the Warden's hand was so close to her he was nearly touching her leg. "I think thirty days ought to do it. It's going to take at least that long for your ribs to heal," he added, and without another word, he turned and slunk from the room.

"He gives me the creeps," Sonia found herself whispering as the pain meds Dr. Cho had administered seeped into her system. Suddenly she couldn't feel the broken ribs or the banged-up nose. "I think a fight with his face can only improve things." Sonia giggled.

"I assume the medicine is taking effect."

"You know, Doctor, I like you," Sonia said, her pain lifting away from her. "I enjoy coming to see you."

"Then trust me when I say you can't do this on your own."

Dr. Cho's hand moved deftly over Sonia's injuries. "I think you need to see the value of your life."

"You have no idea what my life is worth to me. I can fight for what I love." Her eyes moved back to focus on the omamori, and she thought, *I was lucky in love once.*

3

JAMIE

"I CAN'T THANK you enough for your help on the Guevara case," Ali said as she leaned in on bent elbows. The lunch crowd at Pompeii was loud and hurried. Plates and glasses rattled as a busboy cleaned a nearby table.

Jamie forced her eyes onto Ali's face as her unease crackled like static in the air. Trying to focus, she shifted in her seat, flipping her phone face-down on the stiff white tablecloth and pushing it towards the potted succulent in the middle of the table. She couldn't get the damned call out of her head. "It's no problem at all. But you know he was lying." Jamie felt her mouth tip into a wry smile as she looked over at her friend.

"Honey, they're all lying about something," Ali said, waving down their waiter. Her short blond hair was styled smoothly back, her lips painted a deep red. She always went overboard, but it was part of her style. "Coffee." She lifted two fingers toward the waiter and Jamie nodded. "Two, please."

Jamie was often hired by Ali's law firm to assist with their clients' cases either before or after the case had made its way through the court system. Ali, a high-powered criminal defense attorney and old friend of Jamie's, was always hiring the firm where Jamie worked as a polygrapher. At one point, Ali had asked Jamie to come work for her, but Jamie couldn't leave Butch. Working for Ali's law firm would include consulting on cases, investigations, and more than just her polygraph reports. She knew if she took the offer it would keep her in the city for longer periods of time, and she was looking to cut back her time in Arlington.

"How's Drew?" Ali asked.

Jamie automatically glanced down at her finger, with its winking diamond, and flexed it. She still wasn't used to the feel of the ring against her finger or the weight of its implications on her heart. "Good. Fantastic." Jamie felt a familiar warmth spread along with a smile. "Good."

Ali's eyes narrowed perceptively. "Trouble in paradise already?"

Jamie shook her head. A fierce loyalty to the man she loved shifted in her. They weren't in trouble. They had just celebrated their one-year anniversary. Their wedding had been a small private ceremony with only ten guests at the edge of Cedar Lake where she now spent half her week, or tried to at least.

What was bothering Jamie was unrelated to Drew.

"It's nothing really. Just…" Jamie felt a lump form in her throat and washed it down with ice water. A large group left an adjacent table. Their loud voices rose around them and receded as they left the room. She looked down at her phone again before she could stop herself, tempted to turn its face over and peek.

"What is it? What's going on?" Ali's lips pursed in impatience.

Jamie studied her old college friend. They had been roommates their freshman year, just before she'd met her recent ex, Alex Carter. But she didn't want to think about him—not now, and not ever. Alex now worked at Ali's firm, but Ali made a point to never mention him to Jamie. Ali and Jamie had kept in touch throughout the years with trips to Miami or Key West in the winter months, but hadn't planned a trip this year because of Jamie's swift engagement. Having a somewhat shared field, Ali often asked Jamie for her professional opinion. But today, it was Jamie who needed Ali's perspective.

"What's the problem?" Ali asked again with one arched brow.

"Do you remember Nina Nelson?"

An image of Nina's red hair and twisted grimace flashed in Jamie's mind. It was hard to believe they'd been best friends up until that summer at Kring Camp, when Nina became obsessed with one of the camp leaders and mistook a tragic situation for something it wasn't. Years later Nina had snapped from that one incident, and after being arrested for murder and abduction, she'd been committed to a mental institute for the criminally insane.

"The crazy woman who abducted you? Nope," Ali shot back with a smirk.

Jamie felt a short laugh explode from her lungs. She should expect this sarcastic reaction from her friend by now. "Well, she's been contacting me. Letters—that sort of thing. And now…" Jamie twisted the mug of coffee over the glass saucer. "And now she's called me."

"What did she say?" Ali's brow pressed low, pulling her pretty face into a scowl. "She's in a mental hospital, right?"

"Yes, I know. I don't know what the protocols are there for outside communication. I'm going to look into it."

"I can help you with that, if you want," Ali offered, lifting the curved handle of the mug to her lips and staining the rim with a kiss of lipstick.

Jamie had expected the offer, but inwardly cringed to hear it. She needed to handle Nina herself.

"I haven't told Drew."

"Why not?"

Soft music filtered down from a speaker.

"I don't know." She shrugged. "I will—I guess." She didn't want to talk about Nina or any of the related dread she was feeling. She shifted the conversation back to the reason she had asked Ali to meet her for lunch. "I'm going to look into it. But there's something that you might be able to help me with. I have this client I took on through a court order. I noticed on his paperwork that Alex represented him seven years ago, when he was dabbling in pro bono work to see if he liked the criminal side of law." Ali nodded. "His name is Richard Jenkins. It looks like a typical sex offense case. Something like soliciting a minor. But he mentioned a man named Saul D'Luca."

Jamie watched as Ali set her cup down, her eyes narrowing. She leaned away from the table, a not-so-subtle hint that she wanted to escape this topic.

"Jenkins mentioned something about having a guy who has young girls. 'If that's your thing', he told me," Jamie said. Ali nodded, a solemn expression on her face.

Jamie felt her heart pounding, as if she'd accidently found out that her angst was warranted. She didn't want it to be true. In fact, she had gone back and forth about whether she would ask at all. Sometimes it felt like the more she learned about some people the more she wanted to forget.

"He didn't go into a lot of detail, but I wanted your opinion. Is this something I should pursue?" Jamie wasn't even sure why she was asking Ali. Since hearing Jenkins's confession, she felt like her feelings were bursting. Like she needed to act and wanted confirmation on her plan.

"Saul..." Ali began, and stopped. She crossed her arms over her chest, her head tipped to one side. "Saul is a very powerful man."

"Do you know him?" Jamie herself had heard the name a few times but never enough to care. Since her meeting with Jenkins, she'd Googled every lead she could find on Saul D'Luca.

"I don't know him personally. Outside his...business, most

people don't really know him," Ali said. She waved a hand through the air, almost dismissing him. "I would leave it alone, Jamie."

Ali's phone rang and she reached into her purse to retrieve it. Looking down at the screen, she held up a manicured finger to Jamie. "One second. Ali Williams," she said in a cool tone.

Jamie glanced past her out the front windows of the restaurant, watching people hustle past to their busy lives. A woman with shocking red hair walked past, a phone pressed to her ear.

Nina's eerie, haunted voice echoed: "You took everything from me, friend." The last word sounded ground from Nina's teeth. Jamie pictured her twisted features. Was Nina alone in her room at the mental hospital? Pacing the small floor, deciding how she could make Jamie pay for what she presumed was Jamie's fault, for ruining her life all those years ago?

Ali's hand moved up to cover her mouth, a soft gasp escaping. "I told them it was too risky. What the hell were they thinking? This is going to get someone killed." Ali's voice sounded pleading, but with the edge of anger Jamie always saw simmering under the surface. Ali's Type A personality came forward as a low growl rumbled past her lips. "They will track that package, Alex," she hissed, her head turning away from Jamie.

Jamie's breath caught at the sound of his name. She pictured his battered features in her yard, blood spilling from his lips.

"They're a criminal organization, Alex. Not some friendly rich uncle. He'll kill him. This makes no sense. I told Joey if he had paperwork from her it must be hand-delivered to me and only me. Why the hell did they leave it with you? What's the point of Joey disappearing if he's going to send a calling card?" Her hands caught at her throat, absently twisting her thin gold necklace. "I'll come by right now and get it. Don't look at it." A pause. "What do you mean it was opened? Who opened it?"

After a moment, she ended the call as abruptly as she'd answered it. Jamie thought she saw Ali's lip wobble.

"Everything okay?" Jamie automatically asked, but the answer was clearly no. Damage control at work, and it somehow involved Alex.

"I've got to go. Something's come up." Ali stood and frowned. "I'll get you next time," she said and hustled toward the door, nearly running into a couple being seated. "Excuse me," she mumbled, and kept going.

* * *

AN HOUR LATER, Jamie was sitting at her desk, perusing her files and checking her email, when her cell phone rang.

"Hello," Jamie said, looking at the caller I.D. Unknown number.

A breath shivered over the phone line, filling the quiet void for a moment. "Do you miss me, bitch?" Her tone was singsong, as if she were talking to a child, disdain dripping from each word.

Everything seemed to freeze as Jamie's grip tightened on her phone.

"Do. You. Miss. Me?"

Memories of Nina at camp. Nina at the hospital taking care of the sick and injured. Nina killing her lover...Now they were enemies. At least in Nina's eyes.

A feeling of defeat ran through her, marching in a truth she had wanted to avoid. Jamie knew Nina would never give up. "I'll be seeing you soon. You hear me. I'll be seeing you round the corner, bitch." Her voice a whisper now. The hair on the back of Jamie's neck pulled away from her skin like the tethers of a tent.

Jamie pictured the pile of letters hidden away in her desk, the faded postmarks and battered envelopes. The vile suggestions in them. She had wanted to ignore her, but the silent threat of this woman's unbalanced attention sometimes drove her to open them, to find out what Nina had written. She couldn't even tell Drew about them. She didn't have the emotional strength to unpack that now.

"You need help," Jamie said in a loud whisper.

A soft banging sound on the other end of the line grew louder, like a skull smacking a wall, soon drowned out by a relentless laugh. Voices, not Nina's, grew closer to the phone: "She's in here. Nina, honey—" and the phone disconnected.

Jamie sat there looking down at her cell phone as Nina's voice echoed off the walls of her mind. She knew Nina would never be her friend again, but Nina seemed to be getting worse, not better. Her letters were gradually becoming angrier and the neat print turning into the scribbles of a child, her anger visible in the deep gouges and small tears from the pressure of the pencil she used. Jamie could imagine the snap of the lead as she continued to write, frantic to get all the foulness on paper.

She was still holding the phone when it rang again, vibration zipping up her arm. She pictured Nina towering over the crumpled body of a nurse or attendant as she redialed Jamie's number.

But it wasn't her.

"Jamie?" Drew's voice came over the line.

"Hey there, handsome," Jamie said with clear relief.

"What is it? What's wrong?" Drew asked. His voice sounded too far away, a thousand miles at least.

"Nothing." She paused and took a deep breath. "I just miss you."

4

SONIA

SONIA PULLED herself up in bed. She would leave the infirmary today, after three days of Dr. Cho monitoring her cracked rib, among other injuries. She caught her reflection in the shiny surface of the napkin dispenser: her eyes were shades of purple and dark yellow due to her broken nose. Even without the benefit of a proper mirror she could see she looked like a monster from an old horror movie. Her long dark hair was raked into a loose knot on her crown above hollow eyes surrounded with the bloom of waxing bruises. She still felt pain when she took a deep breath, her ribs protesting against the pressure. The good doctor said the pain would last several weeks if she didn't take it easy. This said just after Warden Gibson solemnly relayed that protective custody wasn't currently available and that Sonia would be going back to the dorm.

Dr. Cho was right: Sonia wouldn't be able to take much more of this.

Five years ago, with the help of two investigators and her attorney, Ali Williams, she'd confessed to the brutal murder of her stepsister and best friend, Emma D'Luca. Her plane trip back from Montana, sandwiched between two officers, was exhausting; she hated flying. After only an hour in the air she was hanging over an airsick bag, emptying her stomach. Once they'd landed, she was driven to the police station, an unassuming three-story brick building.

The interrogation room was cool, and goosebumps pricked over her skin from a draft pushing through the grate above her.

"Why were you at Emma's house?" Detective Michaels asked, his pen poised over a legal pad, ready to memorialize her words. He was a solid man with a thick mustache and direct manner.

She felt tears pressing against her eyes. *Do this.*

"She was sleeping with my husband." Her monotone voice sounded foreign to her ears, as if she was hearing herself on an audio recording. She remembered thinking, *That's not me talking.* She pressed on. "I had to confront her about it." Sonia recalled Emma's voice on the phone asking her to come by.

Ali laid her hand over Sonia's. Her touch was tender, but it only added to Sonia's growing agitation. She had to force herself not to shake Ali's hand off.

"What happened once you arrived?" The detective's voice was smooth and friendly. She imagined he would high-five his coworkers later for getting Sonia's quick confession.

I was never supposed to get caught.

"I don't know." Sonia was shaking her head. "We just fought." Tears came then, refusing to abate. "She told me she was sleeping with my husband and…and I killed her."

"What did you use as a weapon?"

There was so much blood. Emma's pretty face frozen, her eyes staring up at Sonia as if any moment they would blink again and she would laugh and smile, like it was all a big joke. The knife, a big one, the kind you'd use to carve a Thanksgiving turkey or a steaming tenderloin, was still sticking out of her like some horrifying magic act.

"A knife. Black handle." Her fingers tightened into a ball on the table.

"I think we need a minute," Ali said, turning to the detective.

He slowly gathered his things: papers, reports, crime scene photos, probably of Emma's body—*so much blood*—and the door closed softly behind him.

"If this was a crime of passion," Ali began, "I can present your case that way. We can get Joey in here to testify—"

"No!" Sonia twisted in her seat to face Ali. "No. He doesn't testify. I'm guilty." Fear flashed through her.

"You have a case—"

"I said no. I'm guilty. I'll plead to the charge and you can mention the affair in sentencing." Sonia was adamant.

Ali looked confused and almost hurt. "Don't you trust me?"

"Yes. I do. But I don't want anyone else involved. He has a new identity, a new life. He needs to stay away from this."

That was five years ago. Now, flanked by two guards, she shuffled back to her cell. The heavy gray doors clicked open at the guard's request. Her stomach quivered at the smell of body oil and funk that hung in the stale air. Groups of women lingered near tables and open cell doorways, their eyes following her slow movement. Ginger, the husky redhead, hitched her chin toward her, winked, mouthed "I'll see you later," and laughed with several others before throwing cards down onto the table. She apparently had the winning hand.

Sonia had learned pretty quickly that she was in the most danger when she was in the pod, a big open area where most of the inmates hung out during the day. Off the main pod were the cells where everyone slept. At 5:30 a.m. the cell doors opened for the day and stayed that way until lights out—or if a lockdown was active. In Sonia's pod, roughly fifty women at one time could be found milling about, watching TV, playing cards or talking among themselves. One could be lulled into a false sense of security while hanging in the pod. It was the first place she was shanked. Just through the tender flesh of her thigh until it was sticking out the back of her leg. The crowd had erupted into chaos and the culprit, a woman named Dani, was never charged. Of course Sonia knew who'd attacked her, but she would never tell. That wasn't how you made friends in places like these. Not that she was trying or that anyone would be her friend anyway, but she did, however, need to stay alive.

Sonia slowly climbed the stairs and moved into her cell, where her eyes fell over her few personal possessions. No pictures of loved ones; instead, a cluster of impression paintings she was working on. Painting helped clear her mind. She imagined her family buried so deep in the textures and colored paint that no one else could see them: her sister Nikki's sharp, pretty features hiding in a peach and tan palate; her father's warm eyes staring out at her in the thick brown folds that only she could see. The paintings were her most precious possessions. Three of them lay taped to the eggshell-colored cement. She occupied the top bunk, the bottom currently vacant. Turnover was a regular thing at Flint Hill.

It had taken a year in local jail to get to the day where she would stand in court and say, "Guilty."

The courtroom had been packed, heat pouring off the bodies in the seats. Saul D'Luca had a large family, one that she was once a part of—stepdaughter to a ruthless man. To most he was a philanthropist, generously allocating money to those in need; a powerful entrepreneur, a gracious host. But to Sonia, he was a killer and a crook. When the commonwealth attorney proffered the evidence of the crime to which Sonia would plead guilty, she felt the force of a thousand deaths wished on her. As she stood next to Ali Williams, her longtime friend, the prolonged tension in her quivering muscles nearly caused her to fall over. Sonia knew all too well what happened when you crossed Saul, family or not.

She pictured his face in the courtroom that day, red with rage, covered in tears that the big man didn't even try to hide. The beautiful Emma D'Luca—his only child, his only heir. And Sonia had taken her away from him. Deputies lined the spaces all around her and she wondered who they were there to protect. Ali had informed her that there would be two security checkpoints each person in the galley would have to maneuver to gain a seat to watch her sentencing. As Sonia stood facing the judge for a terrifying forty minutes, she was sure a bullet would rip through her body at any moment, or a revolt from the galley would rise and swallow her. But it never happened. It turned out Saul had other plans for the woman who killed the light of his life.

"I guess I know where you've been." A soft Southern voice broke through her memory. Sonia nodded to the older black woman who walked inside, her old face dewy and unmarred from the absence of sunlight, fingers stained with ink from the newspapers she handled in the library. She moved inside and leaned against the wall, crossing her arms over her chest. She looked disappointed. "I heard. You okay?"

Sonia nodded for no particular purpose; it was an automatic gesture.

"Been missing you at the library." The old woman took a seat as her eyes followed Sonia, who retreated to her bed. Sonia could hear a soft click as the old woman ground her teeth, a habit of hers.

"Had to get cleared."

"Why you doing this, child?" Harriet asked with a sweep of her hand.

"Not because it's fun, that's for damned sure," Sonia said bitterly. "I have no choice. You know that."

"I know you think that."

"I don't need help. At least not in here." Sonia was adamant, but she wasn't sure she actually knew what the hell she was doing. Look how far her actions had gotten her. No privacy or control over her own life, and eleven beatings since the day she'd claimed this bed four years ago. Ginger and her crew were getting bolder, with no fear of retaliation or repercussion from the Warden because they knew she wouldn't snitch.

"What are you thinking about?" Harriet asked.

Sonia shook her head and inhaled, and the sharp pain reminded her she wasn't dead yet. "I was thinking about Saul," she said, the words spilling out. She couldn't help but want to unburden herself to the only friend she had. As it was, Harriet had a bit of pull around Flint Hill Corrections. She had the distinction, after all, of being an inmate here since the year they opened, in the early 1990s, when law enforcement was directed to wage war on drugs and those who peddled them. She'd been here ever since with barely a grumble. On Sundays she was permitted to speak with her grandchildren from the other side of a thick glass wall, wishing she could hold them just one time.

"Did you get that stuff I told you about?" Sonia asked, wanting to change the subject.

"Yeah, I did," Harriet said, handing over an envelope. "My essay. Facts of the case. My family on the outside." The old woman almost smiled, her hope tentative as fear held her back.

In another life, Sonia had gone to law school. In this life, she was a novice jailhouse lawyer to the few who asked for her help in looking up court cases or filing appeals after their families decided they couldn't afford a real lawyer. Harriet's appeal had been Sonia's idea, and the woman had taken a bit of convincing.

"I don't know why you're wasting your time," Harriet said.

"It's not a waste of time. You don't deserve to be here. You need to take advantage of this reform bill," Sonia said, looking over the paperwork Harriet had given her. "This is good. Real good. I'll get to work on it right away."

Harriet finally smiled. "Thanks for this."

* * *

LATER THAT NIGHT, Sonia sat and listened to the murmured whispers that seemed to seep through the walls. She couldn't focus enough to understand what she was hearing as her thoughts moved back to Saul.

He didn't want her dead: he wanted to toy with her like a cat bats at a mouse after it's been wounded. A swat here, a poke there, just enough to keep her in a constant state of panic. She knew he would get her one of these days. And she could honestly say she didn't blame him at all.

5

SONIA

SONIA'S CHEST pulled up to the table where an antiquated computer rested, her feet tucked under the chair. Internet was heavily monitored at the prison. The site history was stored and reviewed, no social media access, no privacy. Once she understood that, she'd been on a much better footing.

A guard stationed near the door flipped through a magazine, looking up every few minutes. Bookshelves lined the walls, no aisles where people could hide, giving guards the ability to monitor all inmates. Clusters of tables were arranged in the center of the room where Sonia sat.

She moved her mouse to the search bar and entered his name. *Joey Rossi.*

The thought of him used to evoke large bubbles in her chest: she loved him so much. His dazzling smile, his charm and his sense of humor. He was her everything. She tried to remember the last time she saw his face, the last time she touched him. She didn't want to remember the phone call filled with tears and goodbyes. His voice: "What did you do, Sonia? The police are here. Don't come home." She didn't even get a chance to explain.

Several old news articles popped up on the screen and she scanned through the headlines for anything new.

Former employee of Saul D'Luca, Joey Rossi, disappears; sister-in-law pleads guilty to the murder of Emma D'Luca.

Joey Rossi in hiding.

Joey Rossi sighting.

There seemed to be an underground group trying to locate people who'd dropped off the grid. Perhaps it was the challenge of finding such a person, a grownup's version of hide and seek. Bored people looking for something to do. She was relieved that there were no new articles. He was still hidden.

She had known Joey her entire life. Growing up in the same neighborhood, she often saw him strutting around with two of his closest friends.

Nikki, Sonia's sister, would tease her.

"You like him," Nikki sang as they lay in their bunk beds. The night was dark beyond the window and Sonia couldn't help wondering where Joey was, what he was doing. It was impossible to avoid him; his house was two down from hers.

"Maybe. It's none of your business," Sonia shot back. She didn't need a lecture from her big sister.

"I'm gonna tell him," Nikki proclaimed in the stillness.

Sonia's breath caught in her throat. She didn't want Joey to know that when they walked home from school together her heart raced, or that his winks made her melt just a little. He couldn't know she liked him; it would get weird. She bit her tongue. Nikki was stubborn. If she knew her words affected Sonia as much as they had, Nikki would follow through on her threat.

"Go ahead. I don't like him, but say what you want." Sonia's tone was defiant.

When Joey asked her out the next day, she nearly tripped on the perfectly level sidewalk. She knew she was wrong; Nikki had told him anyways.

"Wanna come over to my house this weekend?" he said, and she felt her forehead crease as she avoided his eyes.

"What?" Her heart stuttering in her chest.

"Do you want to meet my folks?"

"Oh—um. I guess that would be okay, if I ask my mom." Sonia had sounded like such a kid, even though she was almost sixteen. She was still getting used to her new living arrangements; her newly-widowed mother had recently married Saul, adding a stepfather and stepsister to the household.

Nearly five years later, Joey and Sonia had a big wedding at St. John's Church in town, and everyone had been there. Including Saul, who blessed the union of his favorite employee and his beautiful stepdaughter.

Sonia felt a smile on her lips as she remembered the good old days. The days before everything became complicated, when those she loved were still a part of her life.

She'd had to let them all go or put them at risk, too. After seeing Nikki just one time, Sonia had refused all visits at the jail; she'd leave her would-be visitors waiting at an empty window until a guard notified them that Sonia wasn't coming. She would throw their letters in the trash, knowing that if she allowed herself to read them, heartbreak would follow. It was better to cut them out completely. At first her mother wrote weekly. Then the frequency dwindled to once every few months. She still wrote these days, but even less often. Sonia assumed that Saul did not approve.

A chair moved next to her, and she looked up, her heart skipping, as the Warden braced his arms against the back of the chair. The swampy odor of his breath shifted past her hair and she drew back.

"Nice to see you're doing better, Mrs. Rossi," he said, unsmiling.

She nodded at him. A whisper of dread moved over her skin, leaving clammy fingerprints behind. His hawkish face turned to look around the room to see if anyone was in earshot. She knew what he was here to tell her and she was ready for his excuses.

"About tomorrow." He whistled softly. His pale skin was doughy, pockmarked around his chin, stubble dotted up from the lack of a close shave.

"I can't promise we won't miss anything, but I put an extra guard on duty in your pod. I need to tell you—" He paused, a hand rubbing his chin. "The protective custody unit had a water leak. Some three cells flooded, and there are people in that unit that really need to stay up there." Implying *she* didn't.

She gave an abrupt nod.

"I just want you to know that your safety is my highest priority." He looked down at his carefully clipped nails, surveying them in a sort of arrogance. "I'm truly doing everything I can."

A glint off his gold pinky ring caught her eye.

"I understand," she said, a lump rising in her throat. She wanted to set the record straight. But she knew the game, and him knowing she knew didn't change her odds. You couldn't appeal to evil people, nor could she stand the thought of putting herself in a position of rejection with this prick.

"I'm so glad you understand." He shifted beside her and stood, his hand near her face as if he would reach out and touch her, but he didn't. She would physically assault him if he did. He seemed all too happy to have come all the way to the library to share this bad news with her in person. Was he some kind of sadist? As he walked away, her eyes searched for a calendar and confirmed tomorrow was the day. She knew it without looking, but her brain was trying to register what would happen this year.

She shut down the browser and moved toward a row of books. It wasn't an impressive library, but it was stocked well enough for her to find what she was looking for. Classics, mostly. Things she would never have found the time to read in her life outside of prison. So many things she would have done differently.

When she got weepy, she reminded herself she was here for a reason, and it was her choice.

D—she was looking for D this time around. Dumas...*The Count of Monte Cristo*. She lifted the heavy volume from the shelf. Its jacket was free from dust. It had been moved recently, and she knew by whom. Flipping through, she found a sheet of crisp white paper wedged inside, and after looking around she plucked it out. Taking out her own prewritten note from her pocket, she pushed it between the pages, replaced the book and moved on. Everyone appeared oblivious to her existence as she made her way back to her chair.

Opening the folded paper, she read it:

"Gang— 3-7. R and N on shift tomorrow. Watch your back."

Yes, tomorrow was going to be an interesting day.

As she walked back to her cell, flanked by two guards, she thought of the note she had received and what it meant.

Tomorrow might finally be the day she died.

6
___

SONIA

Sonia's muscles wouldn't relax even while lying on her lumpy mattress. A fog-covered first light lay beyond the small window, her cell dark except for the steady red flash of the camera mounted in the corner. Sometimes she felt like she was aboard a spaceship, drifting through some kind of void. Or maybe that was her wish so she could detach herself from this reality.

Calls from other women could be heard occasionally in the night as they traded secrets in the open. A threat, a meetup, a complaint about a guard on the block. Mack's name was mentioned at least once a night. He was well liked by the woman, and they boasted about trying to have sex with him. Some even claimed they had, but Sonia knew they were lying. She pictured Mack McKenny smiling, not now, but back in sixth grade English class. She'd had the biggest crush on him then, his lanky figure not yet filled out. They had been friends until one day: the day Jared ruined it.

"You like the black kid?" Jared had taunted. "Bet your dad would love that." His laughter expanded to the group behind him after he shot them a look.

She'd wanted to speak, to tell him he was an asshole, but, to her shame, she was too scared. Scared of what they would say, of being ostracized from the group. She was hardly popular, but it could be worse. She could be shunned.

That day she had run from the school, five classes before Christmas vacation began. At thirteen years old, her emotions were dragging her in every different direction. Could the kids at school be right? Would her father disapprove of a boy simply because of the color of his skin? No—she couldn't believe that. Her dad was a caring, loving person, and Jared was just projecting his own hatred of those who weren't like him. The truth was, Mack was a better person than Jared and Jared couldn't stand it. Mack was smarter, cuter, and better at football.

She dashed toward the tree-line that bordered the school property, separating it from the surrounding neighborhoods. A trail, well-worn from kids cutting across it on their way to class or to the playground during the summer months, laced through the trees. The sodden woods flashed past her as she tried to outrun her guilt, and Jared's laughter. Why hadn't she stood up for her friend? She couldn't see maintaining their uncomplicated relationship after this.

Suddenly her ankle rolled along a bare root twisting out of the earth, and she stumbled onto the damp, cold ground. Wind whipped at her face, causing tears to form in her eyes. Mack deserved a good friend, not her—not the coward she turned out to be.

The sun cracked through the clouds and streamed through the tree's spindly naked branches; their rigid shadows sprang up around her as she lay on the ground and contemplated her options. Her mother would be home, preparing for holiday guests who were arriving the coming weekend. Sonia pictured her mother's disappointed—or worse, angry—features as the school called to inform her that Sonia had skipped after second period.

Sonia didn't want to deal with it; not yet, anyway. When she got home, she decided, she'd stay in the shed out back. The trail through the woods led right into her backyard, a neighborhood of typical two-story homes at the edge of a cul-de-sac. The house was big and silent as she made a run for the shed, shut the door behind her, and looked out the small window facing the house, certain that she had made it undetected.

The shed smelled of sawdust and a weak strawberry air freshener she had taken from her father's Volvo. Pillows and blankets were piled near a battery-operated lantern she used as a reading light. Their father had converted the shed over the summer, and Nikki had joined her for about a month in the fort. But now Nikki was a drag, always sulking in her room after school, no time to hang out with her little sister.

A shadow near the back of the house caught her eye. Dread trickled into her as she thought that maybe she had been caught. She moved toward the window slowly, taking in the two figures that appeared on the deck. The first she recognized right away as her mother: a slight frame and dark hair, leaning back, her arms braced against the rail. Another shadow, a man Sonia had seen a few times before, leaned in and kissed her. *Kissed her mom!*

Sonia blinked back at them, unsure of what she was seeing.

Her mother was kissing a man who wasn't her father. Sonia's heart thumped harder and her belly flipped and flopped. She tried to reconcile the action. It was a goodbye kiss, yes, like her Aunt Dee always did before she left. But then the man leaned in and Sonia had to squeeze her eyes shut at the display. Not a goodbye kiss. Her mother was cheating with a man Sonia would come to know all too well after her father's death a year later.

She wanted to tell her father the moment he came home, but she didn't want to ruin his Christmas. Throughout that last year of his life, Sonia approached him frequently, ready to tell him what she'd seen that December day, but she always backed out; she didn't want to be the one to break his heart. Just like when she used to pretend Santa was real, even after she knew he wasn't. She perpetuated the lie for her parents' sake.

Now, as Sonia lay in her cell, she could hear the women around her gossiping. "I would break off a piece of that and he wouldn't know what hit him," came a declaration, followed by an eruption of laughter.

"I believe that," called another woman, followed by a second wave of laughter.

The day she arrived at Flint Hill, Sonia was shuffling through a line to receive her prison issued clothes when she finally looked up and saw him. Mack didn't smile, only glanced back at her. She absently wondered if he recognized her.

His first cryptic message hadn't come for over a year, and only after her second attack. It was in a book he told her she'd left in the library. *The Count of Monte Cristo*.

"Watch out for Janet" was the extent of the message. Two weeks later, Janet instigated an attack on Sonia during rec time in the yard.

On a whim, Sonia decided to leave a message in the book. Two simple words that had been burning in her since that day at school:

"I'm sorry."

When he sent back a question mark, she smiled. It would be like him to forget others' shortcomings. His messages soon grew more detailed, with premonitions for coming attacks that turned out to be forecasted in the pairing-up of correction officers. Sonia had a sinking feeling when she realized the Warden must know about what was happening. Then his visits started. Dropping by to check her cell, or other implied forms of harassment.

And now this, Mack's most recent note, telling her a group of three to seven women were going to gang up on her, and the pair-up of the guards was not in her favor. Good old Remmy at it again so soon. Sonia wasn't even healed from the last attack.

But today was special.

Sonia often thought of what life had been like before she crossed the threshold of Emma's door that day. She wanted to be with Joey forever, to have a family, if IVF worked out, to pay bills, see the world...all the things that used to matter. Now she was just trying to survive.

A toilet flushed, drowning out the whispers.

Now she had the perpetual fear of being murdered, beaten at the whim of her stepfather's influence, and a deep loneliness that yawned over all of her. She couldn't remember what the tender touch of another human being felt like. A hug, a kiss, a hand-shake. Instead, she would cower at a loud sound or a shadow moving too quickly. She would scan a room, never stopping until she had a wall to her back. This was what Saul wanted: not to kill her, but to make her suffer. Her mind would count as she walked, always by twos. A distraction to confront the chronic stress. It was like she was standing in a field holding a lightning rod during a storm: at any time, she could be struck. She'd created an exercise of sliding down from her bed at night to check her cell door to be sure it was secure. Some nights this ritual would happen four to eight times, but always in even numbers.

As she listened to the whispers around her, she had never felt so lonely. Every night, the only luxury she had was to remember the smell of Christmas dinner, or the warm embrace of her mother's hug, or the soft kiss of her husband. But the memories were fading, moving away from her. Her memories were now scarred by pain and fear, repressing the smells, tastes and sounds of her old life. She had to wonder why she was hanging on at all. But the nagging voice inside told her that her life wasn't over yet. Most of the time, the voice sounded like Harriet. A soft, loving chide.

"You can't give up yet, child." Her perceptive glance would demand Sonia's attention. And Harriet was right, but it didn't make what Sonia had to do any easier. There was a time she'd

allowed herself to lie in the cell and cry because her mind was begging for a release, but she had become hardened by what was happening to her.

A shadow flickered over her bed, and she looked up. Zoey, a new face on the block, looked in on her. Without a word, she stared into Sonia's cell, her eyes scraping over each of Sonia's meager possessions. Was she one of the good ones? After a moment, the guard continued down the line.

Sonia closed her eyes and tried to picture something beautiful, something happy, but her heart hurt when his face flashed in her mind. She looked over at the painting next to her head and let her fingers trail over the rough surface. She stared into his face but it was melding into something she didn't recognize. Someday this would just be a painting to her, and he would be gone forever. *I love you—*

7

JAMIE

"I FEEL sick over what I've done." Jenkins cried, making his belly heave and shake. "Since Beth was born, I can't look at her without thinking of those girls." Tears streamed down his round face as he swiped at them with a meaty hand, displaying dark tufts of hair on his knuckles.

Jamie sat across from Jenkins's hulking form, so large that the chair he sat on looked like it belonged in the children's section of the library. There was a subtle greasy odor in the air: Jenkins, a night cook at a local diner, must have just gotten off work this morning. He'd been early to the scheduled meeting, smoking a cigarette on the street in front of her office when she arrived.

"Jill really loves me, too. I don't think she would if she knew," he said, almost angrily.

She kept her body still and her tongue tamed as Jenkins poured out his guilt. On his third visit to her office his façade cracked, and his blubbering confession was recorded on her laptop, which she used during these sessions. He hadn't noticed or didn't care that she was documenting everything he said.

"At first I tried to tell myself it wasn't a big deal. They were almost eighteen. At least the girls I saw. They just needed money like the rest of us." His nose dripped, and as he spoke spittle popped and flew, his eyes not meeting her steady stare. His posture was rigid until the tears began, and then his shoulders rolled into a slump as his head hung toward his chest. An unrelenting awkwardness always followed the moment when Jamie's clients began to cry. Was she expected to feel bad for him? She didn't.

"I can't tell Jill. She'll leave me. Then I won't be able to see Beth, the only reason I have to live." The big man was speaking of his newborn daughter and soon-to-be wife. He kept insisting he didn't know what Jill saw in him. Sure, she wasn't the best-looking woman he had been with, but she was sweet, and despite the extra layer of fat on her she was beautiful to him. She was seven years younger than his forty-one years. And he'd never thought he would have a child, let alone get married, after being released from prison two years ago. He couldn't bring himself to tell her the truth: that he was put in jail for soliciting sex from underage girls. He told himself he lied for her benefit, but any fool could see it was self-preservation that drove his actions.

"They were almost eighteen, I'm sure of it. They couldn't have been that young," he argued, perhaps to himself. "But Jill won't understand, and maybe I didn't either until Beth was born. I couldn't imagine a man touching her. Not my child."

Jamie hadn't even gone over her routine questions with Jenkins before he broke into a pity party. His court-ordered rehabilitation included polygraphs to assess if he was lying about any of his past sexual misconduct or current court orders, such as joining the sex offender registry and certain other restrictions, like no internet use and trespassing on school properties.

"I'm not here to judge you," Jamie said levelly, though she was doing just that. How could he reason away what he had done?

Ever since he'd mentioned Saul, in their last session, she

couldn't help thinking she had to do something about this bastard who sold young girls for sex. *Stop, Jamie.* Most of the things she found on the internet about D'Luca appeared harmless. Of course, he was rich, so he could simply have one hell of a P.R. person.

"You're so easy to talk to." He managed a glance in her direction, and even with her self-control she felt herself withering under his eyes. It wasn't possible for this man to possess such ignorance about the girls he was having sex with. He must know that they hadn't participated of their own free will and that they couldn't legally consent.

She tried to convince herself her own history had nothing to do with her longing to investigate Saul D'Luca, but that would be a lie. The thought that innocent girls and boys were being used in this way tortured her daily.

"Let's get started," Jamie said.

* * *

AN HOUR LATER, Jenkins sat stock-still, with the look of a man who just woke from a terrible dream, recapping his crimes.

"Mr. Jenkins, can I ask you how you came to know about these girls?" She was finished administering the polygraph, but what could it hurt if she didn't tell him so?

He cleared his throat as he appeared to consider her question. Finally, he nodded, still facing the wall. "An old friend of mine told me about them. I don't talk to him anymore. He's still downstate." One of his restrictions was not communicating with other felons. "I'm not attractive. I know that. Another reason I'm lucky Jill loves me." He brushed his fingers through thinning hair. "I shouldn't make excuses," he added quickly. "I shouldn't have done it, and I'm truly sorry."

Jamie believed him. He was one of the few offenders who seemed remorseful, but he was also a man unwilling to come to terms with exactly what he had done. Jamie sensed that when he did, he might not be able to handle the repercussions.

"How do you know it was this man that your friend was talking about? Saul D'Luca?" Jamie asked this as if she didn't really care about the answer.

He thought about her question. "Do I have to answer that?"

She shook her head. "No."

"I would rather not say. I don't want him to think I'm a rat."

"What about the girls?" she said, too quickly.

Jenkins turned to face her now, his eyes brash. "I can't think about that anymore. Makes me sick."

What he wasn't willing to admit, and what she heard in his response, was that Richard Jenkins was making this all about him, not the girls, and it made her desire to know what was happening even more unignorable.

8

SONIA

IT WASN'T long after Sonia's father died that Saul D'Luca started showing up at the house, formally. She had pushed the image of him and her mother together out of her mind until she saw Saul at her father's funeral. It was way too sunny for the day she would bury her father, and she felt Mother Nature was betraying them. Her anger spiked so quickly that before she could stop herself, she was running from the quiet group of mourners surrounding the hole in the earth. She had stumbled to another part of the cemetery, near a crop of trees, where she knelt and cried. Was her father looking down on them? Through the crack in the clouds, warm sun flickered through to rest on the ground by her scuffed dress shoes. Could he see Saul's hand resting a little too low when he hugged Sonia's mother, Julie?

No one seemed to notice the change in Sonia except Nikki, who finally brought it up weeks later while in their room. "What's going on with you?"

"What do you mean?" Sonia realized she sounded snotty and bit back more words. It wasn't her sister's fault; Sonia wasn't mad at her. Sonia was mad at *him*. Mad enough that she imagined Saul's body smashed and lifeless between the steering

43

column of his Mercedes instead of her father's in the family Volvo. Or maybe he would fall onto the third rail as he waited for the Metro; he used to ride to work Monday through Friday. She wanted him to pay for taking her father's spot at the dinner table, for asking her mother if she really needed to keep old family pictures out so he had to see them every time he visited. This was all his fault. She wanted to scream that he had no right to erase someone as wonderful as her father.

"You can't hide from me," Nikki said in a mischievous tone. Nikki had never been close to their dad, or at least not as close as he and Sonia had been. She wouldn't understand.

"It's nothing. I'm just sad." Sonia knew she didn't sound sad —she sounded mad. But sometimes that's how pain worked its way out of you. Because if she let her guard down, sadness would flood in and drown her. She would rather be mad, but you had to feed anger, and its usual cost was her peace.

"I get it." Nikki tossed a tennis ball at the wall. Thwack, thwack, thwack. "What do you think of this Saul guy?"

Sonia's answer was quick and required no extra thought. "I don't."

"You don't what?"

"I don't want to think about it. I don't want to talk about it."

Nikki, clearly not reading Sonia's steely reserve, didn't relent. "I like him."

Sonia felt a scream struggling up from her lungs, but Nikki couldn't see her face. After nearly a minute with no sound escaping, she slammed her mouth shut and fled the room. She didn't want her mother to be happy with anyone else—to let Saul steal her family.

It was only a month later that their mother announced she was officially seeing him. Her husband had died only months before, and she couldn't wait to be with someone else. For this, Sonia vowed never to forgive her.

She withdrew into herself, taking dinner in her room,

refusing invitations to get to know Saul and his daughter, Emma. She felt the family was betraying her father, but her mother and Nikki didn't feel the same. In fact, Nikki had taken more than a balanced interest in Saul—she was almost possessive of his attention. It was a transformation Sonia didn't understand.

Five months after Sonia stood by her father's graveside, her mother announced that she and Saul were getting married. There were many nights Sonia contemplated running away before she watched the moving trucks pull up to their house. She had avoided spending too much time with Saul; now she would live in his house, but she solemnly promised it would never be her home.

Emma had walked into her room that day, unnoticed at first, but when Sonia turned from her perch at the window, she was staring straight at the bratty blonde.

"What?" Sonia asked.

Emma tipped her tiny shoulders up and looked around her half-packed room. "Do you need any help?"

"No."

Emma's stare made Sonia shift off her perch at the window.

"I know you don't like us." Emma advanced into the room. "I get it. I don't like the situation either."

Voices echoed up from the bottom of the stairs. Saul was teasing her mother, and her mother actually giggled. Sonia felt her eyes roll and noticed Emma's do the same.

"You don't seem upset," Sonia said.

Emma shrugged. "I don't have the luxury."

The statement was so blasé that Sonia saw Emma differently in that moment. Maybe she could like this strange girl, but she wasn't ready to commit just yet.

"I mean, my dad doesn't really care what anyone thinks. When he sees something he wants, he gets it." Emma said it as though Sonia's mother was a piece of clothing or a romantic getaway, along with the implication that he would someday lose interest. Instead of resenting Emma for the harsh truth, Sonia appreciated her for it. At fourteen, most people thought she was too fragile for the truth, and it had only gotten worse after her fathers' death.

Sonia felt her mouth fall open. When? When had Saul decided he wanted her mother? The image of the stolen kiss that Christmas flashed, unwanted, in her mind. How far was a man like Saul willing to go to get what he wanted?

"What do you mean?" Sonia asked. The drunk driver who had T-boned her father's car had died on the way to the hospital. Sonia had never taken the time to think that someone might have been involved that wanted her father dead. "Would he hurt people to get what he wants?" Sonia shifted toward her new stepsister. Emma's blond hair was neatly pulled back from her face. She seemed to consider the question before Nikki interrupted.

"C'mon, Sonia. We have to load the boxes." Nikki's mouth fell open at the sight of the room. "You didn't even pack!" Appalled, Nikki began throwing books from Sonia's desk into a half-full box. Nikki couldn't move into Saul's house fast enough, and it made Sonia sick. But as she looked back at this curious girl, she wondered if she'd just found a most unlikely ally.

The three began packing, and Sonia heard Emma whisper under her breath, "He *has* hurt people to get what he wants."

9

SONIA

S<small>ONIA</small>'<small>S</small> <small>NERVE</small> endings tingled down her arms and legs while panic ballooned into her chest, making each new breath labored. Today was the day.

She could almost hear the echo of the DJ's voice saying "It's a very special day for a very special girl" as people clambered to the dance floor. The music was loud and upbeat and the room quickly grew hot as Joey's body pressed against hers.

She shoved off the memory as she brushed her teeth by rote, clutching the yellow handle of the brush as she tried to ignore her blooming fear.

The first time she was beat up in prison had been a shock to the system. She'd witnessed fights before, in school, but this was different. Those school fights had lasted a fraction of the time and were tempered with restraint, not the rage she had soon learned flowed through some of the women among whom she lived. When she was attacked, a fight that took a few minutes felt like hours of abuse and required weeks of recovery.

Scars now ravaged her once-smooth skin and her nose was slightly larger from the constant fractures. She'd come to the prison already scarred, her right leg never completely healed from the car accident that led to her arrest. Anyone who was paying attention would notice the stuttered gait that gave away this weakness.

She stared into the dirty mirror, and a desperate, scared woman gazed back.

She winced and sucked air through her mouth as she pressed on the bridge of her nose. Murmuring could be heard outside her cell from women nearby. A whisper began, low at first, but climbing to reach her ears: "Green light go, on 216. Green light go, on 216."

It was soft and almost childlike, and its echo sent a shiver through her. Green light was code for a hit, and 216 was her cell number. It was like note-passing among the inmates, only she was meant to hear it. Someone had decided it was time for her to die.

The morning light caught the edge of one of her paintings and she stared back at a likeness only she could see.

"I miss you," she whispered. "I'm not done yet."

LATER IN THE AFTERNOON, Mack walked into the library, where Sonia had her paperwork laid out. His brown skin was smooth and shaved and his hazel eyes leveled on her. A smile, though small, pulled at his lips, and her heart skipped as he approached.

"You've got a visitor," he said.

She shook her head. "Tell her to go away." Sonia pictured her mother sitting in the empty room, and a buried emotion niggled in her chest, or maybe it was just her cracked rib. She wondered what her mother looked like now; older and grayer, probably.

"It's not your mom," Mack said, leaving Sonia's mouth hanging. He never spoke intimately to her in person even as their letters had become more informal. She stumbled on her words and felt her cheeks grow hot as he seemed to read her thoughts.

"Who?"

"Your lawyer, Ms. Williams. She said its urgent," Mack said in a tone suggesting he was delivering a phone message to his boss. His delivery was all wrong, and she found herself wishing there was emotion attached to the message.

Stupid girl. Get it together, already. He isn't in love with you. He just warns you about women trying to kill you, probably out of a feeling of obligation.

In another life, a much less complicated one, she could have fallen in love with Mack, maybe had a few children and argued about finances or why she always stole the covers.

She rose from her chair on shaky legs and followed him. Her eyes constantly scanning her surroundings, listening for the soft sound of sneakers approaching.

"I thought you were off today." She recalled hearing the gossip at breakfast.

"Nah. Picked up some O.T."

"Oh, who's out?" *Let it be Remmy, please, God, let it be Remmy.*

"Michael, up in intake." He raised a brow as they approached a door: someone could be listening. He hit the call button on the wall. "Door 75," he said into the speaker. The door clicked, and he pushed through, holding it open for her.

Ali wasn't supposed to come see her, was she? Her heart tripped as the soft edges of her prison-issued Keds scuffed along the hall.

"Door 38," Mack's deep voice said. Another click and she was ushered into the visiting area. He led her to a cubicle with partitions for privacy, as much as could be afforded. The walls had ears here, and those ears didn't give a damn about Sonia Rossi.

Ali smiled weakly at her from the other side of the window, then frowned, probably surveying the yellowing bruises that painted the dips of Sonia's eyes. Sonia wanted to laugh at the idea that she used to care what she looked like: expertly applying makeup on her face, shopping for slinky outfits for her husband.

"What the hell happened?" Ali waved toward Sonia but looked at Mack, who backed out of the room without a word. "What's this?" Ali turned her eyes on Sonia and gestured toward her face. "Who did this?"

Sonia's shoulder quirked up and down. She was more interested in whatever had brought on this unexpected visit.

Ali's lips pressed together in a thin line.

"Never mind," Sonia said.

"You know we could sue their asses." Ali shook her head, her disgust obvious in the lines drawn across her face.

A brief silence grew between them, and Sonia felt a slow-moving emotion rising in her, inflating her chest and threatening to send her spiraling out of control. It had been two years since she'd last seen Ali, though she had kept in touch over the years. An in-person visit must mean trouble. Sonia couldn't handle anything else today.

"We have a problem," Ali began, getting down to business quickly. "This was delivered to my office last week." She pressed the title page of a thick document up to the glass. As Sonia's eyes scanned the print, a low buzzing began in her ears. Her fingers grew clammy as they rested on the cold steel shelf bolted to the wall just below the window. She couldn't pull her eyes away from the paper. Was this a sick joke?

"Son of a bitch," Sonia said. "Who's seen this?"

"I don't want you to worry about it. It's his own fault. You would think a guy hiding out would know better."

"Who's seen it?" Sonia dragged her damp palms down her jumpsuit. After all this time, how the hell could Joey be so stupid? Was he so confident he wouldn't be found that he couldn't help himself?

"Someone from the firm accidentally opened it. It was dropped off in Alex's office, not mine."

"You said you required hand delivery to *you* only." Sonia felt her temper rising. It wasn't Ali's fault, but who else could she blame right now? "Who the hell is this Alex guy?"

"I know. I know. I'm sorry. The delivery person didn't read the requirements for receipt." Ali's face was drained of color, bringing into focus the lines on her pretty face. "Alex is a coworker of mine at the firm."

"Tell Joey he has to move." That was the only solution to their problem and she needed Ali to make the call now.

"I'm working on it, but Joey's objecting. Said he wants to stay where he is. He has—" Ali averted her eyes from Sonia's. "He says he's getting married as soon as your divorce is final."

A gasp left Sonia's mouth, a reaction unexpected even to her. He was moving on, and she couldn't blame him. He was out there in the actual world, and she was here because of what she had done. It was her choice; no one else made her do it.

"And?" Sonia asked.

"And what?" A look of guilt passed over Ali's features. Sonia was getting very good at reading people; it was one of the few tools of protection she had left.

"And they're going to have a baby," Ali said in a whisper. Her words were the final blow Sonia could withstand for the day. Her eyes slammed shut, and a strangled sound crawled from her throat. A child, a life; all things she would never have.

After several moments, Sonia's mind began shifting back to reality.

Ali pulled out a yellow envelope and laid it on the table: the divorce papers Joey had filed. Tears pooled in Sonia's eyes as she thought of the four years she'd spent here, plus one at the county jail for her trial, and the countless beatings. Most popular girl on the block. And now this. She was faced with the most selfish person in the world whose actions risked throwing it all away. She recalled the voices at dawn that morning and what it meant for her now.

Ali left the paperwork with Sonia so she could read through it after a guard checked it for contraband and staples. God forbid she get ahold of a staple; the entire system would fall.

Ali said she would request Sonia be put in protective custody, a request which Sonia knew the Warden would promptly deny. When Ali asked Sonia how she felt about a transfer, she brushed it off. This was as good a place as any. Besides, the Warden wouldn't entertain a transfer order. She knew that he would reject her lawyer's requests, that she was always placed back into general population because Saul was paying him.

Her leg ached as she walked down the empty corridor on her way back to her cell block. She was hoping it would be Mack taking her back, but it wasn't. Her guard ushered her through a door, nodded to another guard two blocks down and told her to walk to her pod. Sonia heard the low hiss of a voice from somewhere: "In the cut." The guard at the end of the hallway facing her disappeared, out of view. The squeak of sneakers screamed over the polished floor around her. She whirled around, but she was too late. A body nearly twice her size rammed her into an open doorway, and she was falling. Her hip and ribs smashed against something hard. White-hot pain cracked through her body. She tried to protect her face with her hand, but her muscles wouldn't respond to the commands from her brain, or they were trapped somehow. Pain battered her body as fists tenderized every part of her. The crack of a bone, the slap of skin, and the feel of wetness slithered down her face.

Her dizzy thoughts recalled Emma D'Luca's last birthday party. She'd looked so vibrant, so alive. The smell of citrus on her skin. "A very special day for a very special girl." Emma's arm hanging over Joey's, her lips next to his ear. "Happy birthday to you, happy birthday to you. Happy birthday, dear Emma…" Then Sonia was gone.

10

SONIA

IT WAS three days later that Sonia's eyelids fluttered open. Prior to that, her mind was a tangle of flashes, in and out of consciousness; there were loud shouts, shaky movements, voices talking about her condition as if she wasn't there. She lingered under the edge of that restless sleep, or more likely a morphine-induced slumber.

Now her mouth was dry, and her breath was so sour she nearly gagged. When she lifted her head from the pillow pain skittered from each part of her body like the roll of a tide coming in. A cry, or trapped air, released from her dry lips, and she realized she wasn't alone. Mack sat on a chair across the room by the door, head in his hands over his knees. When he heard her, his head jerked up. Exhaustion etched his features. She could see his muscles prepare to propel him across the room but also saw his resistance. She hated that in that moment she wanted his comfort, that she wished he was at her bedside, holding her hand like a damned Hallmark movie.

"You're back." He stood, but didn't make a move toward her. He pulled his cap off like someone paying their respects at a funeral precession, holding it tightly in his grip.

Her throat burned. "Water?"

He looked around, found a plastic cup and filled it in the bathroom. This wasn't the prison infirmary. On the white walls hung hotel room art, posters promoting health, and emergency exit placards. This was a hospital, and Mack must have been assigned to her to ensure she didn't escape. As if that feat was even possible in her state. Her eyes scanned the damage: her right arm was in a sling, and gauze the color of faded yellow lay in patches over her right leg. She shifted slowly and felt the familiar stretching of stitches somewhere on her belly. She did a mental inventory of her level of function and determined it was too early to tell the lasting damage.

They'd got her good this time.

Someone had deployed a taser—she recalled the arcing sound of electricity as her attacker shook loose from her unmoving body. The pain had drowned out any sense of time or surroundings, so much so that she was sure she couldn't identify who'd attacked her nor who had come to her aid.

"You're lucky to be here."

She snorted, a pathetic sound. Lucky. It was probably the last thing she considered herself. When she thought of the tenuous tether she had to this life, she wondered if it was even worth all her suffering. And how good it would feel to let go of that tether and float away like a balloon in a clear summer sky. The one thing that kept her going was something she could never have.

"That came out wrong." He approached the bedside with the cup of water. He used the bed controls to sit her up, and with every inch, her body succumbed to wave after wave of pain. "Do you need some more meds?"

She nodded.

She downplayed this kindness, instead analyzing every inter-action they had at Flint Hill in the last few years to understand his angle. Quiet and watchful, he said nothing to her, but she caught his glances. Sonia could handle herself, and he must have sensed it; instead of intervening outright, he had found a small way to help her, with his warnings.

"Easy." He moved the cup to her lips. "The nurse is on the way." She tried not to look into his eyes, tried and failed. Then the door swung open and a heavy-set nurse shuffled in, her scrubs pulling and stretching around her trunk. An uneasy smile appeared on her face when she saw Mack standing over Sonia.

"Is everything okay?" She halted at the door as if ready to bolt at the first sign of trouble, her eyes moving between the two.

"Just getting her some water," Mack said, setting the water down and retreating to his chair. Sonia couldn't help noticing how care came easy to him.

"You need some more pain meds, hun?" the nurse asked as she checked the machine near Sonia's bed, scribbling some notes on a clipboard that hung nearby.

"Yes, please," Sonia said in a rasp and pointed to her throat. "Why?" was all she managed.

"They had to intubate you. You were touch and go for about a day. Once we got you stable, you seemed to come right around." The nurse pressed buttons on the machines attached to a drip. "To intubate they have to put a tube down there." She motioned to her own throat with a hooked finger.

Sonia bit the inside of her cheek: she felt the impulse to thank the nurse for saving her life, but she was too embarrassed.

"There. You should feel better soon." The nurse turned to Mack. "Your partner's here," she said, pointing out to the hallway, and he nodded but made no move for the door.

The nurse left the room, and Sonia lay back as the drugs slowly seeped into her, cutting away the edges of pain in her limbs and moving into her core. A blissful heat spread its tendril fingers and elevated her over the pain.

"You like to take care of people." Sonia's words were

unchecked by her normal standoffishness, the drugs lowering her inhibition.

"My mother died of cancer two years ago. She lived with me, and I took care of her at the end," Mack said from somewhere across the room.

Sonia's lids grew too heavy to keep open. "I knew you were a good guy." She heard movement somewhere in the room as her mind crawled out of a fog. "I can't remember the attack. I don't know who did this to me. Who saved my ass this time?"

"Remmy." His tone was disdainful. "Just in time, again."

"This is my fight."

"No. No, it isn't your fight, Sonia. We're paid to protect you. We failed not once, not twice, but twelve times, by my count."

"Don't do this to yourself." Her voice seemed to float. He did care.

"I'm going to figure out who's allowing this to happen, and when I do, I'm reporting them to the state board for prosecution."

"I know who it is," she snorted. "Saul D'Luca."

The tick of the clock and slow steady beeps soothed her. Not for the first time, as she drifted off to sleep, she wished she wouldn't wake up.

* * *

SHE WOKE AGAIN, the pain raging as she reached out for the nurse-call remote tied to her bedside rail. Her first fumble for it hit the TV controller and the volume went up a notch, but she ignored it, finally grabbing hold of the device she needed. A different guard sat where Mack had been, a woman she recognized but whose name she had never bothered to learn.

The guard shifted when she realized Sonia was awake. Saying nothing, she pulled out her phone and stared down at it.

The guard's long painted fingernails tapped the screen. The light coming into the window was bright behind the closed off-white curtains. What day was it? How long had she been here?

She thought of the divorce paperwork and her last conversation with Ali. That damned paperwork could lead Saul right to Joey.

The door opened softly and a young male nurse moved in.

"How are we feeling today, Mrs. Rossi?" he asked cheerily.

She nodded, not wanting to test out her throat just yet.

"I think you need to drink some water. It will help with the sore throat." He eyed her hand laying against her throat. She nodded and leaned forward to take the fresh water off the tray. The cold liquid felt like heaven slipping down her throat and caused a coolness to spread in her chest.

"It looks like today is your last day with us. You're being transferred back to Dr. Cho," he said, scanning her chart and writing something down. "Looks like you're out of the woods."

Lucky, she thought bitterly, remembering what Mack had said.

"How long have I been here?" she asked. Her voice was brittle, like dead leaves.

"Seven days." The nurse eyed her with what she assumed was pity. "Do you need more pain medication?"

She shook her head.

"Transport's at six a.m." The female guard spoke up for the first time, snapping gum.

As Sonia rested her head back on the pillow, she imagined some way out of all this. She would never be safe while she was in the system. But her own safety wasn't really the point, after all. She was left with two warring instincts: protection or self-preservation. It could not be both.

She thought of Joey in his new life, with his new wife and baby, working some boring nine-to-five job. She missed her old queen bed and Joey's warm body lying next to hers, the lazy mornings of meaningless conversations. Five years of fear and pain, all for…what had she done it for? When she thought of those divorce papers, of Joey's foolishness in giving away his location, blowing his identity, it was as if none of what she'd suffered in those five years had done any good.

Two, four, six, eight…

"I'll be back with some Jell-O," the nurse said. "I think you should try to eat something today."

Her stomach rumbled at the mention of food, and at the same time, a news anchor on the television, perky and smiling, ruined her desire to eat:

"Authorities say the identity of the man who was tortured and murdered at his Arizona residence has not been released. According to sources, the man had assumed a new identity and may have been hiding out."

Sonia's breath caught as her eyes focused on the TV, where a large question mark on a black backdrop was displayed on half of the screen.

"Neighbors say the man was quiet and had recently moved in with his fiancé," the anchor continued. The camera cut to an interview of a man in a baseball cap, flashing blue and red lights shuttering off the backdrop of cookie-cutter houses behind him. "He was a quiet guy. Kept to himself as far as I know," the man said into the camera, his John Deere tractor hat pulled low over his eyes. "He hadn't been here too long. Maybe a year."

"No," she croaked. *Why did I have to marry such a foolish, selfish man?* "I need my lawyer," she told the guard. "I need her right away."

"Ain't happening. No one can visit you here. It isn't secure," the guard said, not even looking up from her phone. Tap. Tap. Tap.

"Please. I need her. It's important." Sonia could feel her calm dissolving, and her voice, that of a babbling child, betraying her panic.

No. This was all wrong. He couldn't be dead. But she knew, as her eyes skipped around the room, searching for some kind of help, that it was Joey. And what secrets had he unburdened himself of on his way out?

11

JAMIE

JAMIE STRETCHED against Drew's long taut frame. Past the open balcony door of their cabin, resting on the rim of Cedar Lake, flashes of sunlight danced off the surface of the water. The early morning air was saturated with the scent of lilac buds. When Drew found out it was her favorite flower, he'd planted several bushes around the cabin, saying it was an incentive for her to come around more often. Six months later they were married. Now his arms tipped back under his head and his eyes closed. He was sleeping, or at least he wanted her to think he was. She liked watching him sleep. It was a welcome distraction.

She wanted to trace his throat with her tongue, pull close into his arms and lose all her doubts in him, but she knew he wasn't the answer she needed. He was a big part of her life, yes, but he wasn't all of it. And right now, she had some sorting out to do.

She couldn't bring herself to tell him about Nina's recent calls nor the stack of letters she had hidden away in her desk at work. She didn't want to bring them home, into her personal space. She couldn't stand the thought of that filth touching this part of her life. But the vile words and the angry penned threats were eating away at her, and she knew she needed to handle it straight on. Maybe address the medical board at the institute, see if they could help her. She could burn the letters and change her number, but there was something stopping her. Guilt, real or imagined, haunted her—guilt that somehow, she was responsible for Nina's current state. And even though she knew the guilt was all in her head, she felt it just the same. It was Nina who'd decided long ago that Jamie wanted to steal the man of her dreams. She was becoming obsessed with Jamie, and the frequency of her outreach hit a fevered pitch. *You can't reason with irrational people.*

Her thoughts were interrupted by Drew's lips against hers, a moan growing in her throat as he rolled onto her. And she forgot about her guilt for a time.

Later, as Drew was making breakfast, Jamie pulled out her laptop to check her email.

"How's Butch doing?" Drew asked. Shirtless, jeans slung low, he moved with ease around the kitchen. She liked to cook, but she liked to watch him do it more. "What's so funny?" Drew asked, catching her smiling.

"Nothing. Butch is fine. Just a stent. They caught it before he had a full-blown heart attack," she mumbled. Her boss and mentor held a special place in her heart, but Butch loved pastries and bacon. It would be his downfall if he didn't gain control soon. Sure, he had promised life changes the day after being released from the hospital, but she would monitor how long these changes lasted. It didn't help matters much that Butch was nearly seventy years old and stuck in his ways.

A new email in her inbox caught her attention. Saul D'Luca's name in the subject line.

J,

Here's what I could dig up. Not much, seems this guy is very careful.

See you soon,
Butch

THERE WERE two links included in the email. The first was a news article regarding a previous employee of Saul's company, thirty-eight-year-old Devin Laskin. His official job description was Transportation Specialist. The article included the man's confession, wherein he admitted to collecting young girls at the Arizona border and driving them up to Virginia. The man said he didn't know what happened to them once they were dropped off. "I wasn't paid to be nosy. All I did was drive them up. I swear."

The second link was an obituary for the same Devin Laskin, found dead in his jail cell a week before his plea date on the charge of contributing to the delinquency of a minor. An apparent suicide at Minton County jail, according to reports.

"You have any more work that's taking you to Arlington this week?" Drew interrupted her concentration, and she looked up at him. The smell of bacon filled the room, and she felt her stomach rumble. Part of the problem was that Drew made it too easy for her to continue on the way things were. Jamie knew she was taking advantage of how easy it was to be with him, how much he loved her and supported her continuing to work out of Arlington half the week. But she wondered if it bothered him more than he let on. Perhaps she was overlooking the fact that he was a detective for the small town of Cedar Lake, and it kept him busy enough.

"I think I could be persuaded to hang around," Jamie said with a smile. Drew set a plate of eggs and bacon in front of her. "This looks great."

She should've just told him then, but her phone rang in her bag hanging from the back of her chair. She held up a finger and dipped away from the table, grateful for the interruption.

"Hello," she answered.

"Jamie, it's me, Ali. I need your help." Jamie could hear the hum of tires in the background, the whip of air through a window.

"What's up?"

"Can you meet me at Flint Hill Corrections tomorrow?" Ali's voice sounded edgy, not her normal laid-back, don't-care-what-you-think attitude, but more like when she'd skipped out on lunch the other day.

"When? What's this about?" Jamie eased into a chair on the deck facing the lake. A family of ducks paddled about, tipping into the water, their butts to the sky.

"I don't have time to talk about it now. I need your help on an appeal I'm working."

"Sure. I can be there by ten," Jamie said, looking down at her watch and frowning back in Drew's direction. So much for their romantic weekend together.

She ended the call and went back inside. "That was Ali. Something's up. I need to go to Flint Hill tomorrow morning." Jamie kissed his forehead as he chewed. He leaned into her and dropped his head to her chest as if he was listening to her heart-beat. She wanted to tell him everything in that moment, but she couldn't. The words were lodged in her throat. She didn't under-stand why she was keeping this ugly part of her life away from him. But every time she meant to bring it up, she found a reason to let it drop.

She wanted to tell him that sometimes she didn't feel safe, that she hated being away from him even for a night. She wanted to tell him she wanted a family, but she was scared. She envi-sioned the words pouring out of her and the relief she would feel. She imagined telling him she might be pregnant, but instead she kissed him softly and began to eat. She told herself the moment was gone.

12

REAGAN

LIGHT ROLLED OFF THE WATER, its reflection glinting in an undulating pattern on the ceiling above her bed. The throaty hoot of an owl saturated the silence. Reagan listened for any sign of Mason rousing from sleep in his nearby bed.

After three years on the road with Mason, she'd finally allowed them to stay in one place for over two weeks, and she still jumped at unfamiliar sounds. But not the owl. The hoot of the owl soothed her warn nerves.

They'd landed in a small coastal town in Maine, population around 10,000, hundreds of miles away from where they'd started; should the need arise for them to escape again, they were near the Canadian border. There were only two times since Mason's birth that the two of them had gone on the run, but that was because they rarely stayed in one place for too long. It was hard to catch someone or something that didn't ever stop moving.

In these distraction-free moments, Reagan found it hard not to think about her past: all the seconds, minutes, days, weeks and years she'd traveled through to be free. But she wasn't really free. And when she thought of Mason, she knew she wanted him to enjoy the stability that she never had. Not a life spent on the highway, town after town. New people always had questions, and even though she had grown to expect others' curiosity, she could never shed the familiar paranoia that germinated in her mind. In fact, it was increasing with her seemingly good fortune. Had they really managed to escape? She looked around the aging camper. It wasn't much, but the view was priceless. The ocean roiled against the shore, beating in time with her heart, and she'd learned the forest would speak to her through the haunting sounds of its inhabitants, making her feel like this could be their home.

The people hunting her would be looking for a brown-haired, brown-eyed woman traveling alone. Now she wore her platinum-blonde hair at her shoulders, and she hid her thin frame under baggy, unappealing clothes she picked up from local thrift shops. It had taken months to get used to the transformation she saw whenever she caught her faint reflection in a window or mirror.

"Mommy?" Mason's voice was sleep-filled. She heard the soft scratching of his footie pajamas crossing the cracked linoleum toward her.

"Yes, baby," she said, rolling off her bed.

"Were you crying last night?" His small hand dug into one eye as he tried to scratch the sleep away, the other eye trained on her face.

She didn't want him to worry. "I'm fine."

He lifted his arms and she picked him up, which, now that he was six years old, was becoming difficult. He got the height from his father. "What do you want to do today?"

"Do you have to work?" He rested his head against her shoulder.

"No, baby. It's just us today." She smiled as she hugged him close.

She didn't want Mason to grow up like she had, one homeless shelter to the next. State after state, wherever her mother dragged her. She attended fifty different schools before her mother abandoned her in a small town outside of Houston. Reagan knew most people suspected her mother was on the run from an abusive husband, or some other boogeyman. The truth was much less dramatic. Shelby Wilson was poor. Very poor, and even if she worked, they couldn't afford an apartment and a car on terms Shelby was willing to accept. It didn't help that her mother would impulsively buy items they didn't need and, after the evictions, had nowhere to keep.

It was their seventh night at a shelter in Texas when her mother brought up the idea of staying. "Isn't it great here?" her mother asked, her voice begging for Reagan's swift approval. The truth was it was too hot here, the people talked funny, and everything just seemed to slow down.

Reagan answered, "It's great." Only her smile felt flimsy enough to blow off her face. Her mother patted her leg. She stretched out on the cot where she'd slept for the past week. She scanned the room beyond the rows of beds lining the scuffed walls: a mother scratched her arms feverishly while her two young children played with some toys kept in the back. Reagan thought of them like Mickey and Minnie. Cute kids. Was she supposed to think like that when she was just a kid herself? She didn't think of herself as a cute kid.

Sometimes she and her mother wouldn't make it to the shelter before the doors locked at night. On those nights they would sleep in their van. She would huddle on the bench seat in the middle and her mother would recline the passenger seat all the way back so their heads nearly touched.

"Why are you crying?" Mason's voice asked, pulling her from her thoughts. His hands pushed on either side of her face as he stared at her with pouted lips.

"Something in my eye, baby." She gestured toward the kitchenette. "Hungry?"

He nodded his head, dark brown hair flopping into his eyes. She set him on the ground, and he rushed toward the kitchen.

"Time for a haircut." She grabbed her phone and followed him. "Cap'n Crunch?" she asked.

"Yes, please."

She smiled at his manners; he was such a good boy. Her mother always said that even the poor could afford manners.

The crunch of gravel under tires alerted her, and she set the bowl of cereal in front of Mason before bolting to the door. Film around the edges of the glass distorted her view of the trees and road beyond, but she could make out the big black truck pulling into the vacant campsite next door. This was the closest anyone had come to them since they'd arrived four months ago. The campsite she was renting was on the tip of a narrow peninsula surrounded by water. She looked at Mason, who was distracted with his Kindle, and then back to the door to see a man emerge from the cab of his dually truck and survey the surroundings. His eyes quickly looked her way. Reagan couldn't ignore the buzzing of fear. *It's not him, it's not Jeremy.* But she didn't like having anyone nearby.

The man opened his passenger door and a golden-haired dog jumped to the ground and immediately began exploring the site. His nose moved over the ground, his legs propelling him forward as if he couldn't move fast enough. The man looked over at her trailer, and Reagan ducked away from the window. She wasn't sure if he could see her through the film, but she didn't want to get caught looking. Her heart beat faster as she imagined him lumbering over and demanding to know who she thought she was, spying on him. But nothing happened, and when she gathered the courage to look again, the man had his back to her.

She sat on the small bench seat at the table with Mason and pulled out her phone. This morning, like every other morning, she did an internet search: she typed in *Sonia Rossi*.

No news popped up. Relieved, she typed in the next name. *Joey Rossi.*

The headline read: *Arizona Man Murdered: A man now identified as Joey Rossi was found murdered in his home last week in Scottsdale, Arizona.*

Reagan's hand flew up to her lips and smothered a cry. She rushed to the door again and looked out. The man from the next campsite over smiled from the other side, only inches away.

13

SONIA

JOEY WAS DEAD. Sonia had long ago surrendered to the fact that she would never touch him, kiss him, or be held by him again. But knowing he was no longer on the earth magnified the grief she harbored under the surface, in a place she refused to recognize because it made her vulnerable. With each passing day in prison her confidence that Joey had escaped Saul grew, but now she had to stop kidding herself: no one got away from him. The bitter whisper inside of her knew it was those damned divorce papers. Love had killed Joey, again. That meant someone at Ali's office was helping Saul, maybe a law clerk Saul kept on the payroll to keep an eye out for anything addressed to Sonia.

She hit the button for her bed and adjusted herself into an upright position. It was morning. The birth of a new day fell in golden rays beyond the window. The rough clack of a gurney moved down the hall, followed by the squeak of sensible shoes on polished floors. Sonia had been awake for hours, listening to the hushed voices outside her room.

Since seeing the news broadcast last night, she'd thought of little else. How long had the pain lasted for Joey? She was numb, unable to process the full extent of what had happened, but she knew what she needed to do next. The thought caused a swell of stomach acid to churn in her empty stomach.

Scanning the table near her bed, she saw the notebook and pen she'd asked for. She'd tried writing the letter the night before, but her mind was sluggish from the medication. She should have gone back to prison this morning, but the doctor at the hospital wanted to monitor her for one more day.

Sonia leaned forward and was met with a stab of pain emanating from her right hip. Air hissed from her lips as she reached for the paper and, once she grabbed it, she fell heavily back onto the pillow with a dampened thunk.

She'd suffered a long laceration on her abdomen. The doctors told her it was not life threatening, but this information made it no less painful. It was just like Saul to go above and beyond for his precious daughter's birthday—something for Sonia to remember Emma by. What he didn't understand was that Sonia had loved her too, and not because they were forced together by their parents' marriage. She missed the lilting sound of Emma's voice, her contagious laugh, and her unabashed advice.

The smell of cleaning agents and sterile surfaces reminded Sonia of being at the doctor's office years before, when Emma had been waking in the recovery room after her sedation was wearing off. The surgery was a success, the doctors told Sonia. Emma made it through, and they would soon learn if it worked. They were alone, but the muted voices of staff through the door could be heard. Emma, stirring in the bed, looked pale and sleep-haunted, and Sonia felt tears pushing against the back of her eyes as she looked down at her.

"How'd it go?" Emma asked weakly. "Did it work?"

Sonia picked up her hand and squeezed it gently. "It's done."

"We can't tell Dad," she said dreamily; her movements were slow and deliberate. "He can't ever find out."

Sonia nodded. "I promise."

Two months later, Emma was dead.

Sonia stared down at the blank paper. Could she really do this? No more self-righteous indignation to haul around. She would be just as bad as those who harmed her. Worse, even.

She thought of Joey and the last piece of him she had left, and penned a name. Below it, a request, or favor really, followed by information she had committed to memory.

By the time she was done, tears were rolling down to splatter on her shaking fingers. She folded the slip of paper and tucked it into her pillow. She had written it, but that meant nothing. She could hold onto it forever if she decided to. She pictured the paper growing thin and feather-like over time, its black ink fading into blotches of blue like a note found in the pocket of a freshly-washed pair of jeans. She hit the call button.

"How are you feeling today, Mrs. Rossi?" the nurse asked, coming around the sheet pulled around her bed. On the other side sat the female guard she recognized from the other night, the one who had looked in on her cell. She was pale, her nails polished blood-red, contrasting the gray polo shirt she wore. A splinter of light caught on her copper-colored hair, which she'd clearly tried to dye blond. But the dye job couldn't cover up her natural brown color. She stared at Sonia from her seat, unsmiling.

"I could use some more meds, please," Sonia said to the nurse.

"Sure. I was wondering what took you so long." The nurse moved around her bed with a chart in hand, pulling out a sort of key she plugged into the back of a machine. She began typing. "Other than the pain, how are you feeling? Dizzy, sick? I can get you whatever you need." The nurse's soft, round face looked on her with pity.

Sonia spoke as low as she could but doubted the guard could not hear. "Can I get an envelope?"

Sonia's gaze shifted to the guard, who was looking down at her phone again, seemingly unconcerned by the request.

"Sure, sweetie. Let me see what I can find. It might have the hospital's information on it. Is that okay?"

She nodded. "That will be fine, thanks."

The nurse finished up and left, pulling the curtain back around Sonia's bed. A moment later, the guard's shadow approached and pulled it back. "I'd rather have this open," she said. Freckles stained the skin under her green eyes. Her voice was uncertain, unlike most of the other guards at Flint Hill, who used their authority with few boundaries. She sounded conflicted.

Sonia only nodded and put her head back down on her pillow.

"So, who did this to you?" the guard asked.

Sonia turned her eyes on the woman and tried not to smirk. "You must be new."

The guard, whose nametag read "Shaffer", looked back down at her phone but continued speaking. "I'm new to Flint Hill, but not new to corrections. I came from Red Onion." Red Onion was a high security men's prison in Virginia. Not a place Sonia imagined anyone would want to go, let alone this seemingly fragile woman. Sonia assumed she couldn't have had a great experience there based on her looks alone; she was a wholesome kind of beauty, minus the awful dye job.

"Well, I would expect you not to ask silly questions, then. It could get worse for me."

"I get it. But by the looks of you, you may not have another chance. Someone really wants you gone." She took her seat in the corner again, looking over at Sonia. "What did you do to deserve this?"

"You question is presumptuous."

"So, what was it?"

"I guess because I'm still alive." Her voice was so low and broken she almost didn't recognize it herself: it was an echo rising from somewhere inside of her rather than a conscious thought put to words.

"Sometimes that's enough for some people. Guess you killed your husband's lover?"

Obviously, the guard knew more than she let on.

Just then the nurse rounded the corner and handed Sonia an envelope bearing the hospital's insignia.

"What's that for?" the guard asked, standing and making her way to the bed.

"I wrote a letter to my attorney." A lie.

The guard's brow furrowed, and she grabbed the envelope to check for any illicit content. Just an envelope. "Fine." She handed the envelope back to Sonia and returned to her seat.

Sonia pulled the letter out and folded it to fit, then scribbled Ali's name on the face of the envelope, just in case. They weren't allowed to read any attorney/client mail. She folded the flap down and licked it. An ominous feeling moved over her. She might never send the letter out. Better to have it and not need it, but she knew deep down that she would do what needed to be done.

14

JAMIE

FLINT HILL CORRECTIONS was built in the early 1990s to help with overcrowding that had facilities popping up all over the place. State-run, its chafed yellow brick looked dull and unkept, and shiny gates topped with barbed wire surrounded several structures on the nearly ten-acre plot. It was an all-women's penitentiary housing some of the most dangerous women in the state. Home to Sonia Rossi, daughter of a dry cleaner from Arlington, who pleaded guilty to the murder of her husband's mistress five years ago.

Jamie parked her car in the visitor's area.

She had reviewed the email Ali'd sent her last evening to learn more about Sonia Rossi.

But nothing could prepare her for the first impression she got of Sonia when she entered the prison's infirmary and saw Sonia's tiny frame, half-covered in rumpled sheets. Soiled gauze patched recent injuries all over her body and her eyes were sunken and bruised. A nose, recently broken, swelled from what had once been a delicate feature. She was an Italian beauty who now looked more like an extra on the set of *The Walking Dead*. The picture of Sonia that was attached to Ali's recent email looked nothing like the woman lying before her. Today she would have to set aside her immediate sense of pity for this dreadfully injured woman to see what she could observe to assist Ali.

Jamie took the empty seat next to Ali, whose chair was pulled up to the bed.

"This is Jamie Kendal," Ali said to Sonia. "She's going to be helping me with your appeal."

Jamie tried to smile, but it seemed an insensitive gesture in the presence of such suffering. Sonia looked back at her, appraising.

"Hi," Sonia said and turned back to Ali.

"I knew the second I saw those papers this was going to be trouble," Ali said with a knowing shake of her head.

Sonia nodded, folding the edge of the sheet against her index finger. "He always thought he was lucky." Jamie followed Sonia's gaze to a colorful bag hanging next to the doctor, who was working at her desk. "Not lucky in love," Sonia said mournfully.

Ali nodded. "It's him. Tortured and murdered. I would bet my life it was Saul."

"I know it was him." Sonia looked at Jamie with narrowed eyes. "I need protection now. And I need an appeal. Work as quickly as you can. I need to get out of here." The way she spoke was not panicked nor off the cuff. She didn't seem frightened, but exhibited the raw determination of someone putting a plan into action.

Ali was nodding, but Jamie was only confused. Ali hadn't shared how Jamie fit into all of this yet.

"There are some things I can do about your living conditions, but the Warden is a pain in my ass," Ali said. "What grounds are you moving to appeal your conviction?" Her brows met together as she withdrew a legal pad and pen from her bag. A guard who sat soundlessly in the corner perked up at the sight of the writing implement. Perhaps they were fearful that this tiny, broken woman would fight her way free from these walls with an ink pen and her courage.

"Because I didn't kill Emma D'Luca," Sonia said, keeping her eyes level on Ali, seeming to anticipate the reaction that the words would provoke from her attorney. She was right.

"What?" Ali said, her mouth falling open as her pen dropped from her hand, skittering to the floor.

"I didn't kill her, and I have proof," Sonia said, rubbing a rough fingernail against the stiff sheets covering her legs.

"What do you mean, you have proof? Why the hell did you plead guilty?" Ali motioned toward her broken body. "Go through all this…for what?"

"It wasn't for nothing," Sonia said with clear conviction.

Ali's disgusted sigh broke the growing awkward silence.

"I didn't kill her."

"Joey?" Jamie said before she realized she'd uttered the name out loud. She'd heard enough confessions, conducted enough polygraphs, to assume the circumstances. This woman was protecting someone with a determination Jamie had seldom seen before. "You were protecting him," she added as Ali turned to look at her and then back at Sonia, still in shock.

"Is this true?" Ali shook her head. "Because if it is, you don't seem to know what this process is going to entail. You may stay here. They may not accept this. Why—" But she stopped speaking, abruptly stood and started pacing the small space, her heels clicking loudly.

"Why didn't you tell me?" Ali finally demanded.

Sonia frowned and then shrugged. "You have an ethical obligation to represent me. You wouldn't have let me take the fall for someone else."

"You're damned right I wouldn't," Ali snapped back. "All this time. All these years."

Voices in the hall carried past them as a group of inmates shuffled by, their curious eyes looking in.

"They weren't wasted," Sonia said. "But let's get this done. I need to move forward now—today. I need to get out of here, or the next time—" She motioned to her body. "I might not make it. It's not safe here anymore."

"What's our plan?" Jamie asked, less affected by Sonia's declaration than Ali was. "What do you need me to do?" Jamie glanced at Ali, who had the look of someone calculating the success of an appeal or maybe formulating a plan to carry it out.

"I'll start the paperwork on the appeal and pray we get an open-minded judge," Ali said. "This is going to be a mess. I have Javi on staff to help with research and I.T., and Ms. Ming—she's my P.I. I'm going to need to know everything." Ali's eyes appraised Sonia. "Starting with why the hell you would confess to a murder you didn't commit."

15

SONIA

THE DAY EMMA DIED.

Sonia recalled the heat that day. She'd been crouching in her garden in the back yard, yanking weeds between rows of tomato plants, their earthy, metallic scent wafting to her nose, when her phone rang. She pulled off her gloves to answer. "Hey there."

Emma's loud, overwrought voice answered. "Can you come here right away?"

"What's up? What's going on?" Sonia asked, already moving toward the house. Keys, keys, keys. Where were the damned keys? She kicked off her gardening Crocs and pulled on sneakers. Emma's house wasn't far, but whatever it was sounded urgent, and driving would save time.

"It's Saul. I can't believe this is happening," Emma said. *Why was she calling her dad by his first name?* She used to reserve the name for rare occasions, but seemed to be calling him 'Saul' much more often recently.

"Stay on the phone with me. Tell me what's going on," Sonia demanded, her blood pounding in her ears. She heard a muffled sound and a gasp, like air hissing from a leaky tire. Then the phone disconnected.

Sonia looked down at the screen of her phone and cursed. She redialed Emma's number several times on the short drive over, but Emma didn't answer. Parking the car hastily in a visitor's spot, she yanked at the keys to get them out of the ignition, forgetting to put the car in park; the keys wouldn't budge. She slammed the car into park and, fumbling with the keys, dropped them in the footwell as her mind was screaming *You don't have time for this.*

Dashing up the front steps, she tripped and fell to her knees. Her bare skin scraped the second step, blood immediately dripping against the pale gray cement. "Ahh!" she cried in frustration, pulling herself up and cupping her knee with a hand. She hobbled up the last steps to the front door, only then noticing that it was cracked open.

She looked behind her at the neighborhood. Kids were playing on the sidewalk, drawing colorful pictures with chalk. An old woman swept her porch and watched Sonia with an uneasy expression.

She drew in a deep breath.

"Emma!" she called into the silent house. She pushed the door open with one hand and looked around the living room. It was clean, and nothing seemed out of place at first, but then she noticed a tiny trail of blood drops on the white carpet. "Emma, are you okay?"

Sonia's heartbeat cracked through her chest as Gemini, Emma's Yorkie, shot out of the kitchen. Blood smeared his coat and hung to the tufts of his fur. He ran past her and out the open front door before she could grab him. For a split second, she was torn between catching him and walking deeper into the house.

"Emma! It's Sonia." Her voice was pleading now as she rounded the door into the kitchen. Emma lay face up, permanently fixed toward heaven. Her eyes were closed and her pretty face looked peaceful, but the rest of her body was a grotesque

79

display of violence. Saul D'Luca's only daughter lay in a pool of her own blood.

Sonia rushed to her and found herself slipping on the blood-covered floor. Before she could stop herself she was throwing up, narrowly missing the nearby garbage can. Police! She needed to call the police.

A singsong voice came from the doorway, causing Sonia to jump as she looked up. "Emma, look who I found wandering outside. I think he got into some trash—" the woman stopped abruptly when she rounded the corner and let out a scream when her eyes caught sight of Sonia over Emma's body.

"Please call 911," Sonia begged, but the woman was running from the house. Sonia realized only then what the scene must have looked like to this woman. She later learned the woman had agreed to testify that Sonia was at the house and that she probably killed Emma. Sonia's instinct to run had been right.

Sonia blinked the memory away as she looked between Ali and Jamie. "I know this sounds bad for me, but I didn't do it. She was already dead."

Jamie finally broke the silence as Ali processed the information. "You said you had evidence."

"I can get some. As soon as you get me out of here, that is," Sonia corrected.

"What?" Ali blurted, her forehead creased. "Joey did it?"

Sonia was shaking her head. "No. Not Joey." Sonia didn't think Joey had it in him to kill anyone. "He had no reason to kill her, and neither did I." Sonia took a drink of water and pulled herself up to a sitting position. "I knew what it would look like. That's why I ran." She hoped they heard conviction in her voice and not guilt.

"Then who killed her?"

"I don't know. But it wasn't me. I'll take a polygraph. There is no evidence I killed her. No murder weapon, no fingerprints near her."

"There was a murder weapon at the scene. You walked in her blood; they found your footprints in other parts of the house," Ali fired off. Working out the prosecution's case, playing devil's advocate.

Sonia pictured the big black-handled steak knife jutting up... staggering up the stairs, searching.

"You were seen leaving her house. Your blood was on the steps. You pled guilty!" Ali was fully exasperated now. "Saul believes you did it."

"Because Saul needed to believe the killer was caught. Because I was a patsy to save someone else. I don't know who killed Emma, but it wasn't me. Now I need you to help me prove it. Before I die in here."

"What changed?" Jamie asked, her head tilted to one side. "Why now?"

Sonia felt Jamie's intense gaze on her and wondered if this wasn't a mistake. Had she done the wrong thing yet again? "Listen, I don't know who I can trust. But I trust you, Ali." Sonia turned her gaze on her friend. "You've known me almost my entire life. You know my family. I didn't do this, but I had to do what I did."

"But you can't tell me why?" Ali said.

"Why I ran?"

"Yes."

"I ran because I knew what it looked like. I called Joey, and he told me cops were at the house and they knew about Emma. He told me to run."

Ali stared back at her.

"He knew Saul would kill me even if I was found not guilty. I couldn't risk you calling Joey out of hiding to testify and put him in danger too."

"You're protecting someone," Jamie said.

Sonia ignored her. "I was meant to die the other night. Saul must not think I'm worth keeping around anymore." Sonia was reminded of a little neighbor boy who played with bugs under a magnifying glass, and the tiny, charred carcasses he left behind. Perhaps, after pulling off her wings and burning her with the sun, Saul had grown bored. Or maybe he knew her secret after torturing Joey for the truth, and no longer needed her.

* * *

THE ONE THING she missed the most about freedom was the musky smell of summer flowers blowing off the wind. She closed her eyes and felt the warm sun stroke her face, and saw the clouds, soft and white, dotting the sky above. But it was the harsh lights of the prison infirmary that she woke to. Her dream of freedom was a long shot. Ali was right: Sonia's chances didn't look good.

She could hear the Warden's nasal voice carrying down the hall but couldn't decipher what he was saying. Footsteps grew closer. She could recognize most of her dorm guards by the way they walked, the sound their loose keys made smacking their legs, the cadence of their steps. One in particular she always paid close attention to. She heard those footsteps now, walking toward her.

Mack, with his tall, sinewy frame, filled the doorway. Blood marred his cheek, and he glanced at her. A smirk on his face, like he had joined a club.

Dr. Cho looked up from her work. "Fight in Cell Block D?" she asked, standing up. He nodded. "Have a seat," said Dr. Cho. "I'll get you cleaned up."

A moment later the Warden crept through the door. His pervasive gaze traveled over the room and caught sight of Mack.

"Get cleaned up and write that report," he ordered Mack, who nearly ignored his presence. Then he turned his gaze to Sonia. "Mrs. Rossi. My favorite inmate. You're getting ready to move back to general pop. It looks like you're healed up enough.

Moving around?" It didn't seem like he cared for an answer, so she just looked at him. The Warden peered behind him and back to Sonia. "I see you had a visit from your lawyer today," he said with feigned disinterest. He rubbed the bare stubble on his chin and the chafing sound caused an irrational irritation to ignite in her, akin to the way she often felt when she overheard lip-smacking or soup-slurping in the cafeteria. She wanted so badly to tell him it was none of his business—just get out of here. But she bit it back and watched Dr. Cho turn back to cleaning Mack's wound.

"She thinks you need extra protection," the Warden went on. "Threatened a lawsuit, if you can believe it." He snorted. But Sonia saw a flicker of fear in his eyes. He might not think about taxpayer dollars lost, but a lawsuit was a black mark on his reputation, though whether he cared about what others thought of him was unclear.

Still Sonia stayed quiet and listened.

"What are you up to?" he asked in a low tone, his eyes moving over her injuries. "You have a lawsuit set up?"

Ha. Was this guy for real? "What?" Sonia asked, unable to hide her contempt. But she wanted to needle him a little. "The discussions I have with my lawyer are none of your business." She had tried being nice to this guy, and it had gotten her nowhere. She was out of patience. His eyes narrowed on her, and he tilted his head, moving even closer.

"You need to be very careful," he said, so softly she barely heard it herself; she was sure the others didn't hear his threat, but she watched Mack's eyes swing between the two of them, obviously confused by what was taking place.

"Dr. Cho. I think Mrs. Rossi is healed up enough for now. You will do a last check in the morning. She has a new celly she needs to meet." As the Warden spoke, his eyes never left hers. Sonia swallowed back a lump. Great. Moving the devil right in.

With that, the Warden turned on his scuffed brown wingtips and left the room.

"You're all fixed up," Dr. Cho said to Mack.

He stood quickly. "Thanks, Doc," he said, and left without another word.

Sonia pulled herself up in her bed, wincing. Now it would be impossible to protect herself against these women. Her goal had always been to avoid the confrontations, not win them. Winning almost guaranteed the force would be worse the next time. Her idea of what prison would be like before she came here was way off base: it was far worse than she could have imagined.

Dr. Cho moved to her bedside, a sad look on her face. Sonia shrugged at her, unable to do much else. Dr. Cho surveyed her injuries quietly, changing out the soiled gauze and dressing them with deft hands, neither woman stating the obvious: that no one here was going to protect her.

16

SONIA

Sonia was reading at her usual table in the library the following day when she heard Harriet's voice. "I see they got you back in gen pop."

"Just where the Warden wants me, I guess."

Sonia couldn't remember exactly when her friendship with Harriet had begun. It was based on a common love of books and had grown into a sort of maternal relationship. Harriet's natural instinct to nurture those around her was hard to ignore, even for someone as unreachable as Sonia. It woke a need for compassion she had been starving since coming here.

"You ain't gonna die here."

"And neither are you." Sonia shifted to stare at her. "You hear anything back from the appeal?"

The old woman shook her head. "Nah. Nothing yet. But I got a good feeling that maybe this is the year I hold my grandbabies."

This woman didn't deserve to be here. Was justice blind? Did the law demand twenty-plus years for the girlfriend of a drug dealer who got caught holding his drugs? Or was the law so unbending that many good people were still in jail twenty years

85

later for something that people nowadays got probation for? Sonia had never considered these issues until she'd known Harriet, and suddenly injustice had a face, a name, dreams and memories, both good and bad, that formed a human being.

"Tell me about them," Sonia said, putting the book in her lap and giving Harriet her full attention.

"Kevin will be two years old this year." A rare smile moved over Harriet's face. "And Robert will be seven."

"Boys, huh?" What would it be like to never hug one's child again, or never once snuggle your own grandbaby? Harriet was a young mother to a three-year-old boy when she was locked up. With no family willing or able to step up, he was placed in foster care. The new family couldn't find the time to bring her son to see his mother for over ten years. She had missed ten birthdays, yearly holidays and some of the most precious years of her young son's life. In her usual gracious manner, she always said she was thankful her son had found a suitable home, but there was a pain inside her eyes from which Sonia recoiled.

"How's your son?"

Harriet nodded. "He and his wife are doing great. He graduated with his degree in business and I.T. They're doing really well. I don't know how much I like her, but I'm just a prickly old lady." She smiled, revealing her lie.

"You're a great mother and grandmother. We're going to get you out of here," Sonia said. She was not sure how she'd follow through, but she knew she would never give up on this woman. "Let's wait and see what they say about your appeal."

"It's the fourth letter I've sent," Harriet said with one corner of her mouth pinched up.

She was right. The thought made Sonia angry: Harriet had taken the time to write out the letters and research her options, and yet someone might never take the time to read them, despite all the things she'd done since being here, things that made her a better person and more productive to society. Who said she wasn't worth a chance? Was her letter resting in an endless pile of appeals on the desk of some judge, someone who might pick their next charity case at random from the pile? She hoped and prayed that, for Harriet's sake, this wasn't how the system worked.

"What about you? Any children?" Harriet asked.

Sonia didn't like to share parts of herself with others. Especially painful parts. The memory of negative pregnancy tests, doctors' examinations and finally an unwelcome prognosis were topics that had no place in the normal shallow conversations in which she usually engaged. Through it all, Sonia had told herself she didn't care; she was fine. Maybe she didn't even want the responsibility of being a mother. But then why did it hurt so much?

Harriet worked away at cracking her open like a clam, asking little questions here and there. This was a big one, though, and Sonia wasn't expecting it.

She shook her head. "I can't have children." The undercurrent of pain was clear in her tone as she shifted her eyes away from the woman, as if continuing to look at her was like staring into the sun.

Sonia remembered big dinners on Sundays with her sister and parents when her dad was still alive. Before Saul had forced his way into their lives. Parties and family reunions, memories bursting with flavor and bold colors and genuine joy. When she and Joey had gone to the fertility specialist and they told her that her body wasn't up to the task, her heart had shattered. Of course, the doctor had phrased it differently, but that's what she'd heard. It was a wonder Joey even stayed with her. He told her that night that he had an idea, but he had to work out the details before telling her more about it.

She felt the old woman's hand on her shoulder and she was jolted by the overwhelming realization that it was the first caring touch she'd experienced in years, since Ali had hugged her goodbye after Sonia's sentencing back in that packed courtroom. For a long time, she hadn't acknowledged that prison was killing her in more ways than one. She felt the tears building in the back of her eyes and swiped at them with the rough sleeve of her jumpsuit.

Harriet said nothing, just walked away, giving Sonia the space she needed.

Suddenly, a shadow flickered from the corner of her eye. Mack was leaning against a shelf, talking with the freckle-faced guard from the hospital. He was smiling, and when his eyes caught Sonia's he looked away quickly. Like he had just been caught doing something wrong.

Sonia limped over to the shelf where Dumas was nestled among the Ds. It would appear this new guard and Mack were here together. An emotion, unused and forgotten, twitched. Why would he go for her? Though if Sonia was being honest, there were plenty of reasons. How about she wasn't a convict. That was a solid reason. How about she wasn't accused of and hadn't pleaded guilty to killing her husband's lover. Add that to the pros column.

Sonia hadn't told Mack that she was appealing and wondered if the scuttlebutt was going around about it yet. She didn't care who knew, it was immaterial, but she knew she should have told him. He had been such a good friend to her, but she was confident he would have done the same for anyone.

She pulled the book back through the drag marks from its resting place on the shelf.

She worked the pages until she found the note and, without reading it, tucked it away in her bra as she looked around for anyone who might be watching. The library was quiet. Harriet had taken her place near the front, not acknowledging Sonia as she passed. Mack and Freckles had disappeared. Even though the Warden wouldn't give Sonia protective custody, she was assigned guards for her walks to and from laundry and the library on days they could spare the added protection. As if it was a nice thing to do—Warden of the year. The problem lay in which of the guards wouldn't hang her out to dry on a bad day to one of these women who suddenly had a commissary full of money. Thanks to Mack's notes, she knew when to be more aware.

She passed two lines of women on their way to rec, most of whom ignored her as she limped along. The dorm was loud: two card games were going, curse words being shouted regularly, and the players who sat hunched around tables slammed or threw down their cards as the hand came to an end. One woman in particular followed Sonia's gait with her eyes. Since returning to the dorm, Sonia'd been trying to figure out who had instigated the latest attack. As much discomfort as it brought her, she played the scene over and over in her mind, trying to recall any tiny detail she might have initially missed. Nothing came to her. And she was resigned to the fact that she may never know.

Once inside her cell, she lay back on her bunk, facing the open doorway. She pulled the paper from her bra and opened it.

She expected a cryptic note or warning. Maybe a joke or a riddle. But what she found sent a swirl of something through her gut. It was a letter. Not unlike what a man might send a regular woman. Maybe even someone he liked.

As usual, no names were used in greeting or signature.

HI THERE,

I had to get this off my chest. I heard about the attack in the middle of my shift. I can't tell you what I was thinking because I just didn't know. How much longer are you going to go through this? How much can you take? They can move you to another facility. Someplace safer than Flint Hill. You have no friends here.

I know he has it out for you and I know there are others who are not on your side, but don't throw it all away. You act like you have nothing to live for. You do. I want you to know you have a lot to live for, and I wish I could tell you—tell you what that is.

I'm not mad at you. I'm angry at myself for not paying more attention. And I'm working on something, so don't you dare give up.

HEAT MOVED into Sonia's cheeks as she deposited the letter between the mattress and sheet. When she rolled over, she was comforted by the soft crackle of paper. She wanted to tell him she wasn't giving up, either. Not yet. She lay back on the mattress, her body exhausted.

Since her new cellmate, Tammie, had arrived, just as the Warden had promised, the only peace she had in her days had been stolen. Even at night she found herself stymied. She was forced to ignore the impulse to check her door at night and instead stared over at the painting she had moved next to her pillow, searching the folds of color for the hidden faces. Mack's newly forming image was a swirl of deep purple and silver specks.

THE NEXT MORNING, Sonia heard the barred doors roll open in her cell block. Tammie shoved out of bed and shuffled to the door without a word, Sonia just behind her, joining the women who began forming a straight line. Quiet chatter rose as the Warden walked down the row, glancing into cells as he passed. Random inspections.

He pulled up to Sonia and his coffee breath blasted her nose and sent stray hairs flapping against her face. His thinning hair looked greasy, and a dull yellow stained the pits of his white button-down shirt in the harsh light.

"Mrs. Rossi. I hope you're well." He looked behind him at two female COs. "Toss it." And they both advanced into her space.

They lifted her mattress, pulled at her paintings, and searched every visible surface without a word nor a care of how things were left. It didn't take long before one of the female COs brought out the letter from Mack. She had been so stupid to keep it. The Warden smiled as he took the note and scanned it. His face was unreadable, but his temples turned dark pink as he read.

"Who's your pen pal?" he asked, looking up at her.

"It's anonymous," Sonia said, without keeping the petulance from her tone. She had never become accustomed to other people going through her things. Touching them, throwing them around without care, invading her privacy. Nope. It never got easier.

He looked at her as if he wanted to say something, maybe spit in her face, but he chose instead a crocodile smile, revealing the yellow stains on his incisors. "I'll hold on to this," he said, stuffing the paper into his pocket.

"For what reason?"

"Contraband."

"That's a lie," she snapped. The two officers flanking him shifted toward her, ready to act on command. Maybe throw her in the hole for a few days. But that would be a blessing and he knew it, and so he smirked at her and moved on down the line.

"Make sure you write this up," he said to the female on his left, and she nodded. "No rec for a week."

A sinking feeling collapsed in her belly and her hunger disappeared. Not because of the lost rec time, but because she worried about whether Warden Gibson would be able to figure out who Mack was from the letter.

Sonia's fingers curled into her palm as she watched them walk away, but before she could do something stupid, the line shifted toward the cafeteria where they would get breakfast. The lunchroom was Sonia's least favorite place in prison. There were too many bodies pressed in all directions, some watching her, while others whispered in the corners. She had no protection out in the open and no one to watch her back. She'd suffered six of her twelve attacks here.

A harsh whisper came from behind her. Bobbi, a mousy meth-head with whom she had tussled with a few times, stood next to her. Scabs stretched over the visible skin on her arms and her eyes were constantly darting around. Bobbi wasn't a threat, but she did what she was told. Her casual attitude toward Sonia suggested a long life of petty crime.

"Hey, bitch," Bobbi whispered, almost eager, like she couldn't wait to talk to Sonia. Her tone was pleasant, like how you might address a friend whose name was Bitch. "They're watching you."

"Tell me something I don't know," Sonia shot back. The pain in her hip burned down her leg as she limped quickly to keep the line moving. She didn't have time for Bobbi today.

"I'll tell you something you don't know if you get me some cigarettes," she said.

"You're kidding, right?" Sonia felt her breath suspend and just as abruptly start again. "I don't need what you're selling. And I have no friends."

"Oh, you have a friend all right." Sonia recognized the game as Bobbi kept step with her. It didn't matter what Sonia told this tweaker, Bobbi would stab her in the back the first chance she got—but first, Bobbi would try to get something out of it. Sonia had no friends, and everyone knew that—except.

Bobbi watched Sonia's fear register on her face and she gave a tilted smile. "Everyone's got a friend," she teased. Her nails scratched down her arms, the sound amplified by her vigor, like she was rubbing herself with sandpaper. It would appear that Bobbi's payment had come early, and in the form of her favorite high.

When the chatter around them grew louder as the group walked in lockstep, Sonia finally said, "What do you want?"

"I already told you what I want. Some smokes."

"No, I mean why are you talking to me? I have nothing for you," Sonia snapped, losing all patience. She wanted this woman to get on with her threats so she could force down some gelatinous breakfast and move on with her monotonous day.

"I wanted to tell you everyone has friends, that's all. Maybe you need to watch your friends, ya know, keep them close."

Them?

"Maybe bad things happen to people when you're not looking. Like that fine-ass piece of meat you're always watching."

Sonia's head snapped around in time to see a wide grin on Bobbi's face. She wanted to slap it off, teach her a lesson. So that Bobbi would learn she couldn't just walk up to people and threaten them like a recorded greeting card. There were consequences. She pictured sucker-punching Bobbi right in the nose; even if the team of women behind her joined Bobbi's side and beat Sonia bloody, she would at least get in one good shot.

"What do you want?" Sonia could feel her fingers curl into fists. "I don't have any smokes."

"I just wanted to remind you we all have friends and to give you a message."

Sonia's heart tripped in her chest.

"He knows your little secret," Bobbi whispered as the line abruptly stopped. Sonia froze. "And he isn't going to stop until you give him what he wants, what's his."

Then she was gone. Passing her as Sonia's feet refused to move with the line. Women behind her shouldered their way past her as she stood in their way. *What's his.*

17

JAMIE

JAMIE CLEARED her head with the brisk seven-block walk from her office to Ali's. She had pawned off some of her work to Natalie and explained the situation to Butch, then informed Drew that her work would keep her in Arlington for at least one more night. He didn't complain, which somehow made her feel worse. Yes, she had married him, but she hadn't settled down yet.

After exiting the elevator, she was ushered into a large conference room where coffee and cherry pastries were arranged. Ali was flanked by two people near the broad windows filled with the city's backdrop. One, a young man in his mid-twenties sitting behind a computer, looked up briefly to acknowledge her. He wore Buddy Holly glasses perched under wide black eyebrows above a neatly trimmed beard. The other was an older Asian woman clad in all black. Her delicate features were marred with age and her stare was unassuming.

"Glad you could make it," Ali said. Jamie examined her watch to be sure she wasn't later than the agreed upon 9:00 a.m. It would seem they'd gotten an early start, or maybe, given her rumpled appearance and glassy eyes, Ali had slept at the office. "This is Ming—she's my private investigator."

The older woman's mouth twitched into a smile and she gave a gentle nod.

"This is Javi, my I.T. and research assistant. These are our current resources until I know exactly what we are looking for and if we need to bring more people in on this. I would prefer, given what we're dealing with, to keep the team small."

Jamie grabbed one of the bottles of orange juice from the table and took her seat.

Ali looked down at some papers and began. "This case is highly sensitive. I don't want anyone discussing it outside this group. Saul's reach is far and wide. I don't know how he's going to react when he finds out about Sonia's appeal. We can assume it will be just as soon as I file the paperwork later today. He was heavily involved with her prosecution. This may trigger him. Also, I need to add that each of you is agreeing to a risk by joining this case. Feel free to step away if you need to. Saul D'Luca is well known for his ruthless behavior and retaliation methods. We believe Joey Rossi was killed at his order."

They all nodded.

Ali turned to Javi. "Hit it."

Keeping his eyes on his computer, he spoke in a deep, resonant voice. "Saul owns three businesses, all in Virginia. Two consulting firms and a management company. He has connections at the local and federal levels. This may be why there is almost no scrutiny on his businesses. He owns property in four U.S. states and in a few different countries. He divorced his second wife, Julie Angelo, two years ago. Emma was his only child, but his stepdaughter, Nikki Angelo, is said to be involved in some aspects of his work. They are apparently close."

"What about prostitution?" Jamie asked.

Ming's brow raised, and Ali looked to Javi.

"Nothing public, but I wouldn't expect it to be common knowledge if he was involved." Javi's fingers moved with dexterity over the keyboard. "There was, however, a fire at a property in Southern Virginia, a farm. Looks like it was the same year Emma was murdered." His brow furrowed. "It was only a few days before, in fact."

"Cause?" Ming asked.

"Faulty wiring."

"Who reported it?" Jamie asked.

"A neighbor. There was no one at the house, but according to a source of mine in the FBI they were grooming a witness against Saul having something to do with the presence of children at this house."

Ali nodded. "I can get the ball rolling on this, but I think the best way to help Sonia win her appeal is to find out what really happened to Emma D'Luca. I have the details she gave yesterday, and I think we should compare that to the reports." Ali pointed down at several stacks of paper, looking exasperated. Ali was single-minded when she caught a case and was probably already aware of inconsistencies in the reports.

"Because Sonia took a plea, there was only a summary of the evidence at her hearing. I think we should consider that everything the police did after Sonia's confession might be sloppy. I want to go through everything and find out what's true." Ali took a deep breath. "What we know: Emma D'Luca was stabbed to death on July 16, 2013. Two witnesses, fingerprints, and blood put Sonia at the scene. Her cellphone pinged off a tower in the area of Emma's townhouse. According to Sonia, she received a call from Emma that drew her to the house and Emma was in some sort of distress but didn't tell Sonia what was going on. By the time Sonia got there, Emma was already dead."

"It would have only been ten minutes or so," Jamie added.

"There was something." Ali skimmed through the pile of papers. "There was a second blood type in the upstairs bathroom. They couldn't match the blood to either Emma or Sonia, only determined it was female."

The killer?

"Motive," Ali continued. "We need to find out why someone would want to kill her. Then we find our killer. Whoever did it was either very smart about it or didn't fear retaliation from Saul."

"Do you think she's telling the truth?" Ming asked, looking at Jamie. Her voice was much more commanding than her stature. Ali had told Jamie of Ming's background, but Jamie was still surprised by how much her Chinese accent had worn away after all her years in the States. She was granted asylum from the Chinese government nearly twenty years ago, and according to Ali, she had spent most of those years in Boston with extended family.

"I won't know until I talk with her more," Ali replied. "My first impression is that she's desperate. It's hard to judge from that."

Ming nodded.

"This isn't going to be an easy appeal," Ali continued. "There's a lot stacked against her, including her confession. She's in a lot of danger at Flint Hill, so we need to work as quickly as possible."

Jamie nodded. After seeing Sonia's recent injuries, she knew they might run out of time before they were able to prove her case.

Ming spoke up: "She went to Montana for a year?"

"Yes." Ali pulled out a sheet of paper. "Some tiny town near the Canadian border." Ali shifted the paper over to Ming.

"What's in Montana?" Jamie asked.

"Nothing. That might have been the point. Looks like she was living under the alias 'Jennifer Minx'," Javi said.

She knew she was being set up for murder, or at the very least she looked guilty as hell, so she fled. "What about Joey?" Jamie asked.

"He took off the day after Emma was murdered," said Javi. "Fully cooperated with police and had a solid alibi. Changed his

97

name and moved several times before landing in Arizona. Looks like someone tracked him down last week and was just waiting for the right time to take him out. It was pretty grisly. Police think someone was trying to get some sort of information out of him."

"Like what?" Jamie asked.

He shrugged. The gesture made him look younger.

"So, Saul probably learned whatever he needed to know from his interview with Joey," Ali theorized, her tongue clicking loudly in her mouth.

"And that leaves us where?" Ming asked. "I can go out to Montana."

Ali was nodding. "I think that's the best idea. Find out what she was doing during the year she was on the run. Outside of reports and interviews with Sonia, we have enough to work on until you return."

"What about me?" Jamie was already thinking about getting back down to the lake.

"I need a polygraph on Sonia," Ali said, brushing her fingers under her chin. "Do you mind giving me a heads up on the questions you'll be asking her? I want to see if there is anything specific that will help us here."

"Sure. No problem." Since meeting Sonia, Jamie had begun formulating the best approach to find the truth. Sonia appeared to be a straightforward, no-fuss kind of person. But some of her reactions yesterday had seemed practiced, like she had been expecting the questions. Being locked up for five years would give someone like Sonia a lot of time to get her story straight.

"Okay. I think we have a good idea on where to go." Ali turned to Ming. "I'll get your flight taken care of. Check in with me when you land or if anything comes up. Contact the local police and see what you can find out about the driver of the truck who was involved in Sonia's accident."

Ming jotted some notes and packed up her things.

As Ming and Javi disappeared out the door, Alex moved into its frame. Jamie wasn't sure if it was surprise or disappointment she felt at his sudden appearance. She had not expected to see him. In fact, the thought had never even crossed her mind. His face was smoothly shaven and his hair perfectly styled over a wide white smile. Devilishly handsome, or just devilish, to Jamie. He was the proverbial snake in the grass, and none of his charm would ever work on her again. That didn't seem to stop him from wielding it. She recalled watching the press conference after his acquittal in the negligent homicide case of his ex-lover. The same woman whom Jamie considered her best friend had been sleeping with Alex, her fiancé at the time. He had strutted up to the microphone and claimed malicious charges were applied by a reckless detective in the case: Drew Turner. She had wanted to punch his smug face before shutting off the TV.

"Hi," he said, his long slim fingers splayed against the door-frame. She nodded at him, unsmiling. She needed to be clear that they didn't have that kind of friendly relationship. Not after he'd followed her to her hometown a year ago and slunk around her yard like a stalker.

"Ali, there's a package here for you," he said, and excused himself with a subtle wink.

Jamie's eyes skittered away from his—looking nowhere in particular. She was sure this interruption was planned.

"What do you think?" Ali asked.

Jamie had lost track of where the conversation had ended. "About what?"

Ali slouched back in her chair, her expensive suit wrinkling around her shoulders. She was losing weight again. "About Sonia. What's your first instinct about her truthfulness?"

Jamie pursed her lips. "I would have to wait and interview her more, but my first impression is good. She seems convinced that she didn't do it, anyway." Jamie wasn't sure that made sense to Ali, but it was how Jamie liked to approach her cases. "I think she was being honest, but it's very early and I didn't get much time with her."

Ali was nodding, staring into the glass of water she was twisting in one hand, an unreadable expression on her face.

"You know her much better than I," Jamie began. "Didn't you grow up together?"

"Sort of. We're friends still. I have to say, when I heard about the case, I didn't believe it. But Sonia always had a wild streak, that can't be denied. I believed Joey was probably sleeping with Emma—she was a beautiful woman. Everything pointed toward Sonia's guilt. Once they took the death penalty off the table, Sonia jumped at the chance to plead guilty. I was disappointed, but it's what she wanted. It's what she said happened. Ethically, there was nothing I could do."

The weight of Ali's despair visible in her defeated glance, and Jamie couldn't recall a time Ali had looked so…lost.

"I'll call Flint Hill tomorrow and see what we can do about getting that poly and figuring out what happened to Emma." Ali said.

18

SONIA

Jamie was already waiting at one end of the large interview table when Sonia arrived. The room, a hollow box painted pale gray, was windowless and cool. Sonia detected the subtle scent of citrus—it reminded her of Emma. Jamie was dressed smartly in a navy pinstriped pantsuit and silk blouse. She was pretty, with long gold hair that fell past sun-kissed cheeks.

Sonia limped into the room under Jamie's watchful gaze, her gait more pronounced today due to the constant growing ache buried in her bones twitching alive from the rain outside. She'd awoken excited at the prospect of getting the process underway, impatient as she watched dark clouds smother the morning sun just before rain spat from the sky. She wanted to taste its coolness against her tongue and imagined it was sweet, though her common sense told her rain tasted like nothing at all.

"Just have a seat there." Jamie pointed to the chair next to her and turned back to her open notes near piles of folders and a bottle of water. This was the first time Sonia had been in this room, and she absently thought of all the doors she had passed in the last five years oblivious to what was inside them.

A folder labeled "Crime Scene" lay next to her seat and she

wondered if there was some kind of rule that she wasn't allowed to look at it.

As she was pulling her chair out, Sonia noticed a scar on Jamie's cheek: long and thin, like a river drawn on the smoothest map, disappearing out of view under her soft silk shirt.

"How'd you get the scar?"

"An old friend," Jamie said, jotting down something on her lined paper.

Sonia lowered herself into the chair and rested her hands on the table, afraid to look at any of the surrounding paperwork. Heat broke across her shoulders. Sonia was aware that in Virginia polygraphs were not admissible in court, so there must be some other reason Ali had insisted on one.

"Seems more like something an enemy would give you." Sonia had a lot of scars to prove that, each one telling its own brief story. What did Jamie's tell?

"You're looking better," Jamie said looking over at Sonia but ignoring her statement. Her eyes were a shocking green and reminded Sonia of a cat they'd had when she was younger, Mr. Meowgee. He had this annoying habit of attacking people's legs at the dinner table and running away after a good tear in the flesh or cutting at their jeans.

Sonia must have smiled.

"What?" Jamie asked.

"Nothing. Just remembering my other life." A quiet sadness draped over her, like an old favorite blanket lost in a move.

"Well, shall I tell you what to expect or have you taken one of these before?" Jamie asked as she swept her hair behind an ear, revealing more of the scar.

"I know what to expect, but I've never taken one. I've seen stuff on TV."

"Okay. Let's forget about all that and I'll explain to you what I'm going to do." Jamie looked to her for confirmation and Sonia gave a curt nod. "Good. First, we're just going to talk. I'm going to ask you very general questions about yourself, your family, that sort of thing. Then I'm going to ask some more focused questions about the event. There's a skill to what I do, so I hope you'll trust me. This test isn't set up to trick you; it simply uses the physiology of your body's natural responses to line up memories stored in your brain. If there are questions you don't feel comfortable with me asking, or if the phrasing is confusing, we can discuss it before I give you the test on Friday."

"I thought we were doing this today?" Sonia interrupted, aware of her own belligerence. She didn't have time for a long, drawn-out process that might or might not even help with her defense.

"I've only been given two-hour blocks for the interview and one hour for the actual test. The Warden seemed a bit inflexible on time. I would ordinarily have the interview on the same day as the test, but I had to work around him."

"Won't that mess up the results?" Sonia felt herself reaching for reassurance as she rubbed her throbbing hip under the table. "How long is all of this going to take? Will it affect the outcome?" As Sonia lobbed her questions she felt sweat gathering inside her jumpsuit.

Jamie was shaking her head. "A lie today is a lie tomorrow. Go into this with an open mind. Again, I'm not trying to trip you up. I just want you to tell me the truth about everything we discuss. The test will be a fraction of the questions we actually go over. My focus is pinpointed, and there are other techniques I use to gauge your truthfulness."

"Like what?"

"Body language, posture, hidden verbal cues. There's a lot, but don't think about any of that. Just be honest."

Sonia was nodding her head. "Whatever. How long?" Her hands were wedged tightly between her thighs as she bent toward the table, its lip scraping her sternum.

Jamie's demeanor never changed. "I can have the report from your results by Monday."

"Okay." Sonia was nodding, relieved that it wasn't going to take as long as she'd expected. "Let's get on with it then."

Jamie shifted some papers and slowly leaned back into her chair. "Why don't you tell me about yourself? Nothing crazy. Just where you're from, education, family."

Sonia sighed. She hated talking about herself, but she also understood that Jamie was trying to build up a rapport before she started asking questions about killing another human being. "I'm from Northern Virginia. I went to a local community college. By then Joey and I were already married." An ache grew in her at the mention of his name. When they had met, he was so uncompromising about his fate, which he believed was to marry her and love her forever. Or at least that's what she thought he'd believed. "I married Joey when I was only twenty. I was working at a dentist's office. I was a hygienist while taking night classes to eventually go to school to be a lawyer, but…life happened. After we got married, I sort of settled into my job, and decided to give up school for a while, and I just never went back. It was okay because Joey made good money working for Saul's firm."

"What was it that Joey did for Saul?"

"Just office work, I think. He didn't talk about work too much. Just that he made a lot for pushing paper."

"Did he have a degree?"

"Yes. He was an accountant."

Jamie nodded and made a note. Sonia again questioned Jamie's ability—not to get the truth out of her, but to force out something Sonia desperately needed to hide.

"I come from a small family. Mom, Dad and my older sister, Nikki."

"Where are your parents now?"

"My mother married Saul the year after my father died in a

car crash." Her voice sounded disconnected from her raging emotions, just like she'd practiced.

"Sorry for your loss," Jamie said, and her tone was genuine. "I lost a brother," she added as if Sonia might be questioning her sincerity.

"My sister. She's around, but I don't hear from her."

"It says here you refuse visits from your mother and that she used to come up twice a month to see you."

She ignored her surprise at Jamie's statement, and had to assume there'd been a file full of things about herself given to Jamie. "It seems silly that you're asking me things you already know," Sonia snapped.

"It's part of my job in evaluating you. I know you refuse to visit with her, but I don't know why."

Sonia forced a deep breath and determined that she wasn't helping herself with these outbursts, and so far, Jamie was unaffected. She had to keep reminding herself Jamie wasn't out to get her.

"I do that for her protection," Sonia said calmly.

Jamie nodded as if this statement affirmed what she already thought. "Is Saul dangerous?"

A laugh erupted from Sonia before she could stop it. "Is Saul D'Luca dangerous?" She jerked her jumpsuit open to reveal her bare skin beneath. On her chest were scars, big and small, marring most of her pale skin. Stab wounds, bruises and abrasions; some healed, others raw, and more would be tattoos on her forever. A reminder of how much the death of Emma hurt her father.

"Some grieving parents only fantasize about doing this to their child's killer. Saul's living the dream." As she pulled her jumpsuit back over her shoulders the pop of snaps echoed in the room.

"It's not safe for me to visit with my family. It's better for my mother to let me go." Sonia's fingernail traced the edge of the table. She didn't want to believe what she was saying, but it was the truth. "Can you imagine how he would react if he found out his wife was visiting his daughter's killer in prison?"

"They're divorced."

Sonia froze. "What?"

Jamie cleared her throat. "Two years ago, I think."

The fan overhead kicked on with a quiet hum. The shock of this news caused her to miss Jamie's next question. "I'm sorry, what?"

"Are you, or were you ever trying to protect Joey?"

Sonia nodded at the table, refusing to meet Jamie's eyes. "I couldn't let him come and testify in court. His life would've been much shorter if I gave in to Ali's demands to drag him in, but I refused." That was at least half true.

"Tell me about Emma D'Luca."

"A princess. Loved by all."

"Did you love her?"

An image of Emma's beautiful face flashed in a memory. Sonia had been crying, and she felt the weight of Emma's hand on her back.

"He's going to divorce me," Sonia blubbered to her stepsister, wishing she was alone, that her words could be uttered and forgotten in an empty space.

"No, he isn't. He loves you." Emma wore a soft smile as she pushed the hair out of Sonia's eyes. She seemed so sure of what Joey would do, and how he would feel. "I'm going to help you. I think you should tell him what we talked about. I think he'll agree with me," Emma said.

Sonia closed her eyes to the memory.

"Yes," Sonia blurted, her eyes meeting Jamie's again. "Maybe not at first. When I moved into Saul's house, our relationship was more of a collection of mutual understandings. I knew it was really her father I was mad at, but she was an easy target—or so I thought at first. I was only trying to get back at him and prove it was harder than he thought to steal our family."

"Weren't you afraid of him?"

Sonia considered this. "Not at first. I had no actual idea what kind of man Saul was until I found out he killed my father."

"Killed your father?"

Sonia nodded. "Nothing I can prove, but I know he did it."

Jamie took more notes. The scratch of her pen was the loudest sound in the room as Sonia waited.

"When you told the police that Joey was sleeping with Emma, was that a lie?"

Sonia nodded. "I knew it would seem credible. Emma had the type of personality that drew you in and held you hostage." Sonia couldn't help the smile growing on her face as she recalled a forced family function where she and Emma drank too much and hooked their bras onto a replica of the famous *Thinker* by Rodin. Its hard bronzed muscles and smooth lines ensconced in women's wear. A silent protest against her father. She would often complain about how ostentatious his taste was and how he presumed he was cultured for having picked such a piece. Saul valued a lot of things, but knowledge wasn't one of them. He believed in more immediate things, such as power, control and fear.

"We were close. I would stay over at her place while Joey was away on business."

"Why was Joey going on business trips?" Jamie asked.

Sonia shrugged. "Saul valued his opinion. He liked to have him along on new ventures."

"What sort of ventures?"

"I don't know. Business stuff. I didn't ask a lot of questions about Saul's dealings, and you shouldn't, either," Sonia said with a raised brow. "You don't know what you're dealing with."

Jamie's head tilted to the side. "You never wanted children?"

The speed at which Jamie shifted gears must have been a

tactic she used often, to the point of perfection. But Sonia took her time in answering and wondered if it was impeding Jamie's plans. Or maybe this Jamie chick was a good person—Sonia hadn't decided yet.

"No. I have a condition. I can't have children." *Joey would have been such a great father.*

The outer door to the interview room clicked open with no warning and a guard came in.

"I'm sorry, but we have another thirty-five minutes," Jamie said, turning to him.

"No, you don't. Warden said meeting's over," the guard said.

"But…" Jamie began, but Sonia interrupted.

"I'm ready. I just need one minute." She held up an envelope for the guard to see. "For my attorney."

The guard nodded and stepped into the hall, but not out of eyesight.

"Listen." Sonia kept her voice low. "I don't have a lot of time. This isn't going to go how you expect it, and I want you to know you're in danger. I need you to send this letter for me."

Jamie looked at the letter thrust into her face and began shaking her head.

"You don't understand, and I hope you never know what we are dealing with. But you have to do this for me…please. I have no one else. No one I can trust," Sonia begged.

Jamie looked down at Sonia's trembling hand and slowly nodded. "Okay." Her eyes seemed to scan the outside of the envelope as she put it in the stack of papers in her bag. "I'll take care of it."

"Thank you," Sonia said as a wave of adrenaline dumped into her body, causing her lips to shake. She thought about the letter moving through the postal service, into a mailbox, and into the hands of the recipient, and the tiny voice of reason was dead.

19

REAGAN

"MOMMY, WHERE'D YOU GO?" Mason's voice carried through the thin walls of the camper. Reagan grabbed the two plates of sandwiches and grapes and hustled toward the door, pulling it open with two fingers and a pop of her narrow hip. The salty wind rolled away from the ocean and combed through the sea grass, expelling a scent she had come to love. The undulating body of water heaved against its invisible border beyond the steep cliff. Upon first visiting the campsite, she'd been concerned about Mason's safety. The prospect of living next to a cliff with such a young child was worrisome. But Mason was a good boy, and he was never out of her sight for long. Whenever she took on a new job, she made sure it was one where she could take him with her, because she wouldn't use daycares or babysitters.

"I'm coming, I'm coming." She joined him at the picnic table under the yellowing awning. It was warm in the late morning sun, but the air off the ocean was cool. They'd arrived in Maine in mid-winter, when the weather was especially harsh. It was only after an extended stay in a motel that she was able to find the camper for rent. They would have to move on again before winter, though.

She pushed the plate toward him while she settled on the bench. His brown eyes focused on her as his lips drew into a frown.

"I don't want them cut," he whined, picking through his grapes.

"It's not safe for you to eat them whole." She recalled old Mrs. Hillard from the homeless shelter in Texas telling her mother one day that children often died from drowning and choking on things like uncut grapes. It was funny how things like that stayed with someone. After traveling thousands of miles and living in some pretty suspect places, she still recalled this common hazard of grapes to young children. Of all the things to worry about, she whittled it down to grapes—always cut the grapes.

She watched as her neighbor's black truck rolled quietly into his site after being gone all morning.

Max, the handsome solo stranger who had abruptly introduced himself a few days ago, climbed out of his truck. His broad smile was shadowed by scruff on his angular jaw. She tore her eyes away from his chest, hidden under a fitted t-shirt. *You're not a sixteen-year-old girl.*

She couldn't stop thinking about the timing of his arrival, and suspected it was because of her own paranoia. He would have had just enough time to drive from Arizona to Maine…

Ever since finding out Joey Rossi was killed, she knew she and Mason had to be very careful. It was compulsory to move from one place to another at this point, but as she looked out at the vastness of the ocean, she wished they could stay here; this place called out to her. She had already decided their next move would be across the border into Canada and was looking for a way to get her hands on some better forged identification. The I.D. they had now wouldn't hold up to any kind of real scrutiny.

"Nice day for a picnic," Max yelled from his truck as he let his dog out. Charlie shot off toward them like a rocket, his yellow fur shivering with the speed of his approach.

Mason squealed next to her, excited to greet the lab whose tail thumped against the camper wall. A large pink tongue blazed a trial over Mason's plump cheek, and his giggles rose in the air.

"Sorry about that," Max said, staying on the edge of the grass. After startling her the other day, he had been careful to keep his distance. "Charlie!"

The dog's head perked toward his owner, and he seemed torn between staying or obeying. He pulled away not nearly as quickly as he had arrived, looking back over toward Mason several times during his retreat.

"It's okay," Reagan said, watching Max's broad back as he turned to usher Charlie into the camper's screen door. He didn't even bother to lock it while he was away.

She felt guilty for the way she had acted the other day, accusing him of disregarding her privacy when she'd finally opened the door. At first he looked shocked by her reaction, then indifferent. She had only seen him twice since then and he was always friendly. The fact that he was alone bothered her. Well, not completely alone—he had Charlie.

All she really knew about him was his name, and only his first name at that.

"Can we get a dog, Mommy?" Mason's little fingers clamped down over his sandwich and a smear of peanut butter lined his pink lips. The cloying smell rose to her nose.

"Maybe, kiddo," Reagan said, shutting him down gently. If they had to load up into their 2001 Toyota van for months again, the last thing she'd be able to handle was a dog. She understood a dog would bring a constant into Mason's life that he needed, not to mention comfort, but she couldn't commit. The echo of the word *comfort* made her think of her quiet neighbor.

Her phone rang, startling her, and Mason snickered at her

reaction. She shushed him loudly and looked at her phone. Blocked number. There were only a few people who had the number to her burner phone, one of whom was her boss at the hotel where she currently cleaned rooms.

"Hello." Reagan spoke almost in a whisper. Quiet filled the other end. "Hello," she repeated, and was almost ready to hang up when someone spoke.

"Reagan?" The gravelly voice was not familiar to her. She stood from the picnic table and scanned the landscape of wind-beaten trees along the Maine coast, unsure what she was looking for. The sound of crunching gravel rose behind her and she twisted quickly to see Max's large frame in front of her.

"I'm sorry, you have the wrong number," Reagan said, but didn't hang up, captivated by a morose curiosity. Max's hand twitched as if he was holding back some command to move it as he looked at her face.

"I don't think so. I think I have the person I'm looking for."

She pulled the phone back and ended the call quickly, pushing the phone away from her, down the table, with fumbling fingers. She wanted to throw it, hurl it into the water below, but Max's voice broke through: "Is everything okay?"

Charlie barked from behind the closed door of Max's camper. What was he doing here? What did he want?

"I'm fine," she said briskly, taking a seat next to Mason, who continued to eat his sandwich. "Everything's fine." She settled her nose on the top of his head and breathed in the scent of him, grounding herself there.

20

JAMIE

JAMIE ARRIVED at the prison early, anticipating the time it would take her to get through security with all her bags. She should have had an hour and a half with Sonia the day before, but her time had been cut short with no explanation. Sonia had not even argued; it was as if she was expecting this treatment. What else was going on behind these walls? To the system, Sonia was just another murderer, but the prison still needed to protect her. Jamie decided she would subtly ask Sonia about how she was being treated during the second half of her interview. She knew she had to hurry; she was already behind on time.

The door slid open, and with a loud click locked into place. A handsome guard with a nametag reading "M. McKinney" walked toward her. "Ms. Kendal?"

She smiled. "Yes, that's me."

He smiled back. "I need to scan anything you plan on taking back with you." He indicated her bags.

"Yes. Sure. Thank you," she said, pushing her wheeled bag toward him. Drew had teased her relentlessly for the recent purchase, but her shoulder often ached from carrying her two laptops and all the other instruments needed to administer a test.

One day she woke up and decided to hell with her pride and purchase the bag, and she had never looked back.

"Your purse too, please," said the guard, and Jamie handed it over.

"Is Sonia ready?"

He watched a monitor as her purse moved along a conveyor belt. "She's waiting for you."

"What do you think of her?" Jamie asked. His smile was unmoving and the slight shock that registered on his face was fleeting. He probably knew very little about Sonia.

"She's a tough nut, that one. A good person. But who am I?" His arms easily lifted her heavy bag onto the conveyor belt. He seemed to be about to say something but halted when another guard entered the small room. Only when they were alone, after scanning her bags, did he speak again.

"She needs your help, that's for sure." Keys jingled against his thigh as they began walking. "I thought her lawyer was going to try and get her protective custody. She's not safe here."

"Were you the guard who found her after her last attack?"

He shook his head. "Nah, that was my girl Nicole. I asked her to keep an eye out. It's a full-time job, checkin' in on her." He laughed without humor. "Trying to keep her alive."

"Do you know her well?" Jamie blurted.

"I used to. We went to school together." They stopped at a junction and he hit a call button. A man answered. "Door 60," Mack said. The door popped open.

"Small world," Jamie said.

He led her to the same room they had shared before. Sonia was sitting in her chair, staring down into her palms, when Jamie walked in, leaving Mack at the door. She crossed the room with all her bags and pulled out her chair.

"Hello again," Jamie said warmly. "I thought I was early enough to ask the Warden about the interruption last time, but I wasn't. I lodged a complaint after the other day, and I think he was trying to cover his ass." She quickly unpacked the items she might need—notebook, pen and laptop—though she didn't think she was going to use all of them.

"How are you?" Jamie asked as Sonia continued her brooding silence. Mack was right about her being a tough cookie. It would appear Sonia was still intact, with no sign of fresh injuries.

"How do you get on with the Warden?"

Sonia's head slowly turned and her stare seemed to strip away the possibility of any more pleasantries. Like raw emotion shivering under her surface. "Who's asking?"

"I don't ask questions for other people. I know you don't trust me, and probably don't want to, but I'm not on anyone's side. Not even yours. I'm as neutral as they come," Jamie said, marking the date at the top of her legal pad.

Sonia's fingernail traced a tight circle on the table, producing a soft scratching sound."I can appreciate that. I don't need anyone in my corner. Just someone to help me get the truth out there."

"That's good. That's my job. But I also want to make sure you don't die in here." Jamie let the comment hang in the air, waiting to see if Sonia was going to add anything.

"He's a dick, and I think Saul pays him," Sonia said tersely. "The only reason I get this banged up is because he allows it." Her gaze was cool, reminding Jamie of the expression people on public transportation wore to deter other passengers from asking questions or talking to them: *bus face.*

"Well, we agree on that. He's a dick," Jamie said, trying not to smirk but failing.

"Hey." Sonia continued to drag a nail lightly over the table, curling dark hair around her ear with her other hand. "Did you have time to mail that letter?" Keeping her eyes averted, she waited for Jamie's answer. It was clear Sonia was very concerned—even anxious—about asking her.

Jamie nodded. "I dropped it in the first blue box I saw." She had wanted to get rid of it the second Sonia handed it over, but that didn't stop her from looking at the addressee on the envelope. The name *Gennie Smith* was written, with great care, on the front. Jamie had no idea who this woman was, or what urgent message the letter contained, and she hadn't thought again about it until Sonia brought it up.

"Thank you so much. It means…it means a lot to me," Sonia managed to say through obvious discomfort. Appreciation was probably as foreign as the feeling of safety to her.

"Let's get started, shall we?" Jamie asked, smoothing over the awkward moment. "I still need to finish the interview questions we missed yesterday, and then we'll start the test."

"Shoot," Sonia said. Jamie watched as her attitude seemed to shift.

"We were talking about your family. Today, I would like to focus more on your interactions as a family."

Sonia nodded and waited, clearly unwilling to offer unsolicited information. In the quiet of the room, Jamie studied Sonia's face with its tiny lines, its frown marks, and the gold flecks in her brown eyes.

"You were close with Emma?"

"My mother married her father when I was around fourteen. We were only a few years apart. She was older than me—Nikki's age."

"Nikki is your older sister?"

Sonia nodded.

"Are you and Nikki close?"

"No. We haven't spoken in four years. Not since the day after I was sentenced." Roughly a year after her arrest, during which time they never spoke, Sonia confirmed. "I got the sense Nikki didn't want to upset Saul. Or maybe she didn't want to be forced to pick sides."

"Did she mention anything about your situation?"

Something flashed across Sonia's features and she shifted in her seat, propping her bent leg on the edge of her chair.

"You mean, does she think I'm guilty?" Sonia didn't wait for Jamie to respond. "Our relationship was always distant, but once Saul became a part of the family, Nikki changed. She loves him like he's her father. I don't think she's talked about our dad since he died. It made me angry. To answer your question, Nikki and I never discussed what happened to Emma."

"What was it like living with Saul?" She watched as Sonia slumped back in her chair, but Sonia's fingers were clenched, revealing her anxiety. Jamie didn't script her interviews, but she knew what she wanted to ask and was intentionally looping back to Saul.

"I don't know. It was okay, I guess. I didn't spend much time with him. I stayed in my room or visited my friends."

"And Emma?"

"We spent a lot of time together. Not at first, but we found out we had a lot in common. She didn't like her dad either."

"What do you mean?" Absently, Jamie drew her pen to her lips.

"I mean, she knew the kinds of things he did, and she didn't like it. I'm not sure how a person gains a moral compass without a good example, but Emma did it."

"What happened to Emma's mother?"

"She died in a boating accident about two years before Saul met my mom." Sonia's tone was bitter.

Jamie moved on. "Does he have young women around? Prostitutes." She hadn't meant to say it, but there it was. Sonia's eyes narrowed on her, and Jamie shivered. Damned AC blowing on her face.

"How'd you know that?"

At first Jamie assumed Sonia's reaction was borne of anger. But as Jamie studied her features, she sensed something else. Fear?

"How about young girls?"

Sonia nodded, but didn't look up from the table. "Her father was involved with all kinds of things. If he could make money off it, Saul had his hand in it." Sonia leaned over the table on bent elbows. Jamie wondered if her bizarre behavior of avoidance was to appease the guilt of talking about things she didn't want to. Much the same reaction a teenager might exhibit when pulled into the principal's office for smoking pot.

"Do you think Emma knew about the girls?"

"Why did you say 'girls'?" Sonia said, shaking her head.

Jamie hadn't been planning on mentioning Jenkins, but maybe it would soften Sonia up. "I performed polygraphs on a man who was a client of Saul's." Jamie was aware she was taking a lot of liberty with the truth due to her assumptions, but she was sure she was right.

A look of disgust twisted over Sonia's features. "I can't stand that—" She abruptly cut off and changed course. "I think Emma knew, but we never talked about that aspect of his *business*." The last word spat out of her mouth.

"Emma knew about them?" Jamie pushed.

"Yes. I think she did."

"Did her father know she knew about them?"

Sonia looked confused for a moment. "I don't really know what he knew. Once I was old enough to move out I didn't keep up with him at all."

Sensing Sonia's waning cooperation, Jamie shifted subjects. "Let's talk about the day you found Emma."

A nod.

"Walk me through it again." Jamie watched Sonia with trained eyes.

"Are you trying to trick me?" Sonia asked.

"We discussed this already. I'm not against you. Nor am I on your side. I am simply after the truth. I don't want to spring a question on you for the first time during the test. It's not my style. The way this test works is we discuss what I think is relevant and the questions are whittled down to about twenty. You won't know them until I ask, but I won't ask you about anything we haven't discussed. There is a science behind this."

After a deep breath and a weary stare, she began. "I got the call from Emma. She told me she needed me to come to her house. That something had happened."

"You suspected something was wrong?"

Sonia nodded. "I don't know. I didn't really understand what was going on."

"Was the door open or closed?"

"Unlocked, and open. Not a lot, but about an inch." Sonia pinched her fingers to indicate the distance. "I walked through the living room. There was nothing—wait, there was some blood, but I don't remember anything else in there. When I came around the corner, she was lying on the kitchen floor. There was so much blood," Sonia said softly. "And the damned dog barked until he ran out the door."

"Was there a weapon?"

"Yes. A knife." Sonia shook her head. "Maybe—won't that be in the police report?"

Jamie ignored her question. "Did you touch the body? Did you touch Emma?"

A shake of the head.

"It's important you give me a verbal response," Jamie said automatically.

"No." But Sonia didn't look sure. "I must have slipped in the blood—" Her hand hovered in front of her like she was bracing herself.

"Then what did you do?"

Sonia's breath caught in her throat as her eyes stared blankly ahead. "I staggered back and realized I had blood on my shoes." She looked down at the floor. "I'd stepped in the blood and didn't realize it. Then the crazy neighbor came in and started screaming at me."

Jamie was nodding.

"And I think I threw up at one point." Sonia could almost taste the bile. "I left the room and went upstairs."

"Why?"

"I just had to see. I wanted to see for myself."

"What did you have to see?" Jamie reviewed the photos of the bloody footprints trailing up the stairs.

Sonia was shaking her head and kept her eyes on the floor. "There was something I had to find."

21

SONIA

"This is a pneumograph," Jamie said, wrapping two black tubular cords around Sonia's chest. "It measures your breathing." Jamie clipped the cords into place, walked back to her bag and pulled out more items. "Hold out your hand," Jamie said. She placed small pads on the meaty part of Sonia's palm and at the base of her thumb. "These are used for electrodermal reporting— or sweat," Jamie added, smiling. Once the pads were in place, black wires, like the kind from an EKG monitor, were attached.

"Are you ready?"

Sonia took a deep breath. "Is it normal to feel nervous?"

"Yes. I would think so."

Sonia sat still, staring at the wall ahead. This was the day she would prove her innocence. As soon as her false confession passed her lips five years ago, it had been eating away at her like she was living in an alternate universe.

She thought of the handwritten statement she had agreed to write back then, sitting now in some dusty file somewhere. She couldn't even remember what she'd written. Had she told them there was a knife? This wasn't the time to second-guess herself.

Sonia nodded.

"To start, I am going to ask you some generic questions," Jamie said.

Sonia looked over at her. A delicate gold-chained necklace with an intricate metal feather hung over her cream-colored blouse. After their previous visit, Sonia had decided that she liked Jamie. She had a kind of uncomplicated way Sonia gravitated toward. Her words were neither flowery nor meant to cut Sonia down, which she could appreciate. She caught herself making assumptions about Jamie. Maybe she had a husband and a dog. Not a purebred, but a mutt from a local shelter that needed a home. No kids—or was that Sonia projecting?

"Okay," Sonia said.

"I'm going to remind you that these will be closed answer questions. Please answer 'Yes' or 'No' when asked. Please don't shake your head or nod as your answer."

"Yes."

"Is your name Sonia Rossi?"

"Yes."

Jamie adjusted something and Sonia was careful with her movements, reminding herself that Jamie would study body language along with verbal responses. Was anyone ever able to beat one of these tests?

"Do you currently live at Flint Hill Corrections Facility?"

"Yes."

Sonia could hear Jamie typing into her open laptop. Feeling nervous energy welling up inside of her, pressing against her will to remain still, she wanted to tap her foot on the ground, but refrained. What if this failed?

"Is your mother's name Julie Angelo?"

"Yes."

"Did you know Emma D'Luca?"

"Yes." Was her heart beating faster? She tried to clear her head as sweat gathered at her neck; she thought of the electro-thingy acting as a sort of shock collar, detecting her discomfort.

"Did you kill Emma D'Luca?"

She was expecting the question, had rehearsed hearing it over and over, but now that she was asked, she felt her heart skitter.

"No."

More typing.

Focus, Sonia. Her palms were sticky. *What are you afraid of?*

"Did you stab Emma D'Luca?"

Blood. So much blood. Everywhere. It was staining the edges of her white sneakers, splattered on her pristine laces. The house —so quiet until a crash upstairs…

"No."

"Did you take anything from Emma D'Luca's house on the day she was murdered?"

She had raced around, searching frantically for the papers through tear-blurred eyes. Where the hell had she put them? If Saul found those papers, he would never stop hunting her.

"No."

Jamie was moving again. Had Jamie's instruments caught her in a lie? She closed her eyes and forced a deep breath.

"Did you see who killed Emma?"

Someone was in the house with her, upstairs, on the second floor. She walked to the steps, hands shaking. Was she carrying a weapon…a knife? The soft click of a door shutting. All of her senses told her to run…

"No." She felt her fear overshadow her composure, and she wanted to pull the electrodes off her hands and hurl them across the space.

The memory was yawing wider, pulling her back in time to the moment her hand—stained with blood—reached for the knob. She could hear the distinct sound of breathing through the thin wood door.

"Have you ever committed murder?"

Why did this sound like a question they hadn't gone over? Maybe not directly, but indirectly.

"No." She felt her eyelid twitch. The silence in the room roared in her ears. She wanted this to be over. This had been a mistake. She didn't want this woman bouncing around in her head, reading her like a book.

Jamie was writing something down now. What was it? Had she said the wrong thing?

Sonia thought of the doctor's appointment, could almost feel Joey's hand on her arm.

"I'm sorry, Mrs. Rossi, but you'll never have children of your own."

Why was she thinking of that now—at this moment?

She felt the sadness weighting the air around her in the car on the way home. Joey's hand felt heavy on hers and offered no comfort. He had given up. She could sense it in his silence; a heart-wrenching resignation.

"We can adopt," he'd said with little enthusiasm. "You know how many children need a good home?"

Sonia had nodded absently and turned to stare out the window. Suddenly, everywhere she looked, children were there. In buggies and strollers. On picnic tables and on bikes. She was constantly bombarded with children, as if the universe was rubbing it in her face.

Jamie's voice broke through her thoughts. "Did you want to hurt Emma D'Luca?"

"No." *I loved her like a sister.*

Jamie turned the recorder off, and the click echoed in the room. "Is that it?" Sonia asked, daring to look over at her. She expected to see a look of contempt on Jamie's face, but her expression was wholly unreadable. She nodded.

"How'd I do?"

Jamie didn't answer for a long moment. She began removing her equipment from Sonia's chest. As she leaned in, Sonia could smell her citrus perfume. Each time Sonia got a whiff, she saw Emma's sad smile.

"I won't know until I look at all the results," Jamie said, averting her eyes. Was that really how it worked? Couldn't she tell right away? Sonia jumped when she heard the clap of a pen hitting the floor.

"Okay." Sonia's voice shook. "Will you come back? Will I see you again?"

"Yes. I'll come back and talk about the results with you. I'm also helping on other aspects of your case at Ali's request."

"Like what?" Sonia asked, watching as Jamie pulled away the electrodes, leaving small sticky patches on her skin.

"Just going over case information and anything new Ali's P.I. gathers."

"Have you found anything?"

"I'll let Ali handle that. As far as I know, Ming is tracking down people you knew in Montana."

"Why there?" Sonia scooted to the edge of her seat. "I didn't know anyone there."

"I'm sure that's the case, but Ali wanted to check it out." She paused. "Do you know the man who hit your car that day?"

Sonia nodded.

"Who was he?

"Just a guy who worked for Saul."

Jamie considered this, then added, "I think she's trying to follow up on that."

Sonia reached her hand out to touch Jamie's, the action not even crossing her mind before she did it. "You need to stay away from Saul. He's dangerous, and—" She shook her head as Jamie sat in the chair, looking over at her.

"I want to help you," Jamie said. "I don't think you did it, but if that's true, then your best bet of getting out of here is to find out who killed Emma. It's not enough just to do this." Jamie gestured to the laptop. "We need to find out what happened that day and find the person responsible. The police report and investigation were lacking because you pleaded guilty. They were lazy, sloppy, and they probably missed a lot. If we can put the pieces together, you can get your life back. Or at least be free."

Sonia was nodding her head. She was unprepared for the conviction she heard and felt from Jamie. "I need to talk to you and Ali. Go over what you found and see if I can shed any light on it."

Jamie nodded. "That's a good idea. After I get this report taken care of, I'll have a better idea of what questions we need to be asking."

"I guess that's it then?" Sonia sat back, realizing she was still touching Jamie's arm.

"For now."

Right on cue, the door popped open and two guards stood on the other side: one to take Sonia and another to walk Jamie out.

Sonia nodded and stood. "See you soon."

In the hallway, the female guard looked at her. "Arms on the wall." Sonia did as she was told. The horrible humiliation of having another person's hands all over her body never got any easier.

On the walk back to her block Sonia found herself hoping Jamie wasn't as good at her job as Sonia thought she was.

22

JAMIE

"How'd it go with our girl?" Ali asked as Jamie walked through her doorway. Ali was ensconced behind a stained cherrywood desk, papers scattered in front of her and a yellow legal pad propped in her hand. There was a hint of lunch lingering in the air—Chinese food, fried rice maybe. Jamie had driven directly here from the prison with all her equipment, eager to get started on her report. "I'm surprised you don't want to go back home and take care of this report. Avoiding someone?"

Jamie walked in and dropped onto the dark red sofa. The window beyond Ali's desk was filled with the gleaming, angular structures of the city. The late afternoon sun hung high in a crisp blue sky. "I never understood why people don't face their desks out." Jamie raised her hand to encompass the view. Ali turned to look at it for a moment and looked back at Jamie.

"Because it would distract me all day," Ali said.

"Maybe you could use the break," Jamie said, noticing the dark shadows around Ali's eyes, but Ali promptly waved off her concern.

"I'm going to stay to get some work done in the city," Jamie said. "And no, I'm not ignoring Drew. I just need some time to figure out what to tell him."

Ali took a deep breath. "Tell him about what?"

Jamie could recall the echo of sadistic laughter on her voicemail at work. Her phone's steady blinking light triggered her whenever she came back into the office after an absence. She knew what was recorded even before listening. Some Mondays she would have to delete twenty or more messages, recorded at all hours of the day and night. Some were delivered in an eerie strangled kind of whisper, as if Nina were hiding under a blanket with a flashlight illuminating her crazed grin. How was she calling her in the middle of the night? The security at her facility might not be as secure as it should be.

"Well, for starters, Nina is still calling. And...I never mentioned I would be helping you out here," Jamie added. It was just too easy to have two lives: one here in Arlington and one in Cedar Lake with Drew.

"And Alex..." Ali's thought dangled between them. Jamie looked away, toward the doorway, and caught sight of him standing there.

"Gossiping about me again, Ali?" Alex's smooth voice goaded Jamie, and she sat up straighter and shot her eyes away from him. She felt her jaw muscles tighten as she stared past Ali, trying to disappear. She hated that he'd overheard them talking about him. He didn't deserve any attention—even the negative kind.

Ali was unfazed by his sudden appearance. They acted more like brother and sister than coworkers. It had been that way since college.

"What is it, Alex?" Ali's voice cut through the office.

"Ming's here to see you."

Jamie finally looked over at Alex and noticed he was staring at her. He winked. Her stomach twisted into a heavy knot that sunk to her feet, sending a flash of anger gurgling up through her.

"Why are you telling me? I have Kia," Ali said, referring to her assistant, who was standing behind Alex in the hallway. He only shrugged and walked off.

This was the second time he had found a reason to interrupt them, and it was proving to be more than a little annoying.

Kia led Ming in, and the older woman took a seat.

"What do you have for us?" Ali asked before Ming could even get comfortable.

"I think we need to have a meeting. Get on the same page with everything going on." Ming seemed anxious.

Jamie was nodding in agreement. "That's good. Maybe Monday? I'll have my report back by then. I think we may have a whole other issue on our hands once I'm able to analyze the data." She thought of some results she had seen in actual time and was disappointed. She wanted to trust Sonia so badly she might have let that taint her first impression of the woman.

Ming abruptly stood, went softly to the open door and closed it before returning to her seat, both Ali's and Jamie's eyes following her movements.

"What is it?" Ali asked. Ming's anxiety seemed contagious.

"I found two people who were connected to Sonia in Montana," Ming replied, wringing her hands on her lap. "Her landlord, Alfred Wozniack," Ming said from memory. "The other was a fifty-seven-year-old woman named Mildred Collins."

"Okay. And how did she know Mildred?" Ali asked.

"I don't know. There are no obvious ties I can see. But Sonia visited Mildred's home frequently and spent time with her. They could have met anywhere; you'll need to ask Sonia that."

Jamie found herself biting her lip. "What have you learned?"

"They are both dead. Their bodies were found yesterday." Ming looked between both women. "Police are investigating both as possible homicides."

Silence pierced the room as all three women processed this information. Dead—no, worse. Murdered.

"Why kill a landlord and a random woman?" Ali asked herself aloud.

Jamie didn't say it, but her first instinct screamed Saul. But what possible connection could he have to these people?

Ali's slim fingers steepled under her strong chin. "Well, damn," she finally said. "It could be a coincidence. An old woman and Sonia's ex-landlord—doesn't make a lot of sense yet. Keep digging." Ali looked at Ming, who nodded. "What about Sonia?" Ali said to Jamie.

"Sonia told me today that the Warden is sneaky. She thinks he's on the take, but I have no idea if it's true or not," Jamie said, knowing she might sound a bit paranoid. She still wasn't fully aware of what she was dealing with here.

"Okay. Okay. We need to keep this group tight. I don't want Saul finding out about any of our intentions," Ali said. "If either of you want to back out now, I understand." Ali let her statement hang in the air. No one spoke. "Okay, then. I'll contact Javi. I'm going to let him in on what's going on. From now on we watch our backs closely."

Jamie felt a new push to tell Drew about her involvement in this case. She couldn't keep him in the dark if there was any real possibility of harm coming to them.

"I know there are people in this office I can't trust," Ali said as she began chewing the edge of her nail. "So we only run things by the team. No one else."

All three women exchanged knowing glances.

"I need to see if we can't get a statement from the detectives investigating these two recent deaths. Maybe give them a heads up that it could be related to the Joey Rossi hit or Saul D'Luca."

Jamie agreed. "Maybe that would put them in good graces with us, but I'm not sure what they can share."

Ali sighed. "You're probably right, but we can try. I'll talk with Javi, see if he found anything."

"This just got ugly really quick," Jamie said.

23

SONIA

IT WAS past visiting hours when the guard came to get her. Shadows filled the visitors' room behind the glass partition, her footfalls the only sound as she paced a path on the floor.

"I'm not going," she'd told the guard who came for her.

Walker, a middle-aged disaster of a man, had stood over her while she slowly folded her last load of laundry for the day. He was panting, as though he had just climbed ten flights of stairs or run a marathon rather than walking twenty steps. "Yes. You are."

She didn't want to see anyone, had previously refused every visit, but it would appear they weren't giving her a choice. Sonia felt her mouth hang open as Walker smiled to reveal crooked teeth. It wasn't often a man like him could assert authority. She pictured his life outside of work, filled with adult movies and TV dinners—definitely a Hungry Man kind of guy.

It was only when she began walking next to him that she thought to physically refuse by grabbing a doorframe. But when she did, he shoved her shoulder so hard she fell into the wall. He laughed as she whimpered from the jolt. The rest of the walk was taken in silence as waves of anger blasted her. Two, four, six, eight...

Who was here to see her? Her mother was the only person who'd tried since Sonia had arrived at Flint Hill. The last time she'd laid eyes on Julie Angelo was when she was sitting on the other side of this glass, three years ago. Her purse pulled up onto her lap, black hair woven with white-gray, her face drawn into a frown and her eyes glossy with tears. When their eyes connected, Sonia had felt a jolt of emotion, and turned away quickly.

Now, the other room still empty, she wondered why the Warden had her brought down here. What did he have up his sleeve now?

She chewed on her thumbnail as she caught sight of the camera mounted in the corner of the room blinking down at her.

The door to the other room opened slowly, and her heart dropped. It was her mother. Her hair more gray than black now, her skin tan from the sun and wrinkled with age. Sonia's mouth dried out as she watched her mother drift to the chair next to the window. She was still beautiful in a quiet way.

I won't talk to her. If I just ignore her, she will be forced to leave.

On closer inspection, Sonia saw the residue of dried tears under her mother's eyes. She took a seat and clutched her bag, just as she had three years ago.

Sonia felt wetness slide down her cheeks. Her mother didn't arrange this—that only left...

She forced herself over to the chair and sat. Julie was trying not to look through the glass at her daughter but it seemed she couldn't help herself. Her knuckles were white from clutching her bag and she flinched when the door opened behind her.

This time a portly man entered and walked slowly to the seat next to her mother. Sonia felt a scream bubbling up from inside of her, but clamped her mouth down so it wouldn't escape.

"Hello, Sonia. It's been a long time," Saul said. His voice was smooth, but it grated against all Sonia's fears. He was here, sitting in front of her, next to her mother. "I wish I could say it's nice to see you."

"What do you want?" she demanded. She had meant for it to come out level and uncaring, but it didn't. And, like a shark smelling blood, a smile parted his lips.

"I wanted to see you again. I heard you were refusing to see Julie," Saul purred, as if he cared at all about the human sitting next to him. He was a professional liar and a con man. He looked different in many ways. A red hue colored his plump cheeks and an extra fifty pounds on his once lean figure made him look older than he was. He looked... tired. Julie shifted away from him in her seat and turned her face toward the floor.

"Did you know we got divorced? I'm sure that upsets you. Seeing as how you gave me such a warm welcome into the family all those years ago." After a moment of hovering, his hand lowered to her mother's thigh, and Julie cringed at the touch.

The hairs pulled against the nape of Sonia's neck. "I heard." Sonia's voice was strong and bordering defiant now, just how she had meant it to sound moments ago.

He nodded at her. "Did you get into a fight?" His face twisted with pity, his hand rising to cover his heart.

"Why are you here? To torture me? I didn't kill your daughter." Her words came out angry, and she felt a scowl hanging on her face. She couldn't get him mad; she couldn't afford courage now. A tiny voice told her that there was a reason he'd brought her mother here tonight.

"I just want to talk," Saul said, smoothing his thinning hair back on his head and looking over at Julie. He clasped her elbow almost lovingly, and she jerked away from him, the first open act of defiance towards the man Sonia had ever seen from her.

"Tell me what you want," Sonia said.

He cut right to the chase. "I want what's mine. I want what you took from me. I won't live without it. You're a common thief, you know that." His eyes shone with excitement and Sonia couldn't imagine what was going through his head—didn't want to.

"Where is *she*?" Saul asked.

The silence was deafening. Heat flashed over and through her as she was forced to look away from his stern gaze, answering all of his doubt. *She. Her. Where is she?*

"She's not your property." Sonia's fingers curled into a fist against the countertop.

Saul wore a grave expression. "I'm not going to hurt her."

Sonia shook her head in sharp movements, her eyes narrowing in resolve.

"I'm going to let you visit with your mother one last time," he said, and the words pierced Sonia's heart—Saul's point clearly made.

He stood and walked out silently, and when the door closed Sonia pressed her hand to the glass with an overwhelming sense of urgency.

"This is not your fault, baby," her mother declared.

"Mom." She felt the walls closing in on her; they had no more time left. "I didn't let you visit because it wasn't safe!" Sonia was yelling now. She couldn't let Saul hurt her mother like he had her father. She could not choose, and he must know that. "I saw you kissing him. It was Christmas, and I'd skipped school. I was so mad because Dad was still alive, and I was mad at you for doing that to him." The words came tumbling out. She needed to clear it all up before she lost her.

"I'm so sorry," her mother said.

"No. No. No," Sonia cried.

"Shhhh. It's okay, baby," Julie cooed, as if talking to a child. "This isn't your fault. Don't you dare do that to me. Don't you dare take this on yourself like all the other things."

"I didn't do it, Mom, I didn't kill her."

Julie's expression didn't change, making it clear she'd never believed it to begin with. "I will always love you. No matter what. But there is evil in this world that we cannot control. If anything happens to me, you remember one thing: I will be with your father and we will both be watching over you," she whispered through her tears. "And this is not your fault. You and your sister are the best things that ever happened to me after I met your father. I loved him very much. Please believe that. Be strong, because I'm going away, and it isn't your fault. Don't you dare give this beast what he wants," she snarled as she held her hand up to the glass, and Sonia instinctively raised hers again to meet it, the glass pane separating their palms.

The foggy handprint remained after Julie stood.

"Mom, there's so much I want to tell you."

Her mother shook her head slowly. "Remember the good times. And you get out of this place and you get your sister away from him. I love you," she said, and turned and walked out the door.

As she sat in the silent room, Sonia felt the same way she had that long-ago Christmas, the first time Saul had stolen her mother away. Dread, heavy and debilitating, took hold of her. She knew this would be the last time she saw her mother alive.

24

REAGAN

It was over nine years ago that she was wandering that small town in Texas. Her mother had been gone for three days, and Mrs. Hillard, at the shelter, was asking questions.

"Where's your mom? She ain't been around?" Her blue eyes reminded Reagan of the ice coating the roads of Milwaukee when she and her mother had passed through, so cold she shivered at the memory, even though the Texas heat burned around her. Mrs. Hillard ran a tight ship, kicking out the junkies and criminals when she found out about them, and, apparently, watching for unattended youth.

"She's…" Reagan bit her lip. She had come up with some excuse beforehand, but it was hiding now in her brain as those blue eyes stared down at her. The woman's liver-spotted hands splayed over her solid hips. She looked somewhere between mad and worried. Yes, worried. "I don't know," Reagan admitted, looking down at her secondhand Nikes, cracked with wear. Her big toes were pushing at the front edge, leaving them callused. She was nearly fifteen, and her mother was having a hard time affording secondhand clothes with her growth spurts. She was hoping to go a few more weeks before Mrs. Hillard noticed that

Shelby Wilson had gone missing, because Reagan knew they would send her straight to foster care.

"How long?" Mrs. Hillard's eyebrows rose.

"I think a few nights now." She glanced away from the woman's stare. Mrs. Hillard could sniff out a lie like a Texas Ranger.

"Where was the last place you saw her?"

"Here." She pointed to the floor. "The other day, before she went to work. Monica said she would watch me; Mom was paying her." She thought of Monica's threats about her mother's missed payments.

"You're too young to be on your own," Mrs. Hillard said. "I can't believe none of the other employees said anything." Reagan knew Mrs. Hillard was the only person here who paid any attention to the residents of the shelter. She knew who was hiding from an abusive spouse, who was selling whatever they could to afford a habit, and which children's parents didn't come back at night. Mrs. Hillard would regularly call the authorities and then Reagan would never see those adults or children again. But she'd never thought it would be her. Her mother wasn't a junkie, and she loved Reagan.

"You're too pretty to have no protection," Mrs. Hillard said knowingly. Her eyes crept over the other shelter residents, as if someone was scheming to prey on Reagan right now.

"Please don't call the cops. Please, Mrs. Hillard. They'll take me away and when my mom comes back for me, I'll be gone and she won't be able to find me." She begged with everything she had, no shame, no holding back. She wrung her fingers with the force of her will to change this old lady's mind but saw no mercy in Mrs. Hillard's eyes.

"I'm sorry, honey," she said reaching for the phone, but before she could dial Reagan was running for the door. "Come back!" Mrs. Hillard cried, but Reagan was already pushing into the Texas heat, the sun at the horizon and sinking into the West.

Dusk. It always frightened her to be out at dark. Her mother had always warned her that the bad people came out at night. As she fled down the street, her eyes watched the corners where people were lingering, with secret handshakes and half-hugs as they traded money for drugs, weird moans coming from dark alleys. But she was too scared to stay at the shelter and get hauled off by the police. Her mother would come back for her.

She ran until she felt blisters on her feet from those tight sneakers, and found a quiet place in the city near an old ceme-tery. When she was too tired to keep her eyes open any longer, she fell into a restless sleep.

When she woke, her stomach groaned, and she thought of the hot food they would have at the shelter. She could look around the parking lot and see if Hillard's car was in its usual spot, and if it wasn't, she could go back in, just to grab some food and see if her mom had showed up yet. Slowly, she shook the dead leaves and mulch from her clothes and headed back toward the shelter. It was early; the sun had not yet broken over the sky when she noticed a car idling near the curb. The driver leaned against the hood as a hot ember from his cigarette flashed in the darkness. She lowered her head as she passed him.

"Need a place to stay?" he asked.

She shook her head and moved faster past his cowboy boots. He was a big man, taller than she was by at least a foot and built like some of the men from the shelter. Day workers, they called themselves, lean with muscle. But this man looked at her differ-ently; she didn't like it.

"I bet you do. Where's your family?" He was walking beside her now, keeping step with her.

She thought of darting down an alley, but who knew what she would run into down there? He was big, so he probably wasn't as fast as her.

"Good looking girl like you. You're always alone." It was a statement, not a question, and she realized it wasn't the first time this man had noticed her. She felt his fingers grab her arm. She was prepared to scream, her lungs expanding with an impossible amount of air, when he lifted a finger to his lips, and the shock of this caused her scream to expel in a hiss of surprise. A gun rested in the waistband of his pants; the threat was clear.

"I think I'll give you a place to stay." He jerked her by the arm toward his car.

On the two-day trip, she pictured herself fighting him off in ten different scenarios. Kicking, punching and plowing him over. Or maybe a stranger would rescue her and she would run off to the shelter where her mother would be waiting. But none of those things happened. And she wouldn't have thought it then, but the worst was yet to come. A large farm in Virginia would be her new home. A place where terrible things happened. The place where she would first meet Saul D'Luca.

* * *

It was 1:00 in the morning and the moon was bright in the sky when Reagan rolled out of bed. She could see the light peeking through the small window above her bed. She pulled on her robe and left the camper. The ground was cool beneath her naked feet as she climbed across large stones set above the roaring ocean a hundred feet below, the ground dropping swiftly into the darkness beyond as the sounds of the ocean echoed up.

"Nice night for a walk," came a voice from nearby.

Reagan jumped, searching in the darkness around her for the source. She placed the voice before she saw the pale outline of his face twenty feet away. His legs were propped against the rocks as he reclined, looking up at the stars. "I think we should start over."

She pulled her robe tighter as a shiver stole through her.

"My name is Max Randal. It's nice to meet you—again."

She let a moment go by as her heart settled back into a normal rhythm. "I'm Reagan."

"Reagan. Where are you from?"

"Why are you out here?" she asked in response.

"Why are you out here?" he echoed.

"I couldn't sleep." She shifted away from him, always on guard.

"I couldn't sleep either." He looked over at her now. His eyes reflected the light of the camper beyond. "Charlie has woofies."

Reagan felt her forehead crinkle. "What are woofies?"

"Dreams. He's a big dreamer, that dog. He growls and half-barks in his dreams and kicks his legs." Max laughed. "It's the cutest damned thing, but it wakes me up all the time." His hair was dark and short, his broad shoulders pulled back as he lifted the long neck of a beer bottle to his lips.

"Where are you from, Max?"

"I asked you first."

"Milwaukee, Phoenix, Nashville—you name it, I've been there. I think it would be harder for me to find a place I haven't been." She snorted softly.

He nodded. "Canada. Want a beer?" he asked, tipping one toward her.

She shook her head. "I don't drink, in case I need to drive." As in leave this place in the middle of the night because some psychopath named Saul D'Luca found us.

"I'm sorry I scared you the other day. I just wanted to say hello. Mason, he looks like a great kid."

"He is," Reagan agreed. The breeze rippled past her and her hair swirled around her cheeks.

"How long are you staying?" Max asked.

Reagan only shook her head. The rock was still warm under her feet from the day's sunlight, its texture rough against her bare soles.

"I'll cook you both dinner some time if that's okay. Charlie would love the company."

Reagan felt a smile take root on her face. "Maybe. Why are you here in the States?"

He let out a breath. "See the world. Run from my past—I don't know." He snickered like he was joking, but she'd noticed the sadness in his tone.

"Me too," she whispered, and glanced over at him. Heat flooded her cheeks, and she stood up. "I'm heading inside," she said. "See you tomorrow?"

A wide smile on his face. "You bet."

As she lay in bed that night, trying to shut her mind off and go to sleep, she pictured Max's broad smile and wondered, not for the first time, if she could trust him.

25

JAMIE

JAMIE HAD her paperwork spread out on the conference table before Ali showed up. The room was quiet and the sun rose against the glass, casting a warm light. She had slept at her apartment again, and the message she got from Drew this morning had melted her:

"Hey. It's me. You wanna tell me what's going on? Is it something I did? Call me back. I love you and miss you."

What the hell was her problem? Why didn't she just tell him about Nina and that she had taken a temporary job with Ali's firm?

His husky voice echoed in her mind as she tried to concentrate on how she would approach the results of Sonia's polygraph.

Sonia had lied. Jamie had known this the day she gave Sonia her polygraph, but the results were different than she'd suspected. In her detailed notes from that day, she'd written that she did perceive deception—but not on the question that was causing her the most concern right now.

The door to the room opened with a soft whine and Ming walked in, carrying a large bag over her skinny shoulder. "You're up here early," she said as she found her own place to work at the table.

"You too." Jamie turned back to her report. After she'd finished typing it up the night before, she could think of little else until she received a late-night call from Nina. Her breath blasting into the phone as if she were hyperventilating. Then her voice cracked into loud, reckless screams. It took her back to that shadowy basement in the woods…

When she finally woke, she was disoriented and panicked. At first, she was overwhelmed by a certainty that she was in danger that morphed into the echo of those eerie screams.

"What did you find out?" Ali said, moving into the room and slamming the door behind her. Her movement was a surge of energy like a live wire as she refused to take a seat at the table, a steaming cup of coffee in one hand and her cell phone gripped in the other, her heavy footfalls muted by the decorative rug.

Ming spoke first. "I may have something. There were reports from a neighbor in Montana that I interviewed over the phone. Apparently Sonia didn't live alone, as her lease specified, but because her landlord was recently killed, I can't confirm this with him."

Jamie wasn't surprised to learn that Ming had read the entire lease; the woman left no stone unturned.

Ali muttered, "His death must have something to do with Sonia."

"Why would she have people living with her if she was on the run? It makes no sense," Jamie said. "Did she need money? That's not so far-fetched."

Ming shrugged. "The neighbor said he was sure she lived there with a younger woman and a baby."

"How young?" Ali asked.

"Early twenties or younger, the neighbor guessed. The baby was a newborn."

A young girl and a baby. Perhaps the girl had gotten pregnant and was kicked out of her house, or was on the run, and Sonia had taken her in. Jamie made a note to ask Sonia about it at the next meeting. She didn't think to ask any questions about that year, assuming it was irrelevant.

"How would the neighbor even see her from his place? I looked at the map of where she lived. She was really off the grid out there." Ali took a sip of her coffee.

"I guess one of the neighbors was paid by the landlord to take cords of wood up in the spring for the heating. It was just the one time he saw them." Ming arched a brow. "He was certain of what he saw."

Ali turned to Jamie. "Did you finish the report?"

"It's not what you want to hear."

Ali sighed and finally dropped into one of the chairs as if she were physically exhausted. "Hit me." Her hand danced in the air above her head, her neck arched back as she stared up at the ceiling.

"She lied. I've concluded from the test results and from observation."

"So, she killed Emma?"

"No."

Ali's head shot up. "I thought you said she lied."

"She did. But not about murdering Emma."

Ali let out a puff of air like she'd been holding her breath. "Explain."

"I asked her a series of questions regarding the murder itself and some details surrounding it. I'm showing issues with three of the questions." Jamie passed the report over to Ali for her to view.

"What the hell am I looking at?" Ali snapped after looking over the stapled pages for the briefest moment.

Using her pen, Jamie pointed out the inconsistencies in Sonia's results. "Okay. This one doesn't help me, and I would argue the other two are irrelevant."

Ali tossed the report back down. "Look, I didn't ask you to be on her side, but don't screw her over with this stuff."

"I'm letting you know she's hiding something from us. If she isn't honest with us, then we can't trust her." Jamie hated stating the obvious. "And we should wonder what she's up to."

"But she doesn't know who killed Emma."

Jamie nodded. "True, but then why hide information from us? What is she trying to do?"

It wasn't to protect Joey, as she'd originally said.

"Okay. I want you to take a ride over to Flint Hill tomorrow and talk with her about this. See what you can find out. I'll go with you."

Jamie nodded.

"And this stuff about living with someone. Dig into that. See if we can't come up with any more witnesses. It's not a coincidence that anyone who knew her in Montana has turned up dead in the last seventy-two hours. We're looking at a short list."

"Is it possible Saul found out?" Jamie asked. "That he's looking for something or someone?"

Ali shook her head but said nothing. She wasn't sure—none of them were.

"He knew about Montana when Sonia was first arrested. What changed?" Ming added.

"Joey." Jamie shifted forward in her seat, elbows braced on the smooth table. "What if Saul had Joey worked over because he had some information Saul wanted?" Everyone was quick to assume Saul wanted revenge; what if it was something else entirely that he was after? She thought of the bloody footprints staining the white fibers of the carpet at Emma's house. There was something in that house that Sonia had been looking for, and maybe she found it.

"We need to be cautious, ladies," Ali warned. "I may have some information coming from Javi. If it's anything that affects what we already know, I'll pass it along."

Both Ming and Jamie nodded.

"Good. And I need to ask, for no reason other than my own peace of mind: have you both been careful? Watching to make sure you aren't being followed home, that sort of thing?"

"Yes," said Ming.

"Yes," Jamie echoed.

"Good. It looks like this may drag out in the courts. I filed the appeal paperwork, but there's a slight issue I'm looking into. We need to get Sonia out of there before she's killed."

Jamie recalled all the scars and marks from years of abuse covering Sonia's skin, and she knew Ali was right. Saul would not stop until that woman was dead.

26

SONIA

SHE LOOKED DOWN at the picture of an opened chest cavity in a five-year-old textbook donated from a university in Alabama. A rust-colored, slippery-looking, tongue-shaped organ peeked out from under the lung. The ropy length of intestines hung below the stomach.

"Rossi!" Remmy shouted. "Visitor."

The library was empty except for the guard at the door. Sonia stood and returned the book to its spot. She was dreading this appointment.

"Hustle up, it's almost break time," Remmy said while appraising her fingernails. Remmy's long steps seem to glide as Sonia hobbled to keep up with the guard's quick strides. "You're like a cat, Rossi. Like a damned cat." She smacked her lips together as they approached the interview room. "Even pussycats die eventually." She opened the door and winked at Sonia as she passed.

"Thanks for the heads up." Sonia's voice dripped with sarcasm.

"What happened to her?" Jamie shot out of her seat as Sonia entered the room.

The guard looked between the two women, her eyes growing wide with feigned surprise. "Our Ms. Rossi is very prone to accidents," Remmy said. Then she turned and walked out.

"What's this?" Jamie waved a hand toward a developing bruise around Sonia's eye.

"I had a visitor the other night." Sonia's lips pressed together in a slight grimace as she made her way to the chair. "You should see the other guy."

"This isn't funny," Jamie snapped. "This is your life."

"What life?" Sonia sensed a sort of hysterical laugh bubbling up inside of her. "This isn't a life, it's a death sentence. A slow, grueling end." Her fingers found the tender flesh where they'd hit her with the taser probes. She liked to feel the pain—it grounded her somehow. After Saul left the other night, Walker had made a snide remark to her, and Sonia couldn't resist. She had punched that asshole right in the nose. Blood sprang past his hand, cupping his face while the other hand reached for his taster. By then Sonia had raised both hands to signal her surrender, but he had fired it anyway.

Unable to help herself, unable to overcome the burning desire to be in the hole, alone to cry, she had let loose. It was worth it. The taser ride had been short. After Dr. Cho cleared her again, she had been taken to solitary, where she curled up for nearly twenty-four hours, the feeling of hopelessness washing over her in waves as she pictured her beautiful mother being murdered by Saul's goons. And only just after she'd unburdened the secret that contributed to such bitterness between them. Should she reach out to Nikki to check on their mother?

Nikki, her big sister. The last time they'd stood face to face was just after Sonia was sentenced to life in prison. She wasn't even sure why Nikki had come, as her loyalty was firmly planted on Saul's side.

"I'll take care of Mom, don't worry about her." Nikki's short, feminine frame, layered in leather, sat in the opposite chair.

Sonia wasn't worried about their mother back then.

"And if you need anything—on the outside. Let me know. I'm there for you."

Sonia was nearly too shocked by the offer to speak. This was unlike her sister, and what did she mean by "need anything on the outside"? These were the sort of niceties normal siblings exchanged, but not them. She'd decided to let the issue drop, but she never forgot about it.

Jamie cleared her throat, forcing Sonia back to the present. "I have the results from your polygraph, and there are a few things I want to go over with you. Along with some additional information on your case."

The report lay before her, but Sonia wouldn't look down at it as she prepared for the accusations.

"You lied," Jamie said, point-blank. "I don't want to sit here and play guessing games with you, because you know you lied."

Sonia knew what the results would show. "I didn't kill her."

"I know that."

"Then why does the rest of it matter?"

"Because I told you I wasn't on anyone's side. I told you I was after the truth." Jamie's voice rose, but she wasn't yelling; it was more of a disheartened rant, as though she were a disappointed mother talking to her teen child.

Sonia could understand that—that she was a disappointment. She remembered her mother's last fleeting glance as Sonia bucked and screamed that Saul was going to kill her mother as four guards dragged her to her cell. She had fought hard, but it was mostly because the physical pain was a release from the emotional pain threatening to take over. This weakness would destroy all the reserve she had left.

"I need a favor," Sonia said.

"What is it this time?"

"I need you to find out about my mother."

"How did you know?" Jamie asked, her eyes narrowing on Sonia.

"How did I know what?"

"Look. I know you feel like there is no one you can trust, but trust me. There was an anonymous call placed last night to the police. To the Feds. I believe she is in some kind of protective custody, but I'm not aware of the details." Her conspiratorial tone closed the conversation and Sonia felt a wave of relief crash through her with such force that she grabbed the lip of the table, for how long she wasn't sure, but Jamie sat silently by as she let all her emotions surge out of her for the second time in so many days.

Finally, she spoke. "I took something out of that house."

Jamie watched her, her head tipping to the side. "What was it? The police found bloody footprints in the office. What were you looking for?"

"I was looking for paperwork about a procedure Emma had. She made me promise not to let her father find out."

"Procedure?"

"You're not listening," Sonia snapped. "I found someone there."

"Who?"

"I don't know when she got there, but she was hiding in the closet. Her name is Reagan—a seventeen-year-old girl."

Sonia remembered walking into the office, frantic to find the paperwork. She'd tried not to disturb anything, so that no one would know she had been there. A noise from the closet had startled her. Her instinct screamed that the killer might still be there. She reached for the sharp letter opener on the desk. She couldn't leave without those documents. Saul would find them…and he would investigate.

She slowly made her way to the closet. She could hear the soft rasp of heavy breathing, accompanied by the pounding of blood in her temples.

"I'm armed," she said. She wanted to sound imposing but only sounded out of breath. The door to the closet was open about half an inch, and she caught the edge of the door with her fingers. The scream that emanated from the closet when she opened the door was high-pitched and frantic. Sonia resisted the urge to cover her ears, so she could wield the letter opener. There, on the floor, among the boxes of shoes, was a young girl. Her pale skin smooth with youth, tears streaming down her cheeks, her hands held high in surrender.

Sonia lowered the letter opener. "I'm not going to hurt you." She backed away from the closet, her heart beating like running rabbits' feet against her ribs, and took in several long breaths. "I'm not going to hurt you," she repeated, and the young girl's breathing quieted.

"My name is Sonia. Are you alone?"

The girl nodded her head vigorously.

"What's your name?"

"Reagan," she whispered.

"Who hurt Emma?" Sonia stepped closer and for the first time she realized this girl could have done it. She surveyed her for blood or any other signs she was involved. Nothing. Sonia reached a hand down to help her up. "I'm not going to hurt you." She didn't know how many times she would have to say it for this girl to believe her.

Reagan slowly took her hand and pulled upright with ease. She was skinny, too skinny, and young.

"We don't have much time," Sonia said.

"Help me," she whispered softly.

Sonia let the girl's hand go and noticed notches of angry skin around her wrist; not fresh but healed over with time. The young girl was cradling her flat belly, and Sonia understood.

"Yes. I'll help you, but we can't stay here. We have to go. We have to run."

The soft click of a pen brought Sonia's thoughts back to the present.

"Who was she?" Jamie asked, leaning toward Sonia. "Where is she now?"

Sonia felt cornered. "Look, I didn't lie to keep myself out of trouble. This girl needed protection. If Saul were to find her…" Sonia inhaled sharply and blew out her breath in a long stream.

"I understand. Our team is working low-key. I don't want anyone to get hurt. Can you tell me anything about her? What was she doing in Emma's townhouse?"

"Emma saved her." Sonia's voice was wistful. She often thought of that day—the day everything had changed—even when she was free and on the run, with a teenager in tow. She went from thinking she would never have a child to being part of a family overnight. She found them a place, a nothing town in the middle of nowhere. She thought they would be safe there. A place where Saul should not have been able to find her. But he did—a testament to his relentless pursuit of her.

"I worked for a hobby shop in town. I kept to myself. I couldn't let anything happen to her again. She'd been taken by one of Saul's men." Sonia spat the sour words. Reagan, sweet girl, deserved a loving family, not to be at the mercy of a deranged pervert like Saul who acted like they had some sort of normal relationship.

"Saul," Jamie whispered.

"I couldn't leave her there, scared and alone. So I took her with me. I knew what people would think. Emma must have called me to help her with Reagan. Saul—he does things. Horrible things to make money." Sonia felt herself shiver. "But I don't think he would ever hurt Emma, no matter what she was up to."

Jamie reached out and squeezed her hand. "It's okay. We're with you."

"I thought you said you don't choose sides."

Jamie shook her head. "You did this for the right reasons, and I might have done the same thing. Does that make sense?"

"I wanted to save her."

"Where is she now?"

Sonia leveled her eyes on Jamie, searching her for any sign that this was a trick. She couldn't trust anyone with this secret. It would not only put Reagan at risk, but Jamie, also.

"I don't know," Sonia said evenly. "I really don't."

Jamie nodded and leaned away. There was something bothering her; Sonia sensed it in her rigid shoulders and blank expression.

"What else did you lie about the other day?"

Sonia should have known it wouldn't be that easy to deflect Jamie's questioning. She'd told her the truth about Reagan, hoping she would let the other issue drop, but Jamie wanted the whole truth.

Finally, Sonia said, "I lied when I said I never killed anyone."

27

JAMIE

THEY WAITED AS LONG as they could before Jamie took over the meeting. Ali ran late sometimes, and Jamie had things she needed to do this afternoon.

"So, I have some recent information that might be helpful," Jamie said, looking between Javi and Ming. "I learned that Sonia was living with a young woman named Reagan in Montana, and that Reagan was in the townhouse with Emma the day she was murdered. I believe Saul kept her as a sex slave, but I don't have any proof yet. Sonia wasn't willing to talk about Reagan beyond that. She only said she found her at Emma's townhouse on the day she was killed."

"Maybe she's the one who killed her," Javi said.

Jamie shook her head. "No, I don't think so. According to Sonia, she was just a frightened kid."

"What's her full name?" Javi asked.

"Sonia didn't say." Jamie frowned.

"Well, does she want our help or not?" Ming asked.

Jamie understood their frustration, but she had to agree with Sonia on this one. Revealing too much about Reagan might put her in danger if Saul found out.

"I can work on locating her. What about the child the neighbor mentioned?" Ming asked.

Jamie shook her head. "She didn't mention a child, and I ran out of time before I could ask. It would be great if you could follow up. Sonia has no idea where she might be. Said she probably ran after Sonia was arrested. As far as I can tell—"

The door pushed open and Alex walked in. "Sorry I'm late. I was just told Ali was a no-show today. The firm will want someone in on this," he said, taking a seat at the head of the conference table next to Jamie. She felt her stomach twist and her forehead wrinkle as the familiar scent of him drifted to her nose. She found herself clenching her fists under the table and forced them open.

Alex looked at her and smiled, seemingly unaware of her aversion to him. She thought he might reach out and touch her, but he thought better of it. She moved her hand onto the table and turned her body to face the others.

"What did I miss?" Alex said, looking around the circle, his expectant manner on display.

Jamie shook her head. "We were told only to discuss this case with Ali."

"Well, Ali isn't here, and this firm is representing Sonia. In fact, I was just given paperwork by her assistant to file in court today," Alex said, holding up a stack of papers as if Jamie needed proof. His eyes studied her, pulling away her careful layers. She looked away in surrender. She needed to resist the urge to challenge him at every turn. She was fully committed to maintaining her professional manner no matter how inappropriate he became.

Jamie looked at Ming and Javi, who seemed unfazed. A lawyer was a lawyer, after all.

"We were just talking about finding Sonia's roommate in Montana," Ming said.

"I wasn't aware she was living with anyone," Alex said. Oh, great. Now she was required to bring him up to speed.

"Did she kill Emma?" Alex asked.

Jamie shook her head. "I think Emma was trying to rescue her." Jamie shifted back to her thought process before Alex could interrupt. "As I was saying, there's nothing on the books that Saul is in any way involved in human trafficking, but I have confirmed through a separate individual that Saul could get young girls for sex." Jamie felt her cheeks heat as Alex watched her.

"Saul D'Luca?" Alex asked, tugging at his tie.

Jamie nodded.

"You don't think he had anything to do with his own daughter's murder, do you?" His look insinuated that the question was meant to chastise rather than garner a response.

"No," Jamie said.

"Good." Alex tapped his pen lightly against the tabletop.

Ignoring Alex's outburst, Ming backtracked to Jamie's statement about Reagan. "She could have come from anywhere. There are a lot of young women brought into the country and sold as sex workers or used as cheap labor for rich people. Was she a nanny, perhaps?"

Jamie had wanted to ask Sonia these questions, but when she'd sensed her shutting down, she backed off. "I don't know where she's from or where she might hide out." Jamie was shaking her head. "Sonia said she had marks on her wrist, like she was restrained. She was scared and didn't talk much for a long time."

"Her name is Reagan? What's her last name?" Javi asked.

Jamie cringed. She didn't want Alex to know all the details. "I'll have to ask Sonia. I'm going to go visit her again tomorrow to see if there is anything else she can remember," Jamie said.

"I'll go with you," Alex offered.

"Ali's going." Jamie glared at him. "Or are you assuming she'll call out tomorrow, too?"

Alex shrugged. "Don't know, but I'm going to be helping with the case from now on. They wanted more hands on deck." He smiled graciously. The sort of smile that trapped the unwitting.

Jamie could feel the bile burning up her throat at the idea of spending even more time with her ex. Was this the exact reason she had avoided telling Drew that she was helping Ali with this case? He didn't like Alex, and Jamie didn't blame him. It wasn't because he was Jamie's ex, but because he was unbalanced, as well as unpredictable.

"Will you excuse me?" Jamie said and let herself out of the conference room, feeling all eyes on her; she couldn't get out fast enough. She pulled her phone out and dialed Ali's number. She didn't know what was going on here, but she wanted to hear it from Ali that Alex would be on the case. She didn't trust him, and with good reason: he had betrayed her more than once. And had only narrowly missed an indictment for leaving the scene without helping a dying woman.

Ali's phone rang right to voicemail. A gurgle of apprehension bubbled up in Jamie. Why wouldn't Ali call her?

Jamie made a beeline to Ali's assistant's office two doors down. Kia's face said it all.

"What's wrong?" Jamie asked. Kia looked exhausted, her normally kempt appearance sliding toward disheveled.

"I can't believe this, right."

"Believe what?" Jamie was missing something. "I don't know what's going on."

Kia's small mouth pursed, and tears threatened the corners of her brown eyes. "Ali's missing."

"What! Since when?"

"Last night. Her husband said she never came home after leaving work." Fresh tears peeled down the young woman's cheeks. "I don't know when she left. She's always working so late. Especially with this recent case." She blotted at the tears with a tissue.

Jamie reached a hand out to touch the woman's arm. "It's okay. I'm sure they'll find her." But panic flashed in her as she processed what this meant. Her mind was trying to control the terror under the surface. Ali...gone. Alive...or dead?

"Alex said he would tell you guys," Kia said, looking left and right as if he was standing nearby, analyzing her delivery.

"He never—" Jamie's voice cut off. "Keep me updated," Jamie said to Kia, and walked back to the meeting. She quietly took her seat and her heartbeat slowed only as she focused on the discussion.

Ming was wrapping up what she'd learned in Montana. Jamie's eyes watched Alex as he nodded in all the right parts and passed out reassuring smiles with a bonus compliment here and there. A show for all to see.

"Is there anything else I need to know about?" Alex asked, his pen poised as if he had just taken copious notes over his still-blank paper. Everyone shook their heads. "Good. You guys work well together. I'll help in any way I can."

Ming and Javi were gathering their things when Alex rose to leave. He apparently noticed that Jamie hadn't moved. "Everything okay?" he asked in a low tone, his head tilted toward hers.

"Why didn't you tell us the police are looking for Ali?" Jamie said loud enough to catch Ming and Javi's attention.

Alex's lips parted in surprise, but he quickly regained his composure. "I was waiting to hear what the police had learned. I didn't want to upset anyone. Do you have a minute? Follow me to my office," Alex said, holding his hand out to guide her. She became so overwhelmed by the desire to roll her eyes that her left eyelid began twitching.

His office was exactly what she expected. Extravagant and

cold. Like him. All clean lines and polished silver, but affording no comfort.

"What is it, Alex? I have a lot of work to catch up on."

"Take it easy. I'm the boss; you won't get in trouble," Alex said intending to come off cute but sounding more controlling.

"I don't work for you or Ali. I'm freelance," Jamie snapped. It was going to be impossible to hide her contempt. For a moment she relished the thought of just going off on him. How great it would feel to watch his confidence melt into a puddle on the floor.

Alex tried to look wounded, but she saw the calculation under the surface. "I wanted to talk to you about this girl Sonia found. Where's she from? How is it she came to know Emma? Is there anything else you can tell me about her?"

"Just what I told everyone already. I'm not hiding anything from you."

Alex paused just a beat before he took a seat behind his massive desk and steepled his thin manicured fingers under his jaw. "We need to work together on this. If Sonia didn't kill Emma, we need to find out who else had a motive. This girl could be the key. We need to find her."

"As I've already said, Sonia doesn't know where she went after she was arrested." Jamie couldn't remember whether or not Alex had been in the room at the time she'd shared this information, but she wasn't feeling very charitable toward him.

He shrugged off her harshness. "I have information that tells me she placed a brief call—less than one minute—at the scene of the accident. To a burner phone."

"Who told you that?" What else was he not telling them?

"It was in one of the police reports. I can't remember which. If she warned this girl to run…" Alex let the thought hang between them.

Then what? Jamie wanted to ask. She's already spent five years in prison for a murder Jamie believed she didn't commit.

"Well, its kidnapping," Alex finally said.

"Bull."

"She took her when she was a teenager. Probably under eighteen years old," Alex said. To an outsider, it might appear he wasn't arguing, but he was. She could recall many fights just like these.

"Whatever, Alex. Have fun trying to get Sonia to trust you when you try to get kidnapping charges on her."

"But she trusts you."

"What are you saying?" Jamie noticed her foot tapping the floor. She wanted out of this office and away from this person.

"I'm saying you can talk to her. Get information. We need it for the case. We're at a dead end."

They were hardly at a dead end. Ming was finding something new every day. She was combing through the police reports and Javi was looking at social media and other digital options. Jamie didn't want to call Javi a hacker, but she didn't ask him how he found out his information.

But instead of bringing up any of her immediate thoughts she found herself asking, "Why haven't you asked about Ali?" She paused, then added, "Have you spoken with the police about her?"

He took on a somber tone as his ego sank under the surface. "Yes. I've been on and off the phone with them since she went missing. We're doing everything we can to locate her."

"We?"

"The firm." He seemed to pout. She wanted to ask him if he cared about Ali or if it was just his duty, but she dropped it.

"I'll give you a heads-up when I go see her, but I think I should go alone. She's very skittish."

"She needs to know who's working on her case."

Jamie's phone chimed. Thank goodness. "I have to take this." She left the office, not giving him a chance to speak again.

"Hello?"

"It's Javi. Check your email."

He ended the call without another word, and Jamie pulled her phone away, perplexed. Javi was a bit odd; she would have to get used to his abrupt manner. It seemed he communicated much better with technology than with humans.

When she opened her email and read what Javi had alerted her to, her mouth fell open. "What the—"

28
SONIA

S<small>UNLIGHT</small> <small>HIT</small> Sonia's skin and spread warmth like hot rocks from a spa. She leaned back, arms extended, eyes closed toward the sky. She was resting on a metal picnic table at the edge of the rec yard listening to voices, birds, and the steady beat of a basketball nearby. She'd recovered her rec privileges today, and her body was thirsty for fresh air and vitamin D. The obnoxious echo of even numbers tumbled in her brain, but they were quieter out here.

"Can never get enough of this." Harriet's voice came from nearby and Sonia opened her eyes to see her walking at the edge of the fence, fingers trailing along the diamond-shaped holes. "Word on the block is you're innocent."

Sonia tipped her head back again. "It's complicated."

"I got time."

"Well, maybe not so complicated. I didn't kill the woman I confessed to killing." Saying it out loud, Sonia realized, made her sound insane. It didn't seem that way all those years ago when she signed statements and made up a story about her husband sleeping with Emma. It felt like something she had to do—that there were no other options available.

Harriet's mouth twisted up on one side when Sonia turned to look at her. "You're too smart to do something stupid like that, child."

"I did what I thought was right and now I'm in a big mess." She let out a deep breath as she caught sight of Ginger's red mane, her green eyes looking over at Sonia while she leaned into Tammie's ear.

"Watch out for that new cellmate of yours. She's looking to make friends."

Sonia smirked.

"Rossi!" A shout came from across the yard. Shaffer and another female guard stood near an open doorway. "Visitor."

"Not again," Sonia muttered as she slowly stood. She couldn't take another surprise visit from Saul.

"Watch yourself," Harriet warned. "Word is Tammie's interested in what they got to offer." She tipped her chin toward the group in the yard and frowned.

The walk was gossip-filled as Sonia shuffled along between the other women. Mack's name was mentioned, and her stomach lurched.

"Who's here to visit me?" she asked the guards.

"Someone from your lawyer's office. Pretty chick," Shaffer said.

Sonia just knew this polygraph was going to backfire. A big lie. A little lie. She had been caught again—she wasn't any good at this. She'd already told them more than she was planning to. And now it was all unraveling.

"Put your hands on the wall," the guard commanded. Sonia was subjected to a search, and they opened the door for her. "You have thirty minutes."

"I was told sixty," Jamie spoke up from the table.

"Thirty minutes," the guard shot back and left the room.

Jamie waved Sonia over to the table, her movements jerky and her cheeks flushed. "We don't have much time," Jamie whispered. She hit a button on her laptop and white noise emanated from the small speaker.

Sonia sat down and leaned in toward the edge of the table. Someone must be dead, or, worse, Saul had found them. "What happened?"

Jamie took a deep breath. "Ali's missing."

"What!" She pictured Ali's pretty, sharp features hanging out of a dumpster, homeless junkies rummaging through her pockets, and she pinched her eyes shut. "Since when?"

"Since sometime last night, after she left work. Sounds like they found some tapes from the parking garage; they're reviewing them."

Sonia began chewing on her thumbnail. "What's being done to find her?"

"There's an open investigation, but that's not all." Jamie looked weary. "They found two bodies."

Sonia let her mouth fall open. "Who?"

"Your old landlord and a woman from your hometown in Montana." Jamie's eyes stayed on Sonia's face, reading her.

"It's him. It's Saul. He must have found out I knew those people."

Jamie softly shushed her. "I don't trust the people in this place. And there's another thing."

Sonia leaned in toward Jamie as she could barely hear her whispering. "Because Ali's missing, the law firm put a man named Alex Carter in charge of your appeal." Jamie took a deep breath. "I don't trust him."

Fear pricked her. "What the hell," Sonia huffed. "What am I supposed to do with that?"

Saul's revenge was closing in on everything: squeezing, crushing her.

"I want to be completely up front with you. I have a past with Alex. I don't believe it's clouding my judgment, but I wanted you to know everything so I don't stain your opinion."

"What should I do?"

Jamie looked at the door and back to Sonia. "Who's paying for your legal defense?"

Sonia had not been expecting this question. There was a flash of guilt as she thought of the life insurance policy she had maintained on her husband.

"Life insurance money."

"From Joey?" Jamie guessed.

Sonia nodded, her gaze cast to the table. "I thought it was the least he could do seeing how I kept him out of the courtroom. I tried to protect him."

"I thought you said you didn't think he did it?"

Sonia let out a low grunt of frustration. "I don't know who did it. I'm telling the truth. I may not have pleaded guilty because of Joey, like I said, but I didn't want him to be dragged to court to testify. I thought if he could stay hidden, he would stay alive." It was the truth. She still loved him.

"So, you pleaded guilty to protect this girl you found?"

Sonia hesitated. Something Jamie didn't fail to notice. "I did it for Joey and for her. I did it for my family, too. There's little that Saul would feel when he finally gets around to killing me, once he's sure I've suffered enough. I doubt he would even blink an eye. I would never be safe."

"And you thought you'd be safe here?" Skepticism poured over each of Jamie's words.

"Joey told me not to go home. I had this girl in my back seat and she was crying and terrified. The cops were already at the house. I didn't know what to do. He told me to clean out the bank account and run. So we ran." Sonia swiped her sleeve against her face to catch the tears of frustration. "I don't care what happens to me, but I need them protected."

"Yeah, about that. Do you know who called the Feds about your mother?"

Sonia started to speak, but Jamie put her finger to her mouth.

"Don't say it. Don't tell a soul if you know. That person will be in danger if anyone finds out."

Sonia nodded.

"I'm going to have to bring Alex with me next time I visit. At least until we find out what happened to Ali. But I have a terrible feeling about his involvement."

"I thought you didn't trust him. If you don't, then I definitely don't. I mean, I don't trust anyone."

"But we need to be smart about this. He's a necessary evil. All we have to do is be careful about what we mention to him. If there is anything he doesn't need to know, don't tell him."

Jamie pulled a single sheet of paper out of her stack. "Which leads me to why I'm here." She pushed a single printed email over to Sonia while keeping her finger to her lips, then tapping the paper.

As Sonia scanned the short email, she knew her worse fear might have been realized. She had to think fast.

"I was going to tell you about him," Sonia said in a low whisper.

"I want you to be very careful what you say to me. To anyone," Jamie said. "I don't want anyone else to get hurt, let alone a child."

Who was going to protect them? There was nowhere Saul couldn't find them; his need for revenge drove him to keep hunting. And if Saul had discovered the truth, it would be worse.

"I want you to know I will never tell." Jamie's hand reached out to squeeze hers. "If he's yours."

Sonia was shaking her head absently. "I can't have children."

Jamie's brow furrowed.

"Mildred delivered Reagan's baby," Sonia said with no emotion at all. Looking past Jamie now, she pictured Reagan reaching out to hold Mason. And all Sonia could think was: Saul's blood ran through this child.

"And now she's dead." Jamie seemed to be thinking out loud.

"Reagan's out there right now, taking care of a young boy all by herself?" Jamie asked.

Sonia felt the familiar prick of pain as she thought of the two of them on their own. They were still better off than they'd ever be with her. She was sure they had evaded Saul for a while by staying on the run, but not for long enough; somehow, he had tracked them down.

"Is Saul hunting them now?" Jamie asked.

Sonia thought of the two bodies recently discovered in Montana. "He won't stop until he finds them."

"Why?" Jamie sounded frustrated. "Why them? Why kill all these people?" But then it seemed to dawn on her. "It's his child." It was a statement, and Sonia lowered her head to stare at her hands.

"She'll be fine. She's older now." Sonia shifted in her seat.

"When I bring Alex here, don't mention the child. Don't mention anything we've discussed."

The door to the room opened. Sonia stood and, with a nod, walked out, defeated.

29

REAGAN

THE FIRST TIME she met Saul, he seemed nice. He was a big man with an angular face and thick black hair. He wore a wedding ring, and she remembered thinking that he must have a family, maybe some kids; he wouldn't hurt her.

She had been wrong. After crying for nearly two days in the car with the man who abducted her, she arrived at the farm. The house was big, with a wide front porch wrapped around the sides. Its white shiplap siding shone in the sunlight while wind licked up the large pin oaks that sprung up over the long green yard. It was just the type of place her mother would hate, claiming the upkeep would be horrendous.

The man stretched out of the car and ducked his head. "Come inside. If you try to run, I'll shoot you and leave you for the coyotes." He said this with no emotion. She pictured the snarling animals feasting on her flesh, their howls ripping into the night. No, she wouldn't run; not yet.

She followed the man inside, where she witnessed silent faces of girls in the halls and through doorways. All young, all different ethnicities, sadness painting their pretty features. She wondered: how had they all gotten here? Wasn't anyone looking for them? She'd bet anything angry Mrs. Hillard would be looking for her—even if out of spite for running away like she had.

That night she met Saul for the first time at dinner. She sat quietly, not touching the roasted chicken before her, wondering absently who had cooked it. What kind of place was this?

"You're very beautiful," Saul said in his gruff voice. "How old are you?"

"Fourteen." Though her body was weak and hungry, she didn't touch the food. She was certain she would throw up anything she managed to eat. Saul was dressed in a button-down shirt and blue jeans, much like a trendy uncle. She felt uncomfortable with the way his eyes studied her, and she looked away.

He leaned back in his chair and sipped at the dark amber liquid in his glass. "Where are you from?"

"Everywhere," she whispered.

"How did Jeremy come across you?" Jeremy. This was the first time she'd learned the name of the man who'd kidnapped her.

"I ran away from a homeless shelter after my mom disappeared. He found me—there." Her voice broke.

"Well, it's my luck." Saul nodded. "I'll take care of you here." He made it sound like he was doing her a favor. It would be her first lesson in his narcissism. She wanted to argue with him—to beg him to let her go back to that dirty shelter in Texas, but she would be wasting her time.

What happened in the days and months following was worse than Reagan could have imagined. Things she learned to block out to survive. She was locked in her room every night. As far as she could tell, there were at least six others in the house: four girls and two boys. During the day they were allowed out of their rooms—only in pairs, and only while Jeremy or some other armed person watched over them. When men were visiting, she would hear the weird noises: yelling, moaning and then inevitably crying. She would pinch her eyes shut and imagine she was back at the homeless shelter. Her head resting against her mother's arms. Her mother's skin always smelled of grease and cinnamon donuts left over from her shift at the diner. "I love you, baby," she would whisper.

Now, in her room all alone, Reagan cried so hard her gut ached. She missed those dingy walls, and the room filled with strangers. And not just because it reminded her of her mother, though it did, but because it was the last taste of freedom she had.

Saul's orders were strict: no one touches Reagan. Could she really escape the same fate as those around her?

When he came to her, it was two months before her sixteenth birthday. She had been at the home for nearly a year with no indication that anyone was looking for her. By then she had learned the horrors of this new life from a girl named Fong, a Chinese national whose parents were caught at the border in Arizona. Fong had run away and was found three days later by a man whose name was Devin.

"Was?" Reagan asked.

"He dead now," Fong said in her quiet voice. It was some-times hard for Reagan to understand her thick accent.

"Did he hurt you?" Reagan asked.

Fong shook her head. "Only drive."

Reagan nodded.

It would take her days to recover from Saul's visits. She imagined killing him, but then what? She wouldn't make it past his armed security. She didn't know where she was, nor did she have any money to aid in her escape. If she ran out of here at night, she was as good as dead in these woods.

Then one day, *she* showed up.

Reagan was in her room, alone. She could hear the gravel crunch under tires and looked out the window to see a sporty silver car. A woman got out and approached Saul, who was waiting on the porch for her. Her face was red and her stride purposeful as she neared him.

"What is this place? Tell me now," she demanded. Saul tried to hug her, but she pushed him away, mumbling something too low for Reagan to hear.

The woman looked up and caught sight of Reagan. A look of shock worked its way over each of her features and Reagan ducked out of view.

"They're children," the woman snarled. There was muffled movement, a slap against skin, loud footsteps over gravel, then a car starting up and rushing away.

A moment later Reagan heard Jeremy's voice: "What do you want me to do about that?"

He was such a lapdog, always trying to make Saul happy. From bringing him young vulnerable women to taking care of his messes.

"You'll do nothing about that. She's my daughter." Saul's voice was hard as steel.

His daughter. Could it be she had no idea what her father did? Jeremy had left Saul on the porch to watch the dust pick up in the wake of the silver sports cars departure. He stood there for a long time, just staring, and she wondered what Saul was thinking.

When Jeremy wasn't on "a run to the border," as he called it, he maintained security at the house with a woman named Spider. Spider was worse than Jeremy. She always walked around sending shifty glances at the girls as though she personally hated all of them. One night, Janet, the most vocal girl of their group, had leaned towards Reagan and whispered. "Rumor has it one girl bit a client. He went on and on to Saul, demanding he kill the bitch. Two days later the girl went for a ride with Spider and never came back." Janet eyed her. "Don't try to run or Saul will send her after you."

That was the sort of thing that happened in movies. Not in real life.

30

SONIA

It was just after Mason was born that Sonia began planning for the day Saul might find them.

Sonia had begun to explain over breakfast at their cabin in Montana. Reagan had looked up from her bowl of cereal, her long brown wavy hair pulled back from her face, just like every day. Reagan did everything she could to hide her remarkable beauty because Saul had made it a curse to her.

"What's that?" Reagan said.

Sonia arranged a big black bag on the table the size of a suitcase, next to the sleeping baby.

"We need to be prepared. I know Saul is looking for me. He'll want to get to me before the police do."

The spoon dropped from Reagan's hand. "How would he find us out here?" She waved her hands, gesturing toward their tiny cabin. "I get lost coming back from the store." In typical Reagan fashion, she lightened the situation with sarcasm.

"It's just in case. You can stay with me or you can break out on your own. It's me he'll be after, and if you feel safer on your own…"

"I want to stay with you." Her voice was weak, nearly whiny.

"You promised to take me to Texas to find my mom."

"Shhh." Sonia stood and went to the girl. She pulled her into a hug, and Reagan hugged her back. "I won't ever leave you," Sonia murmured. "I just want you to know your options. That's all. There's cash and clothes ready to go." She waved toward the bag.

Reagan released her and picked up her spoon. "You wanna take me out driving today? You promised," she added, in case Sonia had forgotten.

At each word Reagan told her about her past, Sonia's heart had bled. To be so used and unloved. Even after all these years, she was still looking for her mother. It was true that Sonia had promised Reagan she'd take her back to Texas, but Sonia knew it was unlikely that Reagan's mother was still there.

Sonia swallowed the lump in her throat. They were always dancing around what-ifs. Planning for the worst. If Sonia ever gave her the word, Reagan was to take the baby and drive as far as she could. "Don't stop for long, keep going. Don't use the phone, trust no one," Sonia had said, but she'd never truly expected for Reagan to have to do any of those things. Sonia wasn't supposed to get caught.

A few months later, Sonia had to make that phone call from the side of a road as she bled and cried and confessed to a murder she didn't commit, so that they might escape. Now, while Sonia lay suffering, scared and emotionally broken on her bunk bed, she pictured Reagan and Mason under the stars, smiling and happy.

The surrounding lights dimmed as the cell doors rolled into place with a succession of loud clicks. By sheer willpower, Sonia had ignored her urge to check her cell door each night. What was the point? She now had to worry about Tammie killing her from inside the cell. They had spoken very little since she moved in, but Sonia noticed how close Tammie and Ginger had gotten.

Tammie rolled off her bunk and used the toilet without a

word. Her lack of modesty led Sonia to assume she had been in jail for a while, or more likely in and out.

A quiet wave of a whispers rose around them, sliced by a loud scream that rang through the dorm. One inmate let loose a trail of curses and a few kicks to her cell door before quieting down.

"What're you in for?" Tammie asked. Sonia rolled over to see the whites of her eyes glossy in the dim light, looking over at her.

"Murder." She didn't reciprocate the question, didn't much care what charges this girl was here on. The goal was to stay in her lane and get the hell out of this dump.

Tammie sank to the floor and began to loosen her braided hair with her fingers. "I got popped for malicious wounding. Nothing like murder, but the judge went on and on about how it coulda been." Her indifference seemed obnoxious, but her voice quivered near the end. She was just a scared girl trying hard to cover up her fear with bravado.

"What are you, like twenty?" Sonia asked.

"Twenty-two."

"What did you do when you were on the outside?"

"Hobbies and stuff?"

"No. For a job."

There was a pause and a shuffle. "I was going to school to be a nurse. Nothing fancy, a certified nursing assistant, but I was pretty good at the schoolwork." Tammie cast her eyes away as if embarrassed.

Sonia felt her brow pull low. She would be lying if she said she wasn't surprised. "You want to keep doing this the rest of your life—sitting in a jail cell?" A lump formed in her throat. *Like me.*

"I got a plan when I'm done here. I gotta do eighteen months."

"Don't come back here." Sonia thought of what it would be

like to squander a second chance. If she made it outside this place someday, she wouldn't so much as speed ever again.

"I ain't a kid," Tammie shot back, getting to her feet. "They offered me things to kick the shit out of you, but I'm the one who's gotta live with you."

A shadow flickered by the door, and Tammie ducked into her bed. A dark outline lingered and looked in on them before continuing down the line.

Sonia considered what Tammie had said and how easy it would be to manipulate a girl like her. What had they promised? Drugs, cigarettes, maybe some money for her commissary. Whatever it was, wasn't enough for the trouble she would get in once she was charged. But the people who put Tammie up to it didn't care what happened to her.

"You don't attack your cellmate," Sonia said in a level, low voice. The moon, with its gauzy, pale rays, shone through their tiny window.

"Because you'd tell on me? You a snitch?" Her youthful voice sounded bitter beyond her years.

"No. Because I won't have to. They'll know it's you. There's only the two of us in here, right? But I don't snitch. If they know it's you, they'll put charges on you," Sonia said, sitting up in bed and sliding down to the floor. "And don't think for a second Ginger didn't think of that first."

Sonia sat on the floor and looked over at Tammie. She was reclining, her face looking up at Sonia's mattress.

"Whatever. I ain't gonna do anything, so you can sleep easy."

"You said you have eighteen months. You said you have a plan. Don't listen to anyone here. They're only going to get you into trouble. Pieces of trash around here don't care about anyone but themselves. They would have set you up for life if you would have listened."

Tammie looked over at her with big round eyes in the dark. "Whatever—drop it, okay. I'll figure it out. I don't smoke anyway, but for some heroin—you're lucky you ain't dead yet." She snickered, but Sonia wondered if she was joking at all.

Sonia took a deep breath. "I think I can help you."

* * *

THE FOLLOWING MORNING, Sonia sat at her usual table in the library, leafing through her science book. The soft flick of pages turning filled the air; three other inmates sat around the room. Mack had missed his regular shift, and Sonia hated that she'd noticed. There was no one she felt comfortable enough to ask about his absence.

"Hey there," Sonia said to Harriet. "How are things?"

"Could be worse."

"Things could always be worse when we're above ground," Sonia said, not having the energy to try today. She was feeling the weight of the knowledge of Reagan and Mason out there with a monster hunting them, along with the utter hopelessness of being stuck here. Nothing she tried to distract herself with seemed to work for very long.

She studied the picture in front of her, memorizing every angle and location. If this was going to work, she would need to be accurate.

"Taking a new interest in the human anatomy?" Harriet said, not looking up from her task of sifting through new books, donations from a local charity.

Sonia shrugged. "I got time."

"Maybe she's studying to be a nurse," Ginger said, coming up behind her. Close enough for Sonia to feel the air brushing past her. Ginger took a seat across from her, flipping the chair around and straddling it. Sonia wondered if Tammie had already run back to Ginger about their talk.

"How's that any of your business?" Harriet remarked.

"I wasn't talking to you, old lady," Ginger snapped. "I was

talking to our resident punching bag over here." Her eyes scanned Sonia's face, and she smiled wide. "That's gonna leave a mark."

Sonia didn't waver.

"Mind your own business," Harriet said again, this time leveling her eyes on Ginger, a silent challenge.

"You don't want to associate yourself with her." Ginger's eyes flicked toward Sonia and back to Harriet. "It's bad for your health." Ginger clucked her tongue and turned back to Sonia. "Why don't you tell me what I want to hear. Did you think about what Bobbie said?"

"Go to hell." Sonia slowly rose, trying to bore her eyes through the woman. She limped over to Harriet and began to gather the books that needed to be put away; she had to get away from Ginger.

"You know he'll find them, anyway," Ginger said, adding, "You could save yourself a lot of pain, and when it's time, I'll personally make sure you go quick."

Sonia was glad her back was to the woman so she couldn't see Sonia flinch from her words. She pulled the books into her arms and walked away. Saul thought he knew what he was chasing; what would he do when he found out it wasn't what he thought all along? There was no way of knowing.

When Sonia went back to the desk, there was only one book left. A classic. *The Odyssey.*

"That's for you to take with you." Harriet pushed the volume toward her. "You might like it. It's on Oprah's list, I think." Harriet winked.

Sonia reached out her hand. "Watch your back. I don't want you getting anything coming my way."

Harriet squeezed Sonia's hand and shook her head. "What's right is right," she said. "I'm not afraid of darkness, child. I was living with it for longer than you been alive. And that girl—that girl is pure darkness."

31

SONIA

"It's nice to meet you," Alex said while looking at his computer screen. She smirked at Jamie, who in turn rolled her eyes. She couldn't help but feel disappointed that Ali wasn't waiting for her. She missed her friend. So much so that on the short walk here she had convinced herself that Ali would be waiting for her when she pushed through the door. And just like all the other times she'd let hope in, when her eyes fell on Jamie and who she presumed to be Alex, it burst.

Sonia sat down in her usual chair. She liked it when Jamie sat in *her* usual chair, but Alex had set up his things there, pushing Jamie to the other side of the table, further away from her, and Sonia wondered if physically separating them was some kind of a tactic.

"We're going to go over some aspects of your case. See what's what. Now that we have the full polygraph report, we know what we're dealing with," Alex said, closing his laptop and making eye contact with Sonia for the first time. He wore silver-rimmed glasses that Sonia wouldn't have been surprised to learn were more for show than function. His hair looked windblown, but in a way that you would want your hair to be windblown, his suit tailored to his athletic build. Sonia took an instant dislike to him. He was a shark but disguised himself as a protector. She should know; she was surrounded by sharks.

"Sure," Sonia said, looking down at her fingernails, avoiding his stare. She absently wondered if extremely attractive people were more needy for attention because they became used to the fawning. Could this man walk into the grocery store without making housewives, at least the straight ones, wish they were going home to him?

"We have conclusive results on your poly that you didn't kill Emma D'Luca," he began cheerily, and she thought for a moment he meant to congratulate her.

Looking between the two, she noticed that Jamie was facing away from him, her posture rigid as she shifted in her seat, twisting the diamond stud in her ear.

"I turned in my report and Alex has reviewed it," Jamie spoke up. "You passed all relevant questions." Jamie managed a slight emphasis on relevant, catching Alex's attention; he threw a glance at her.

"Yes. It would seem you're telling the truth," Alex said, followed by a smile. "Now, we need to find out who really did it. It will be your best defense."

"An innocent person shouldn't have to sit in jail just because they don't know who the real killer is. That's not justice," Sonia shot back. What did justice mean to a man like Alex Carter, she wondered—was it a two-thousand-dollar suit? A Rolex watch?

"Yes. Of course, we're still going to file your appeal, but I know Jamie and Ali must have told you the importance of finding Emma's killer. How much would it benefit your case. You're the one, after all, who pleaded guilty." It was her onus.

Sonia was shaking her head. "File the paperwork. I don't know who killed her."

Jamie spoke up again. "We're looking into several possibili- ties. But as Alex will mention, our private investigator discovered that a woman was found in Emma's townhouse when you went inside." Jamie kept her eyes on Sonia.

"Yeah. I was just trying to help her." Alex was watching her as her fingers sawed at the table's edge to disguise the tremor in them.

"We can work with that," Alex said. "First, tell me what you were looking for."

Sonia stumbled over her tongue. "What?"

Alex's head tipped almost imperceptibly to the side as if he was reading her expression. His jaw shifted. Sonia felt heat move over her chest and she cleared her throat. Had she told Jamie she was looking for something? Yes, she must have, because of the bloody footprints. Her mind was a jumble of stories and lies, too many to sift through.

"You went into Emma's office to find something. What were you looking for?" Alex repeated. She watched his knuckles clench for just a second, then loosen. Perhaps, instead of being on her side, he was trying to trick her.

"I wasn't looking for anything specific. I thought there was someone still in the house. Maybe the killer."

Alex nodded; clearly, he wasn't buying it. "What did you do after you found the girl?"

"I took her with me. She was frightened and asked for my help."

"Who was she? Why was she there?"

"I don't know. She wouldn't talk about it with me, and I let it go. She was clearly traumatized."

He wasn't taking any notes, just studying her face. She felt unease seep into her as she stared back. He was too keen. She thought of blood in the water. He would be circling and circling until he got what he came for. Each question was a taste—until she tripped up and he went in for the kill.

"Look, I'm—we're trying to help you," Jamie said. Alex's hand twitched as he almost reached out for Jamie's, and Sonia recalled their conversation from a few days ago. They had a past together. She couldn't picture a woman as strong and confident as Jamie falling for this bag of trash, even if it did have a handsome exterior. Right now, clearly, he wasn't trying to charm Sonia. He saw her as a useful tool, that was all.

"I know that," Sonia responded. "But I can't help you. I can say her name is Reagan. She was young, maybe sixteen. I was scared for her and she said she had nowhere to go. I was trying to help her, that's all." Sonia was aware she sounded like a broken record, but she didn't know what else to say. Reagan had been a sex slave for a vicious, horrible man who was now hunting her to get what was *his*.

Alex was just about to speak when Jamie cut him off. "Well, we're filing my report and your papers tomorrow. This process can take some time. First, we'll see if a judge will review your case. We're also going to continue to look through the investigative reports and eyewitness accounts to see what the police might have missed. As far as I can tell, it may be a lot. They were focused on your confession and may have missed some things. I'm going to be meeting with the officer who took the report, see what he can remember. Is there anything you can think of that might help us?" Jamie finished.

Sonia thought about the call that had drawn her to the house. Emma was scared. Worried about something. Sonia had assumed it was because Emma had taken Reagan from Saul, but Saul would never hurt Emma. She must have been afraid of someone else—but who?

"What about protective custody?" Sonia asked.

"We tried, but the Warden said you're not in danger," Alex said. She assumed Alex didn't put up a very good argument for her.

Sonia let out a humorless laugh. She'd figured the Warden wasn't going to budge, seeing how he was such a proud man.

And now he had to worry about someone on his staff leaking to the Feds about Sonia's mom being in danger.

"Do you know anything else about my mother?"

Alex glanced at Jamie and back to Sonia. "I'm sorry. I thought Jamie told you."

"Told me what?" Sonia looked at Jamie, who flinched slightly.

"Your mother's body was found this morning."

32

SONIA

ALEX'S TONE WAS MOURNFUL.

Sonia watched as Jamie clutched her chest and stared opened-mouthed at him. He dropped his hand over hers as if to communicate something to Jamie along with a minute shake of his head. All other thoughts dropped away from Sonia.

"There was a body found. It wasn't identified yet, but your mother's car was nearby, abandoned," Alex clarified.

"But you said—" Sonia looked at Jamie. "You said she was safe."

"I didn't know…I didn't hear anything about this until now," Jamie said, clearly confused. "They told me—"

"Told you what? Who?" Alex asked sharply, as if Jamie wasn't in a position to know anything.

Jamie shook her head as her cheeks grew crimson.

A deep desire to scream was rising in Sonia's belly. Just like all good things, love, hope and peace can all evaporate in a split second, and it just so happened that Sonia had lost all three. "I don't want to talk anymore."

"Wait!" Alex jumped up, planting his hands on the table and

leaning towards Sonia. A dogged intensity crackling through his movements. "I need to know about the baby."

Before she could stop herself, her head jerked to face him. It looked as if he wanted to reach out his hand and grab her. The hair on Sonia's arms prickled.

"I'm done here," Sonia said, standing up. Bang, bang. Her fist knocked on the door, sending a wave of pain into her arm.

"Wait. We need your help to find this child. He could be in danger," Alex said as he began rounding the table. A wave of nausea passed through her.

"I'm protecting him. You don't give a damn about anyone but yourself. It's a good thing for me I can read that all over people." She shot a look at Jamie and turned back to the door as the guard pulled it open. "I'm ready to go back now," Sonia said, and walked past the guard and out of the room. When she entered the hall, her hungry lungs expanded to relieve the burning pain that had begun in the room that was suffocating her.

She went to her cell. Her fingers gripped the edge of her painting and tore it away from the cement. She didn't want to cry. She didn't want to feel anything. She could only see her mother's face as she followed Saul out that door the other night. Followed him to her fate. *"It's not your fault."* It sure felt like it was her fault. What could she have done? Turned over Reagan and Mason to a killer? Was she to choose who lived and who died? This thought made her think about the letter.

She was such a poison to those around her. Even though she was just trying to do the right thing.

Her eyes caught on a group of women gathered around a table, some playing cards while others gossiped. Tammie looked straight up at her, Ginger at her side. They were always together outside of lockdown, now.

That kid was putty in Ginger's hands.

But Sonia had bigger problems to worry about. What she needed to do was figure out how to cut the head off the snake.

She thought she had left a cold trail, but it was warm, and heating up with every new witness. Everyone who'd come into contact with her during her short stay in Montana was now a possible leak in her plan. She had to stop the questions and the inquiry.

When the truth came out, Reagan and Mason would never be safe again. Not while Saul was still alive.

Sonia picked up the library book resting on the bed. She was about to put Jamie in that danger again, she knew, and she swallowed the guilt. Jamie had lied to her. She said her mother was safe, but she wasn't. Was it possible Jamie really didn't know anything about her mother's situation and might have just lied about it to get Sonia talking?

Sonia pulled out a piece of paper and a pen and began to write. Just one name across the blank page. She would request an envelope and give it to Jamie next time she saw her, no matter what kind of target it put on Jamie's back.

33

JAMIE

JAMIE HAD CONTACTED Ali's husband on her ride home.

"The police are working on locating her SUV," Mark said in a raspy voice. "I just don't get it—she was happy, or at least I thought she was."

Did Mark think Ali had left him? She wanted to console him and tell him it was going to be alright, but she couldn't.

She heard a young boy in the background and knew it must be Sammy, Ali's four-year-old son.

"Is that Mommy?" Sammy called out, and Jamie's heart shattered. She told Mark to keep her apprised of any developments and that she had spoken with investigators earlier that day. They hadn't given her any answers, but she was able to mention to them that her current case might have something to do with Ali's disappearance.

Now, Jamie studied the shoreline. Its usual peacefulness was disrupted by the screeching of a mother bird warding off a predator, and intermittent shadows flashed onto the deck as vultures circled overhead. Drew was still at work, and she was using the quiet to think over what she knew. And what she didn't.

What the hell was Alex thinking, blindsiding her at the visit with Sonia earlier? It would have been prudent to share with her the information about Sonia's mother's death before telling Sonia. Unless he was using the information to knock Sonia off her guard and charge in with the question about this child. Sonia's response was just what he had wanted. He'd tried to hide his smug satisfaction, but Jamie was aware of how Alex acted when he thought he had won. Jamie would have asked why he ambushed her with news of Sonia's mother after the meeting, but she had driven separately, using the excuse that she was heading back to Cedar Lake to take care of some business. She couldn't get away from Alex fast enough. On the drive, she decided that as soon as Drew got home, she would tell him about working with Alex.

Since getting home she had made several fruitless phone calls to try and confirm the death of Julie Angelo, and now found herself staring off into the lake. Its glossy surface rippled from something underneath the water, sloshing against the battered wood of the deck.

It was evident to her that Alex had forced her back to square one with Sonia. She could see it in Sonia's last glance—Jamie had lost her, and she didn't blame Sonia for it. The trust they had formed was so tenuous and fragile.

Her phone rang once and abruptly stopped, immediately causing Jamie to think of Nina calling— The phone displayed a missed call from Javi. But when she called him back, he didn't answer. She put the phone down, only to have it begin ringing again almost immediately, as though he had been screening her call.

"Hello."

"It's Javi…" His tone was awkward, like he couldn't decide if it was a question or a statement. It made her smile.

"Yes, Javi. My service is spotty out here. What's up?"

"I remember what Ali said about keeping things quiet. I

found something I think you need to see in person. Are you able to meet?"

Jamie sat up straight in her chair. This was the most interaction she'd ever had with this quiet coworker. She was hopeful that he mentioned Ali's name. Maybe they'd found something.

"Yes. When? Where?"

"Arlington. Public library on North Quincy street."

"Yes. Is 7:30 okay?" Jamie looked down at her watch, calculating drive time and traffic in Northern Virginia to be sure she was giving herself enough time.

"I'll be there." He hung up.

Jamie felt her pulse quicken. Javi was not the dramatic type. If something had him this concerned, it must be big, and it was obviously not on Alex's radar. Jamie had never shared her mistrust of Alex with Ming and Javi. It was merely a suspicion—she would need to get proof before sharing her thoughts with them. She needed evidence that Alex was trying to help Saul track down the girl from the closet. Whoever she was, she was important to Saul.

"Honey, I'm home!" Drew's deep voice bellowed from the front door. Hearing it, her heart skipped.

"I'm out back," she called.

"I bet you are. Wearing your birthday suit, I hope." He rounded the corner with his eyes closed and his arms outstretched like someone asked to join their own surprise party. When he opened his eyes, he smiled widely. "Or sweatpants— almost as sexy."

He dropped down on his knees next to her chair and kissed her, his hand holding her face to his. When he finally pulled away, she was nearly breathless.

"You're early. I was going to change."

His fingers found the edge of her pants and traced along her belly. "I missed you, Mrs. Turner," he said as he pulled away. "I'll show you how much if you come inside."

"Wait," Jamie said. She was losing her nerve as she looked over at him. "I need to tell you something." He froze at her expression. She felt her heart flutter as she raced to find the words.

"I've been working with Ali." Her fists tightened. "On an appeal for a woman named Sonia Rossi."

His eyes narrowed. "Okay."

"Ali—works with Alex. I've had to see him on several occasions." The sun sank behind a cloud muting the light.

He nodded solemnly. "Okay."

"I'm sorry I didn't tell you sooner."

At least when she was working with Ali, she was near a friend. Now that she was forced to spend time with Alex, she was suffocating slowly in bad energy. As much as she tried to deny it, Alex was getting under her skin. Poisoning her.

"That's fine. Just don't hang out alone with him," Drew said. "I don't trust that guy." His breezy attitude had her puzzled. Had she worried for nothing?

"There's more." She cleared her throat. "Ali's been missing for three days now."

Drew's eyebrows shot up. "How?"

Jamie shook her head. "No one knows yet. The police are investigating."

"Wait. Who's Sonia Rossi?" Drew asked, backtracking, his analytical mind realizing he'd skipped over the important part.

"A woman who pleaded guilty to a murder about five years ago."

"Rossi. Rossi. Why does that name sound familiar?" He seemed to be talking to himself as he visibly tore through his memory.

"Joey Rossi was her husband."

He snapped his fingers. "The Emma D'Luca murder?"

Jamie nodded. She could see the dots beginning to connect in

Drew's head. "You're working with the woman who confessed to killing Emma D'Luca?"

The case was well known in Virginia. More because of Saul than Emma. She'd led a quiet life, made generous charitable contributions, and had a good reputation—unlike her father, who was known for his intimidation and illegitimate business dealings. Shortly after her murder, Saul had poured at least some of his assets into a charity bearing his daughter's name to offer a cash reward for any information leading to Sonia's location. The thought was to put some hard-up people on her trail and avoid the police. Saul wanted to get to her first.

Be on the lookout for a woman traveling alone. Brown hair and eyes. If found, contact the number listed below.

No doubt the number led to a seedy hotline for paid killers.

"That's—" Drew's words fell off. He looked out over the water, not in the manner of a man enjoying the scenery, but as one scanning the shadowy reaches of the shore where a man or woman might lurk, watching them.

"It's fine, Drew. I'm being very careful." Jamie stood and walked to him but stopped short at seeing his expression.

"And Ali—she's probably missing because of this case."

It wasn't a question, but Jamie felt compelled to respond. "We don't know that."

"What can I do to help?" he asked, walking to her and pulling her hips into his. He hugged her close, and for a long time she didn't answer. She just relaxed against his embrace, relieved she had married such a good man.

"You think you could get any information on Saul's business dealings?" Jamie asked.

"For you, anything," he whispered.

* * *

JAMIE HAD STAYED at Cedar Lake for as long as she could, but she was fast approaching her meet time with Javi.

During the two-hour drive she kept thinking of all the reasons Javi would need to see her in person. None of them were good.

A snarl of traffic choked her exit for twenty minutes while a tow truck removed a disabled vehicle. She sent Javi a text saying that she would be running a few minutes behind.

When she finally found a parking space at the library, it was raining. Water slapped her cheeks despite her umbrella as she ran down the street and entered the library, thirty minutes late. She spotted Javi sitting just near the entry, looking at her when her eyes fell on his. He didn't smile, only closed up his laptop and walked to her.

"Second floor," he said. "Follow me." She silently followed him up the wide staircase. Its aging red carpet displayed outlines of wet shoe prints. Some sort of clean laundry air freshener scented the cool air but couldn't mask the smell of aged paper.

Once they'd passed rows of books to reach an abandoned corner of the second floor, Javi took a seat at a table. There were no other people in sight.

Jamie sat across from him and blurted, "What's this about?"

Javi's eyes examined the area before he turned the laptop screen toward Jamie. On the screen, she was staring at a face, grainy and half in the shadows of the darkened interior of an SUV. It was a woman with dark hair and sharp features. She looked at Javi. "What am I looking at?"

"This is the woman who followed Ali out of the parking garage the last night she was seen."

Jamie felt a prickle of fear move over her skin. "Who is she?"

"Her name is Nikki Angelo. She's Saul D'Luca's stepdaughter. Sonia's—"

"I know who Nikki is," she cut in. "Where'd you get this tape?"

"I don't think Alex is telling us the truth. I think he knows what happened to Ali. This was emailed to him the morning after her disappearance from someone in building security. He deleted it and didn't forward it to anyone—that includes the police."

Jamie tried to sort through what he was saying. Why would Alex first not mention Ali's disappearance, and then proceed to hide this video? She had specifically asked Alex for any new information about Ali, and he'd said there was none.

"He never told me about this. Did he tell you?" Javi asked, not making eye contact with her.

"No, he didn't mention anything. Why are you hacking his email?"

Javi looked around again, his edginess causing her to do the same. She could only imagine what others might think of their shady behavior, but they were still alone.

"Ali asked me to, if…if anything happened to her," Javi said, looking at the computer screen again. "I think she knew someone was following her. That she might—come up missing." Jamie recalled with perfect clarity Ali's disheveled appearance and distracted attention. Maybe someone warned her off, but she kept pushing.

Javi's words caused a sinking feeling in her chest. She realized she was drumming her foot on the floor and stopped. *"Is that Mommy?"* Why would Ali risk it?

"What do we do? Can we go to the police with this?"

Javi looked worried by her suggestion and explained that this course of action would implicate him in his breach of Alex's email.

"They have to look into this woman," Jamie said. "Tell me about her."

Again, Javi blanched, his lips twisting into a frown. "On the books, she's his stepdaughter. Off the books, some say she's the reason people fear him so much. She's close to his operation, and is assumed to be the one who carried out some of his more brutal acts to get people to stay in line. They call her The Spider and she lives with a woman, roommate or girlfriend, I'm not sure. Name is Gennie Smith."

Jamie's breath suspended in her lungs. The letter she sent for Sonia, to Gennie Smith…that letter was somehow connected to Sonia's sister. But why use Jamie to send a letter to her own sister?

"'More brutal acts'? Like killing her own brother-in-law? Abducting Ali and…" Jamie shifted in her seat, unable to finish the thought. "Does Sonia know about this? About what her sister might be doing?"

Javi shrugged his shoulders as he continued to work on his computer.

"Is Saul trying to stop the appeal? It will go forward even if Ali's—dead." Jamie hated saying the word aloud, but what she'd said was true; as long as Ali was missing, Alex would handle the case. Jamie's heart shuddered; Alex had found his way onto Sonia's case through Ali's disappearance, hadn't he? She'd already contemplated the idea that he was a mole, but could he be involved in Ali's disappearance? No. He wouldn't do that— they were good friends.

Javi shook his head. "I don't worry about those things. You should talk to Ming."

"Okay. Okay," Jamie chanted, looking around, inwardly trying to think of a plan. "Is there any way to anonymously get this to police? So they have the information, and can go question Nikki?"

Javi nodded. "Yes, but they may not take it seriously."

"We have to try. It can't be too late."

Javi nodded and began typing, his fingers fluttering over the keys.

Jamie wasn't sure her brain could handle anything else. She just wanted to be home with Drew, wrapped in his arms.

"I'll get together with Ming and see what we can find out." Jamie rubbed her cheeks. "We need to keep Alex out of this. He's after something and it has to do with this child." Jamie stopped short of any further explanation, wanting to keep Sonia's secret.

She had a bigger issue, and his name was Alex Carter. How much of an issue he was—that remained to be determined

34

SONIA

SONIA DROPPED the yellow-handled toothbrush down her sleeve and into her waiting palm as she sat at a table in the rec yard. Shouts and murmurs carried in the mid-afternoon breeze as Sonia watched two guards lounging near the door. A piercing laugh from one guard could be heard over the repeated scraping of the hard plastic handle against the table leg.

She thought of all the people she had lost at the hand of Saul D'Luca. Her father, warm and kind, the most important man in her youth, killed so he could take his wife. Then Joey, the man she'd vowed to love forever, tortured and murdered. Saul had stolen her sister Nikki with his charm and lies. Nikki might as well be dead. And now he wanted Reagan and Mason. The only reason she kept herself alive. The only reason she was in this dump was so that Saul would never learn of baby Mason's existence. But it was too late now.

She dragged the hard plastic back and forth over the metal leg.

From the corner of her eyes, she watched as Tammie walked past, silently glancing at Sonia. She was careful to hide the toothbrush until she was gone. Tammie avoided Sonia outside of their cell. Probably afraid of the repercussions from Ginger and her crew.

Sonia continued to sharpen her weapon, knowing she would need to use it very soon.

35

SONIA

Sonia had not been expecting another visit from Jamie so soon. The breeze was warm and smelled of fresh cut grass under an overcast sky. Jamie was sitting in the outdoor visiting area that looked much like a dog run.

"How are you?" Jamie asked as Sonia walked along the fence to a metal table with benches attached.

Sonia didn't answer; she wanted Jamie to know she was still pissed at her.

"About your mother."

It was as if Jamie was reading her mind, and Sonia didn't like it. She didn't want anyone else in her headspace.

"What about her?" Sonia said, trying to sound uninterested to prove Jamie couldn't hurt her. She had been able to tell by the look on Jamie's face at the time that she didn't know anything about Julie; Alex had sprung it on both of them. The real question was, what did he stand to gain from the declaration? Some sort of sick, twisted cooperation? If so, he was on a whole other level, and she had grossly misjudged him.

It was only then that Sonia noticed Jamie's clothes: jeans and a t-shirt, no makeup, messy hair. This must be Jamie's distressed look.

"I don't know where she is," Jamie said. "But the body they found has not yet been identified. I think Alex—" Jamie stopped short of finishing. She got up and started pacing. "I don't know why he said what he did."

"I know you didn't know."

Jamie nodded. "I've spoken with the local police. They just said the Feds are involved and couldn't tell me anything else— no one can tell me anything." She seemed to mutter to herself as Sonia watched.

"That guy's a prick." Sonia recalled Alex's smooth suit and manicured fingernails. His assuming air which made her want to leap over the table and choke him with his three-hundred-dollar tie. Perhaps her feelings had not been so strong at their first meeting, but they had progressed since then. The more she dwelled on their meeting, the more Alex's words dripped with disdain and his mannerisms were painted with arrogance.

"How much does he know about Mason?" Alex had said *"he."*

"Mason?"

Sonia moved to the table and sat. "The baby—Reagan's son."

"He doesn't know anything, I don't think. Just what Ming told us in the meeting—that she lived with you and a baby. That's it." Jamie blew out a breath. "I wanted to ask you—who else might Saul use against you?"

Sonia made a show of taking time to think before she answered. "I can't think of anyone," she said, trying to sound flippant. The truth was much darker. Who was safe from Saul when it came to getting what he wanted? No one. *Not even you, Jamie.*

"What about Ali?" Jamie asked.

"What about her? Have they found her?"

Jamie shook her head.

"It's probably Saul." She hated how nonchalant she sounded. Had her situation pulled all of her human empathy from her? That she could speak of her friend's danger so briskly made her stomach ache.

"But why? Why does he want her? Does she know something?"

Sonia looked back at Jamie, unflinching. She wanted to trust this woman, but in the end, it was too much to risk, and Sonia had made several mistakes already. She had been misguided to think a single call to her sister would draw no attention, but in less time than it took the FBI to track a phone call he had managed to find Sonia.

"I don't know," Sonia said.

Jamie walked back to the table and pulled a paper from her bag, which was resting on the tabletop. The picture was low-quality, but looking closely, Sonia could tell who it was.

"Do you know her?"

"It's Nikki, my sister."

Jamie seemed relieved when Sonia said it. Was this a test?

"She followed Ali out of the parking garage the night she disappeared," Jamie said.

"I'm sure she's also the one that got Joey." There it was again! So calloused. Sonia would have thought some kind of hidden emotion would come through, but it didn't. There was no emotion there, just a well of forgotten memories. Dead and buried under bitterness and guilt. She was playing chess with people's lives and she had to decide which pieces to sacrifice and which to keep. She wanted to scream; this wasn't a game. But when someone puts a board in front of you and holds your king hostage, what can you do but play along, hoping you can stay one move ahead?

Jamie's face paled in the muted light as clouds covered the

sun. She had no idea what she was dealing with—not yet, anyway.

Sonia continued. "Saul will use her for the personal jobs. Things he can't trust anyone else to take care of." Sonia drew a circle with her finger on the table.

"She's your sister." There was bewilderment in Jamie's voice, searching for explanation. "How could she do that to you, your husband and your friend?"

Sonia slumped forward onto the table. "My sister was never very close with our real dad. When my father was killed and my mother moved us in with Saul, Nikki became very attached to Saul. Fascinated by what he did and how he was treated." She looked down at the rough edge of her thumbnail. "She idolized him then, and I doubt things have changed much."

"What kind of person is she?"

"Ruthless. She cares for no one." Sonia didn't like talking about Nikki. Even after all she had done to Sonia, speaking ill of her sister felt like a betrayal. "We haven't spoken."

"Who's Gennie Smith?"

"Who?" Sonia cleared her throat. Damn, she was a bad liar.

"The letter you asked me to send—it was addressed to a Gennie Smith. Who is she?" Jamie's arms snaked around her waist. She wasn't moving anymore but studying Sonia intently.

"Nikki's girlfriend."

"What was in that letter?"

"It was a greeting. Nothing, really, just…" Sonia looked away. "I asked her to stop all this." She spread her arms in front of her. She finally felt her emotions crack like an iceberg dividing down the middle and with a heavy heart realized it was only because she had gotten caught again—not because she cared.

"Let me help you."

"So you can be next?" Sonia was shaking her head. "I think I've done enough damage for now, don't you?" She looked out over the empty yard. An overwhelming feeling of fear crowded her, pushing against her walls, begging to come in.

"He knows I'm working for you. Doesn't that already put me in danger? Reagan needs my help. Let me help *her*," Jamie's voice pleaded. Each new word was like a crack to Sonia's reserve, a pickaxe to her carefully placed walls.

"I can't help you find them, because then he finds them, and then it's over. As long as he doesn't know where they are, they have a chance. Once he finds them—I know what he'll do."

"Who's Mason?" Jamie asked.

Sonia's eyes flickered from hers. Who was Mason? There was an easy way to answer the question. "Reagan's son." No big deal, just having a conversation. "She was so early in her pregnancy when I found her that I doubt anyone knew about it. But if Saul found out…"

Jamie was nodding. "You believe the child is Saul's son?"

The breeze lifted Sonia's hair away from her face and tickled against her cheek. "Maybe. Look, I don't know. Reagan didn't want to talk about what happened to her at the farm."

"The farm?" Jamie asked.

"Yes. It was where Saul kept these young women."

"Did you tell anyone? Notify the police?"

Sonia rolled a pen over the table. "I placed an anonymous call a few days later. After we were on the run. According to news reports, the place was burned to the ground." She blew out a breath. "He was always one move ahead of everyone."

"Did you ever tell Joey about Reagan?"

Sonia recalled that day: Reagan lay in the back seat, a blanket pulled over her body as they drove away. They had nothing, not even a toothbrush or change of clothes. Sonia had gone to the nearest ATM and emptied their bank account after her call to Joey. They had been on the run for a week before Sonia thought to buy a burner phone and call him. But when she called his cell, it was off. By then police were looking for her, the main suspect in Emma's murder. She had no way of knowing where Joey was.

"The last time I spoke with him was just after I left Emma's house that day. He didn't know about Reagan." Sonia was sure of that.

"How did Saul find out about the child, then?"

"I don't know. I have no way of knowing that information." Sonia looked away. "What are you going to do about Nikki?"

Jamie bit her lip. "We got the picture of Nikki to the authorities. Now we wait and see if they go talk to her."

"Ali will already be dead. You need to know that."

Two hours later Sonia was in the library, skimming through a magazine, when Harriet finally appeared. At the sight of her Sonia let out a mental breath of relief. Her thoughts bounced back to Ali. Just like that, another one bites the dust. She'd never thought her plan would claim so many casualties, but she still would have gone through with it. She didn't know when this commitment to them formed, but she would do anything for Reagan and Mason. She needed to get out of here, and her sense of urgency was increasing every day.

"I may have good news soon," Harriet said, unsmiling.

"Appeal?"

"Looks favorable," the older woman said, busying herself with a stack of returns as if what she'd said wasn't the best news Sonia had heard in years. "Someone read it, at least."

"This is amazing news." Sonia's voice was high pitched. She wanted to hug Harriet but refrained.

"What about you?" Harriet asked. "What's going on with your case?"

"I don't want you involved any more than you talking to me involves you."

"I'm not afraid of those women," she scoffed.

Sonia put down her magazine and looked Harriet in the eye. "I don't know what I would do if you don't live a free woman again." Harriet's eyes shifted away, and Sonia thought she saw a slick sheen on them. "You deserve this. And it's about damn time this was made right." Just as she finished speaking, she watched the Warden walk in, his beady eyes finding hers as he moved swiftly across the room.

"Aren't you the popular one recently," he said. His hubris apparent in his lifted chin and piercing gaze.

She felt her eyes narrow on his, though she never consciously made the effort. A pounding began behind her eyes and she pinched the bridge of her nose. Like the same bitter fruit leaving the same bad aftertaste, he was here to harass her again.

"I don't know what you mean," Sonia said.

"Come with me," he ordered and turned on his heels. Sonia shot Harriet a quizzical look and followed. Her heartbeat faster when she thought of Mack. The Warden must have found out about the letters. Or maybe that Mack had notified the Feds about her mother.

The Warden, with his quick steps, led her back to the interview room. She felt her brow furrow in confusion. Then dread moved over her. Was this another special visit? She wasn't sure she could handle another one of those.

What else could he use as leverage against her now that her mother was out of the picture? But it wasn't Saul who sat at the head of the table. It was Alex, smiling like the shark he was. One who smelled blood in the water.

36

SONIA

"HAVE A SEAT," Alex said in a pleasant tone. His hand signaled toward the chair next to him. He was just as dapper as the last time she had seen him. His hair and suit so put together—his cologne somehow smelled of wealth. "It's nice to see you again," Alex said, and began looking through some of his paperwork. "I have some papers I need you to look over for the appeal. Some things I'll need you to sign." He pulled his pen out and handed it to her. His actions suggested that no hostility lingered from their last meeting, but she found herself repulsed by him still.

She hadn't put much thought toward what his involvement in the case would be like. She had assumed that once she made her declaration of innocence and took a polygraph, they would let her go. A new thought dawned on her like a bad dream: what if they didn't let her out even though she didn't kill Emma? When she'd decided her only option was to lie and go to jail, she'd thought she would be here forever; she didn't have a plan to get back out.

"Okay," Sonia said, looking over the paperwork he placed in front of her.

"So, I heard you had a visitor today," Alex said evenly.

She didn't respond. Instead, she looked over the papers he gave her, reading each word slowly: her recent written statement of what she said happened the day Emma was murdered, the polygraph report, and some other case notes from a woman named Ming. She couldn't help but wonder if she'd covered all her tracks or if this Ming woman had found anything Sonia didn't intend for anyone to find.

"When you're done looking over those," Alex said, "let me know, and we can discuss what's going to happen next."

Sonia thought he was trying to appear at ease, but there was a rough energy in his movements a hint of annoyance in his voice. He seemed—angry.

"Okay," Sonia said. "There are some things here that are incorrect."

"Just circle it and we'll go over it," he said with a wave of his hand.

"Don't you want to know what's wrong with it?"

Alex cleared his throat. "How often would you say Jamie comes to visit you?"

"A few times," Sonia said with intentional vagueness.

"Why do you think that is? I mean, what are you two talking about?"

Sonia shrugged. "The case. Who I think killed Emma—just stuff." Sonia thought her answer sounded like something a teenager might say to their parents when they were caught sneaking into the house after a night of partying. More than subtle hinting that it was none of his business.

"I asked her about my mother," Sonia said, watching his expression transform: his eyes narrowing, his cheeks pulling just a bit tighter.

"And what did she say?"

Sonia wanted to tell him that she said you're a douchebag,

and not to trust you—not that Jamie even needed to warn her. But instead, she said, "That they haven't identified the body you told me was my mother's." She did not try to hide the contempt in her voice.

He nodded as though he was trying to calm a hysterical person. "I'm trying to help you. I guess my information was bad, and I'm so glad Jamie cleared that up with you. Hopefully your mother is in a safe place. It's a good thing someone here thought to call the Feds in. I would hate to think of what might have happened." He clapped loudly in mock celebration.

What odd behavior. Sonia placed her elbows on the table, her back rod-straight, trying to make her small frame as large as possible. She wasn't afraid of this clown, and he needed to know it.

"I don't know what you're doing, but stop it," Sonia said in a hushed tone.

Alex took the papers from her, glancing at the corrections Sonia had made. "It looks like all of these are wrong. I'm going to have my team go over everything with a fine-tooth comb. I don't want this appeal rejected because of typos." His voice dripped with feigned sweetness. And just like that the façade dropped away.

She pictured jumping from her seat and smashing her fist into his face, breaking teeth, splitting lips, and leaving scars.

"It's going to take a while longer now," Alex continued. "I'm sure that's okay, because we're talking about the rest of your life. We need to get you out of here so you can make sure Reagan's safe."

Alex's mention of Reagan made Sonia flinch before she could stop herself.

He picked up the paperwork and made a show of straightening it. "I'm sure she'll be fine wherever she is. Somewhere safe—and far away. I think you should tell me where you think she might be. She could be a witness to the murder."

Sonia shook her head. "No way in hell would I tell you, even if I did know."

"Suit yourself," he said, sitting back and resting his clasped hands on his chest. "You should have special protections in here because of your snitching, too. It's sad. I know the Warden said you recently fingered one of your previous attackers." Alex pulled another sheet of paper out of his briefcase. Ginger's mugshot stared up at her.

Sonia's heart beat fast as she looked down at the picture. "Nope, wasn't her."

"I have your statement right here. They didn't ask you to sign it because of your physical condition after the altercation. Looks like you're lucky to be alive."

Sonia jerked up from her seat, walked to the door and began pounding.

"I'll see you in a few weeks. Once I get all these typos taken care of," Alex said as the door swung open and she rushed out. "And for your protection, I'm the only visitor you are now allowed to see. Got to keep you safe."

The Warden wasn't waiting in the hall for her. He had turned tail and ran. She knew he could be devious, but she had no idea he would sink to this level.

The word would get out about the statement she had supposedly written. Then someone would try to kill her. All it took was one rumor, and the fact that Ginger was no longer on the block. They had probably moved her to the hole and told everyone it was because of Sonia's accusation.

As she joined the pod she took extra care to watch others around her. The looks she garnered from several of the woman loitering around were harsh, but no harsher than usual. Maybe the word wasn't out yet, but that didn't put her at ease.

"Where the hell you been?" Tammie asked when Sonia entered the cell. Tammie had become much more vocal since their first talk, but Sonia knew Ginger had her nails in her. She hadn't had a good night's sleep since her new roommate arrived, always listening to the creak of the mattress below her.

"Library," Sonia said and went to her bed to lay down.

Tammie left without another word, leaving Sonia to wonder what the girl knew and what she might do with that knowledge.

37

REAGAN

REAGAN WATCHED as Mason tore across the small space between the campsites, his cries chasing after him. Max and Charlie were just setting up their breakfast on the table under a red-striped awning. The wind was wild, racing off the coast, and the water building on the ocean's waves, capped white, bent and tumbled into frothing water that licked up the shore.

"How's it going, bud?" Max asked Mason, who fell to his knees next to Charlie, the eager beast.

"Doggy," Mason cried. Charlie greeted him with kisses and a wagging tail.

"He really wants his own dog," Reagan said, approaching with a mug of hot tea in hand.

"Join us." Max spread a hand toward the table. "Can I get you some cereal? It took me all morning to make."

Reagan smiled. Max was easy to be around, and it didn't hurt that she found him attractive. She never considered having a regular relationship with a man. For the first time ever, she'd spent extra time on her appearance that morning: she'd brushed her hair for half an hour and pinched her cheeks before coming out to see Max.

"Sure." She turned to the boy. "Mason, go easy on him."

"The wind was crazy last night," Max observed, looking out over the swelling tide.

"It reminded me of Washington State. The beaches there are quite beautiful." The wind lashed again and the teabag string flailed against her mug. "It's a bit cooler here."

He turned back to look at her, studied her face. "You look—different today."

She turned away from him, suddenly wondering if she had overdone it. She didn't want him to notice that she noticed him. The fact that he was detected her extra effort made her cheeks grow hot.

"Where are you going to go next?" He took a drink of coffee from his mug and kept his eyes on her.

She shrugged. "Not sure yet."

"We have a new neighbor." Max hitched his chin toward a newly occupied campsite, where a small pop-up trailer was erected next to a screened-in tent. No sign of its occupants.

"Looks like it's a singles party." Max laughed. A nice sound.

"What do you mean?" Reagan asked, not taking her eyes off the campsite.

"Just a man, like me and Charlie here," Max said, scrubbing the dogs ear. Charlie ground his head back into Max's hand and growled a low sound of pleasure.

Just a man—like Max. Reagan tried to tell herself that nothing was strange about that fact. Maybe he was fishing. A lot of people left their families at home to go fishing. There were other simple explanations, too, but none of them purged the growing shadow of dread.

"I have to work today," Reagan said absently as she turned to watch Mason fawning over the dog. The hair on the back of her neck shifted as she watched his tiny fingers petting the dog's golden fur. In a split second, she pictured someone taking him away from her. She imagined a vehicle's red taillights glowing and fading into the surrounding darkness with his pale face pressed to the window. Her heart ached at the brief thought and she knew she would have him sleep next to her that night. That would be two nights in a row. He didn't complain; he liked to be doted on and fussed over. He ate it up.

Reagan stood abruptly. "We have to go, Mason."

"How about dinner?" Max asked as they turned back toward the camper.

She felt a blush rise on her cheeks, suddenly feeling self-conscious. "I'm heading into work."

"Need me to watch Mason?"

Reagan stopped walking, and the wind whispered in her ear. She tried to ignore all the warnings she was getting. Who was this new arrival? Could she trust Max? Maybe she could trust him for dinner, but she sure as hell wasn't going to leave Mason with him.

"He comes with me, but thanks."

"Must make it hard for you to get your work done." Max was stretching his lean body over the table when she turned to face him, Charlie lying at his feet.

"It's no bother for me. I like the company." She had worked at the Anchorage Hotel for three months, and the truth was that her supervisors didn't know she was bringing Mason along on her shifts; she didn't know what they would think of it. She might even get fired over it, but that was a risk she was willing to take. "Maybe on dinner." Reagan said and walked back to their camper, her steps a bit lighter.

* * *

TWO HOURS LATER, Reagan was hunched over on all fours as she pulled up the duvet to look under the bed in Room 110. Mason sat quietly in the corner at a table, playing a game on her phone. Every so often he would giggle at something, then fall silent again. An hour into her shift, she was still thinking about Max. She kept going over and over their earlier interactions and what each little thing might mean. After years of running, she hadn't thought this day would ever come. After years of personal torture at the hands of Saul, she was shocked to learn that she could ever see a man in any other light besides a predator. It had taken her a long time to realize she was punishing all men with this mindset, instead of the one responsible for her pain.

"I'm hungry," Mason said, looking over the phone at her.

"There's food in the cooler." A small bag she brought with their lunch hung from her cart. He got up and walked to it, pulling it down to the floor where he could inspect the contents. Reagan stood back up and swiped at her jeans. The edge of the curtain was folded in on itself and she adjusted it. Her eyes moved over the parking lot as a big shiny truck stopped outside the office and a man slid out. He wore a plaid button-down shirt and jeans. His jaw was fuzzy from stubble and his cheeks pinched and red. Her heart seized in her chest as she recognized Jeremy. It was the first time she had seen him in over six years, but she would never forget his face. He was walking to the front desk, where he would ask for her, no doubt. Watching his familiar movements, her mind was racing so fast she was frozen in place.

She hadn't given her employer her real name, but it would be easy enough for Jeremy to describe her if his first line of questioning was rebuffed. Clearly he already knew where to look.

Her van was parked in the rear lot, and she grabbed Mason's hand and yanked—too hard. Adrenaline, mad and frantic, forced its way through her veins.

"Mommy, that hurts." Mason tried to pull away, but she tightened her grip.

"We need to go. Mommy needs you to be nice and quiet," Reagan whispered as she peered out through the curtains. Jeremy was still in the office, his broad back to the large window. She hauled her purse and the food bag over her shoulder and pulled Mason out the door. The first-floor walkway was covered, and she moved as fast as she could with Mason's short strides. She was half dragging, half carrying him when the van came into view.

She must have messed up. It had been so long. She had crisscrossed the country, using several different aliases. She had done everything Sonia had told her to. All but one thing: she had kept the burner phone Sonia had given her, the one Sonia had called on the day of the accident. Sonia's pain-filled voice: "*Safekeeping...*" The word that set it all in motion. Sonia was in prison for the rest of her life, but Reagan had gotten soft; she secretly hoped it would ring one day and Sonia would be on the other end. Safekeeping—the safe word. Sonia told her she would use it: "Don't trust anyone unless they used the safe word."

She heard the bell from the office ring as someone exited or entered, but she didn't look back. Her focus was on getting Mason into the van and getting as far away from this man as possible.

With shaking hands, she buckled him into his car seat, taking twice the usual amount of time as her fingers slipped off the buckle in her haste.

"Are you okay, Mommy?" Mason's small hand grasped hers.

She nodded and closed his door. Moving into the driver's seat, she slammed the door and locked the car. Fumbling, she dropped the keys. *Slow and steady.*

Just as she sat upright and slammed the keys into the ignition, two big hands clapped against her window. Beyond the glass, Jeremy smiled at her. She froze, staring at his features, feeling the familiar pull to hide; to run. Panic pushing her in all directions.

"He just wants the kid." Jeremy pointed at Mason. "I'll let you go, but I'm taking the boy."

"Who is he?" Mason's little voice shook. "Is he going to hurt us?"

She started the van, and the hands drew back and hit the window with such force she flinched back from it, expecting the glass to shatter into her lap.

"Oh, Reagan. I can see what you're thinking. You want to run. But I can promise you that's a bad idea. Because if you do I'll catch up to you, and I'll make you hurt so bad." His voice was soft, his mouth turned up into an expectant smirk.

She threw the van into drive and stomped the gas pedal. The van jumped forward while Jeremy fell back. A trial of curses exploded from him as he took off toward his truck. Tears pricked at her eyes and her hand twisted against the steering wheel. Faster and faster she drove, until she realized she had nowhere to go.

38

JAMIE

JAMIE WAS the last to arrive at their meeting. Alex was waiting at the head of the table while Ming and Javi looked over paperwork set before them.

"Sorry I'm late." Jamie tossed her bag onto a chair and sat down.

Alex gave a swift nod and started in. "That's all right, you're worth the wait."

Jamie's eyes darted across everyone's faces and they turned from her, avoiding her eyes.

"As I was saying." He cleared his throat. "We need to find out about this Reagan and her child."

Jamie's muscles froze at the mention of that name. Something wasn't right; nervous energy was pouring off Alex's normal calm.

"This is an appeal for Sonia." Jamie felt her gut tighten. "This girl has nothing to do with that."

The room felt too hot and she pulled at her silk blouse. She had seen this look on Alex before: on the night he broke into her apartment and cooked her dinner. A man unwilling to take no for an answer. She had stood up to him then, and she was more than willing to do it again.

"Yes, she does," Alex argued.

When Jamie was ten years old, she and Trevor, her twin brother, had stumbled across a nest of rat snakes at the lake. Black bodies clumped in a slithering mass. After a moment of inertia, the snakes became aggressive, moving out of the nest to push them back. Alex was apparently all out of charm and was going to come right at them now.

"She could have seen who did this. What better way to prove her innocence than to find the real killer? This has been our strategy all along."

"Sonia said Reagan didn't see anything."

"You and Sonia do a lot of chatting," Alex said, sharply. Javi and Ming both looked at Alex, and he took a deep breath. "Look. I'm under a lot of pressure to take care of this quickly."

"She won't tell you where they are. You're wasting your time."

"Then you guys find her. I want all of your focus shifted to finding this girl. I'll get us some more resources if we need them. That's now our main focus."

Jamie felt a wave of anxiety move through her. He was pushing too hard.

"I think we can handle it," Ming spoke up. "I found something."

Jamie's eyes blinked rapidly as she willed the older woman to remain quiet—*don't tell him anything.*

Alex stood, walked over to Ming, and took the empty seat near her. His arm cocked against the table, his head resting in his hand. "What did you find?"

The move was so abrupt Jamie felt her mouth hanging open.

"When I was in Montana, I went to Sonia's old workplace. One of the staff gave me a tour and sent this to me afterwards because she thought it would be helpful." Ming pulled out a small picture with a pin-hole at the top. It showed several people around a table with a birthday cake. Sonia was in the upper right corner with a smile on her lips—clearly pregnant.

What the hell was this? Jamie looked at Alex, whose expression remained indifferent.

"You knew about this," Jamie accused.

Alex frowned. "Knew about what? That she's lied to us once again? Not news, sweetheart."

His words grated her, a nearly physical pain. "Please use my name when referring to me." She practically ground her molars 'til they cracked.

He smirked and kept going. "I had some information that suggested Sonia was pregnant before she left Virginia. I had no idea she carried the baby to term."

"We don't know that she did." After the words left Jamie's mouth, she realized her mistake. He might not know that Reagan had been pregnant at the time as well—or maybe that was a lie too.

Jamie grabbed the picture and studied it. Sonia's smile was genuine. Jamie had never seen her smile like that. Her cheeks were fuller, unmarred by physical abuse. She'd said she couldn't have children, and Jamie had believed her. But now the pieces were falling into place. Sonia hadn't run to protect Joey…she ran because she knew she was pregnant and she didn't want Saul to find out. A child for a child; it made sense. It would explain why she pleaded guilty to a murder she didn't commit: to keep his birth a secret. It could have been that Joey was the only other person who knew about the baby, and when Saul's men got to him, he talked.

Jamie's eyes narrowed on Alex. "Who told you that Sonia was pregnant?"

Alex shook his head, his faux-happy facade melting away to near contempt at her question. He didn't respond to it. "What else do we have, people?" Alex said, clapping his hands loudly.

Ming and Javi looked at Jamie.

"Come on," he said. "We've been working this case for weeks. Are you really telling me that's it?"

When no one else spoke, he stood. "I've got meetings the rest of the day. Let's follow this lead on Reagan and the baby. I want to hear something soon," he added before he left the room.

After the door closed, Jamie spoke. "We need to derail this. Something isn't right."

Javi finally looked up from his computer at her. "Why would he not tell us about this before if he knew?"

Jamie was nodding and ignoring the grumble in her stomach. "I have a feeling there are a lot of things he isn't telling us." She thought about the video of Nikki.

"Javi, have you found any medical records for the birth?" Jamie asked.

"I wasn't looking for them because I didn't know."

"Yeah, sorry." Jamie silently told herself to slow down. "We need to see if there's any record of that birth. One of the murder victims in Sonia's sphere was Mildred Scott. She was a midwife." Fear sparked to life in her. Was Saul tracking down the baby and killing the witnesses along the way?

"Mildred had her own midwife practice for twenty years. Home births, no meds type thing," Ming said as she looked over her notes, "Quiet, no enemies."

"How did she die?"

"Stabbed; house was ransacked."

"Tortured?"

"No."

It could just be thieves, but they had to keep every option open.

"Why does Saul want this child so badly?" Jamie asked.

Ming shook her head. "Revenge?"

That was Jamie's first thought, too. Perhaps she was overanalyzing; usually, people did things for the most obvious reasons.

Jamie thought back to her conversation with Sonia about the child, and how standoffish Sonia had been. How careful and practiced her answers seemed.

Then Javi offered a rare piece of insight: "Maybe we should not try to find this child. I think it would put them in danger," Jamie pursed her lips. "We need a plan."

Ming nodded. "I'll look into all the medical records Javi can get his hands on. Do I need to make another trip to Montana?"

"No. I think everything we need is right here." Jamie sat up straight in her chair. For a brief moment she felt a loss of confidence in her ability to detect deceit. Sonia was cunning and a good liar, but Jamie had wanted to believe her. Whatever it was, they would have to keep Alex in the dark. She felt the need to warn someone...but who? Ali was missing, Sonia was in perpetual danger, and this other woman and child were in the wind.

One thing was for certain: Alex was working on Saul's team, and he was no longer trying to hide it.

39

SONIA

IT WAS NEARLY 6:30 when they began filing into line for breakfast. Exhaustion caused Sonia to stumble twice on the short walk, the soles of her shoes catching on the ground under her lazy legs. The voices of women in line bumped and fell down into Sonia's head, generating a quiet rumble.

Her thoughts kept circling back to her meeting with Alex yesterday. The Warden had stopped by afterwards to confirm her visitors list was now restricted. "For your own safety," he purred.

This left her with only one option. If it failed, she would die here.

She watched Mack walking four steps ahead of her, monitoring her group as they were guided to the cafeteria. She ignored the tingle she felt when she looked at him, recognizing now how much she anticipated his presence.

As she waited in the food line, Mack took up a position by the door, monitoring silently. He hadn't looked in her direction since passing her cell this morning, no matter how much she willed him to.

The bland smell of oatmeal was overpowered by cinnamon and raisins drifting to her nose as food was passed to the woman in front of her. Trays banged against the rails and bags of juice were passed out.

"He's got a nice ass," Tammie said, coming up beside her.

Sonia shook her head. "Whatever." She made a show of looking over the rest of the room.

"I'm a short-timer. Think he's into white chicks?" Tammie continued.

Sonia did not want to have this conversation with her. On the outside women were generally treated like meat, but in here, she felt sorry for the harassment someone like Mack got on a daily basis. She could see he didn't like the added attention. Maybe Sonia was jealous, because the fact of the matter was, she was in the same boat as all these other women when it came to her chances with Mack. Zero. He certainly didn't need an ego boost from a bunch of sex-starved women.

She imagined a conversation with him about it. Both of them laughing, him putting his hand on her arm. Then he would lean in to kiss her—

A punch in her rib brought the cafeteria back into focus. Pain like a hot poker being shoved between the thin flat bones grew as if a hot glass of water was spilling down her back. She jerked around to see Tammie sinking away into a sea of faces, lines etched across her forehead. At least she'd taken Sonia's advice and waited until they were out of the cell. She just might get away with it—this time.

Sonia sank to her knees and tried to reach around to grab at the stabbing pain emanating in her back but her arms couldn't reach it.

Two guards shoved their way into the women surrounding her on the floor. The large group swallowed Tammie's small figure, protecting her like a cocoon.

"Get a stretcher," a female guard yelled. "Everyone line up on the wall. Everyone line up!"

Sonia heard the squeak of sneakers on the floor as they all

scrambled back. Like the sound of a high school basketball game.

"Sonia, stay with me." It was Mack's voice. Warm, like a stream soaking up the sun's rays on a summer day. They were fifteen years old again, in English class where their fingers had accidentally touched, his eyes darting from hers and a blush kissing her cheeks. All their fumbling.

"We have to stop meeting like this," she said and felt a smile on her face. Her vision was blurring, and the pain flared. "Maybe one of these times I won't be savable." She was babbling, unsure what had let loose her tongue. She sagged against him, unable to lay back, and she thought she felt his embrace.

"You're not going anywhere except an ambulance." Mack said it with so much confidence, she felt safe enough to let her eyes close. She trusted him, and she sailed off over a rough sea of pain.

THERE WAS an intense light focused on her face; a myriad of voices floated on the surrounding air. She couldn't tell what they were saying or what it all meant. In and out she rose and sank like a shipping lane marker bobbing with the current. Something was holding her up, pulling her to the surface. Finally, she broke through, and looked around at the hospital room and the guard at the end of her bed.

Mack sat in a chair, staring at her. She opened her mouth to speak, but it was so dry she only produced a cough. Her throat felt lined with cotton balls, but her body was blissfully without pain.

Mack stood and moved to her bedside, handing her a glass of water. She tried to sit up, but she didn't have the energy. She feebly felt around for the button to adjust the bed, but Mack already had it in his hand and pushed the control button.

"Who did this to you?" A scowl on his handsome face.

Sonia shook her head. The cool water felt like a blessing, traveling down her throat and loosening her tongue. "I don't give up my sources."

"This is bull. One of these days you're going to die. Do you want that?" Mack growled.

At one point she might have wanted that, but now, with an end in sight, she needed to stay alive. "I wasn't expecting it," Sonia said. "I can't be on guard every moment, you know that. It's all of them against me. And now that the Warden started the rumor that I wrote up a statement against Ginger, they're all gunning for me."

"He did this!" Mack's jaw flexed.

"Does he know what you did? About my mother?" Mack looked behind him. Sonia felt her pulse jump—he was the one who called the feds about her mother. "Because if he knows, you're in danger."

"Don't worry about me. I can take care of myself."

"I thought…because you were gone, I thought something happened to you," Sonia said. In her head the statement hadn't sounded as emotion-filled as when she said it out loud. Had their small pen pal relationship meant so much to her? Or was she just so desperate for a friend that she'd latched onto him, inferring things that weren't there?

"Don't worry about me. You have enough to worry about." His brown eyes softened. "How is the appeal? Did your lawyer give you a timeframe?" Energy was pouring off him as he fired his questions.

"The Warden won't let me have visitors now." A barking laugh erupted out of her mouth. Was this what it felt like to lose it? "Who's working the night shift?" Sonia managed to ask.

"Jerry. I think someone's still pissed at him for his extended light duty. He's scheduled here all week."

"The back again?"

Mack shrugged. "I don't know."

"You really think I'll be here a week?" Sonia looked down at her still body and wondered what the damage was.

"And how is our patient today?" a woman asked, coming through the door. Her white coat hung from her small frame; glasses perched on the end of her nose. She couldn't be much older than Sonia. The scent of eucalyptus wafted off her skin as she leaned over Sonia. "You're awake," she said, smiling.

Sonia nodded.

"How are you feeling? How's the pain?" she asked as she looked over a file hanging at the end of Sonia's bed.

"Fine," Sonia said, wishing that the doctor would just leave.

"You're lucky that—what is it? a shiv?—didn't puncture your liver. It was right up there," she said almost joyfully.

Sonia felt her brow crease. Shank. She remembered all the scraping to get it just right. Traveling the length of the metal table leg to sharpen the tip.

"I'm going to have the nurse come in and get you cleaned up." Her eyes darted to Mack and back to Sonia. "Okay?"

Sonia nodded, feeling her cheeks grow warm. He would have to leave, but she couldn't stop the thoughts before they entered her brain.

After the doctor disappeared out the doorway, she looked at Mack. "I'm not going to die on the inside." Her fingers gripped the sheets. "Do you remember school?" She felt a smile on her lips as she closed her eyes. "I had such a crush on you. I wanted to tell you, but I thought the others would make fun of me."

"Why are you telling me this now?"

"Because I'm sorry I was a shit."

The nurse walked in and Mack retreated to his chair as she pulled the curtain around the bed. The last thing Sonia thought of was the bright yellow handle of the toothbrush she had been crafting for a week that was found stabbed into her back.

40

JAMIE

Jamie was happy to make it back to Cedar Lake, but thoughts of Alex kept puncturing her normal peace. His wrinkled appearance and wild eyes kept circling in her mind like turkey vultures searching for the dead or dying.

She woke early the next day and got up, leaving Drew in bed, his bare chest peeking out from tangled sheets. God, she loved that man. She pulled out her phone and dialed Flint Hill to make an appointment.

"Sonia Rossi was put on a restricted visitors list," she was informed.

"By whom?" Jamie sat up quickly, straddling the lounge chair.

"I'm not at liberty to discuss those decisions," came the practiced response.

Alex strikes again.

Jamie began looking through the files Ming had sent her, and some medical paperwork from Mildred Scott's office that Javi'd found. There were two places where Sonia's alias appeared in the text. Whoever doctored these records had missed two vital spots, giving away Sonia as the patient. Not Reagan. And if

Jamie was able to find this information, so could Saul. Giving credence to Jamie's assumption that it was revenge Saul was after. Or what if Saul's goal was to take the boy as sort of a replacement for the child he'd lost?

The mother's date of birth, noted on the birth certificate, put her at thirty-two today. The mother's named was listed as Jennifer Minx. Everything else in the documents identified Tyler Minx as the mother of one Mason Minx. This must be Reagan's alias.

Jamie picked up her phone and dialed the number of Cal Riffin. Cal was Sonia's neighbor in Montana, the one Ming had spoken to on her trip. As it rang, she cursed softly. She'd forgotten about the time difference; it would be very early in Montana. She was getting ready to hang up and try later when a man's rough voice answered.

"Hello."

"Mr. Riffin, please."

"Is this a sales call? Cause I ain't interested."

"No—please don't hang up. My name is Jamie and I'm a friend of your old neighbor, Jennifer."

He grunted.

"I just wanted to ask you a few questions."

"Make it quick. I got work to do." His voice sounded like he had something pinched between his teeth.

Jamie nodded, though he couldn't see her. "Was Jennifer pregnant when she lived next to you?"

"Yup. Sure was. Went all the way and had herself a boy, I think," he said, seeming to soften a bit.

"Do you remember her living with someone?"

"A brown-haired girl." The sound of a lighter cracking to life came over the phone. "I just got done telling some other lady all this."

"Do you remember if she was pregnant too, or just Jennifer?"

"Jenn, I think. I didn't pay too much attention, but the other one always wore baggy clothes, so maybe."

"Thank you. One other question. Do you remember them having any visitors at the house? Men or women?"

"I only saw one other person out there ever. It musta been the day after they took off, leavin' unpaid rent. She was small, dark hair. Not much else I can tell you."

"You mean a woman showed up at the house after they moved out?"

The man blew out a breath. "It was the day after I saw the young one tear outta there like the place was on fire. Like it was dine-and-dash time. Then this lady shows up, looking around the outside of the place. Mighta broke in, I don't know. I went and checked it out the next day. Place was locked up tight."

If the woman looking around was Nikki, as Jamie suspected, Saul had known about the baby five years ago. It was a miracle Reagan had made it this far.

"Thanks, Mr. Riffin. Have a nice day."

She tossed her phone down and went through all the medical paperwork Javi was able to find. Some initial work-up at her OB-GYN: *Patient complaint: inability to conceive. Has been trying for two years with no success. Referred for IVF. Women's Clinic.*

Jamie picked up her laptop and shot Javi an email asking him to look into anything he could find about this Women's Clinic.

It was only two minutes before she got a response:

"I gave all this to Alex this morning and it was accompanied by an attachment."

Alex had this information but he wasn't sharing? Each new development in this case seemed to be old news to Alex, and she had a feeling she knew why.

Jamie looked over the paperwork. Sonia and Joey Rossi began their IVF consultation two years before Sonia went on the run.

Sonia wasn't lying when she said they had issues. They looked to be unresolvable ones.

Jamie heard Drew whistling as he made his way downstairs.

"Looks like someone had some fun last night." He winked.

She yawned.

Drew pulled up to the counter and began leafing through the mail. "Does this mean you're going to be staying out here instead of driving up to the city the rest of the week?"

She looked over at his hopeful expression. "Maybe."

He tore at another envelope as she looked back at her computer.

"What's this?" He held up a single nearly blank sheet of paper.

"I don't know." Jamie stood and walked to him. She took one look at the envelope and her heart sank. She had forgotten to drop Sonia's letter in the mailbox.

"I was supposed to mail that out for Sonia," she said, reaching for the paper.

Drew's expression was confused. She looked down at the words printed on the paper: two words, one name. Alex Carter.

"I don't understand," Jamie said, her fingers brushed her lips. Why would Sonia want this mailed out, and what did it mean?

His face softened a bit. "Do you really think it's such a good idea to be sending mail out for her? There's a reason she was using you and not the mail system."

Jamie was shaking her head. "There is no one else she can trust." As she said it, she looked back down at the paper. Sonia had pressed the letter into her hand at their last meeting. Not unlike the first time. She recalled their words:

"No. I can't do this again."

Sonia pulled the letter back. "It's just to Nikki." Her trembling finger pointed to the name on the front.

Jamie shook her head. "I can't—"

"Please! He's going to try to kill my mother. I need Nikki to

know, to understand she's in danger, so she can help her. Maybe talk to Saul."

But this letter didn't have anything to do with her mother.

"What does Alex have to do with this?" Drew asked.

"I don't know. I can't think." She looked away from Drew and the paper. "This is the second letter I agreed to send for her."

"What was in the first one?"

"I don't know. I didn't open it." Her tone was petulant.

"I wish you'd consider getting out of this case." He padded across the kitchen, leaving a space between them. He leaned back against the counter and looked at her. "You're being played."

It wasn't a question, more like a statement. She wanted to tell him he was wrong. That she was smart enough to know if that was true. She had spent her career testing people with a polygraph machine and learning the ins and outs of "tells". She knew what she was doing. Didn't she? But as she rested her hip against the countertop, she thought of all the lies Sonia had told her. Lies Jamie had believed.

41

SONIA

Sonia heard Jamie's voice before she saw her.

"I need to see her. I'm working with her lawyer and this is a time-sensitive matter," Jamie argued.

"I'll need to talk with my supervisor."

Someone huffed loudly.

"It'll take five minutes, maybe less," Jamie urged, followed by silence. Then she was entering Sonia's room. Pushing through the door looking like a caged animal just let loose.

"I didn't expect to see you so soon," Sonia murmured. Jamie's hair was wild, and her eyes seemed to zero in on Sonia, causing her to sit up as much as she could without the assistance of her adjustable bed.

"We need to talk," Jamie said. For a crazy moment Sonia thought Jamie was going to strike her. But instead, she threw her bag down and began pacing the length of the room. "Alex is trying to block anyone from coming to visit you. Including me."

It was unnerving to watch her track the floor in her sneakers, her usual business attire replaced by jeans and a t-shirt. Like she had just finished gardening or running errands. Like whatever was going on was so urgent, it had pulled her away right in the middle of something.

"What's going on?" Sonia asked. "You're making me nervous."

"Alex just moved in and took it all over." Her hands raked through her hair. "I need answers from you."

"What kind of answers?"

"IVF?"

"What about it?" Her heart stuttered. "I went there. It didn't work."

"I can't help you if you continue to lie to me." Jamie stopped pacing, pulled a picture out of her bag and slammed it on the tray table. "I know Mason's your son."

Sonia wouldn't look, couldn't. She didn't want to see whatever it was staring back at her.

"Look at it," Jamie growled. "Come on—look."

"No."

"Look at the picture, Sonia!"

She felt her mouth drying out. She peered down, just a quick look, and saw herself with an expression long lost. It could have been happiness, hope, or maybe contentment written on her smile and in her eyes.

She had assumed this was coming. Saul had known ever since he sent Nikki to kill Joey. Joey probably told her within the first hour of the interrogation. Or maybe Saul had sent someone else. Nikki was too close to it all. He could be a paranoid old man, especially when it came to anything involving his precious daughter.

"Yes. I gave birth to Mason." She wished she could pull the words back in. Say he was her son, but it sounded all wrong. After she went on the run, and had Reagan to take care of, and Joey was gone, she didn't feel like she had a family for a very long time. Then, when she went away to prison, the dream moved away for good. She couldn't allow that hope into her life.

It would destroy her from the inside out. Chewing on the fat and spitting out the bone.

What if she had been there for his first tooth, to tuck him in at night and tell him the boogie man wasn't real? What if she could hug him and hold him and tell him how much she loved him? What if she could tell him about the sacrifice she had made to keep him safe? And warn him that the bad man was coming? Instead she fell asleep every night next to a painting that hid his face yet kept its contours in her mind. The color of his eyes dotting the paper's edge, the brilliance of his voice nestled in the folds. She missed him so much, but she couldn't cry over it: to let the emotions in was equivalent to letting them take over. They would ravage what was left of her like vultures.

"I couldn't tell anyone, you understand. I can't trust anyone when it comes to them." Fat tears streamed down her cheeks.

"So you were pregnant. That's why you ran?"

Sonia looked down at her open palms and nodded.

She recalled rushing Reagan out to her car that day. All the thoughts playing through her mind. What the hell was she going to do? She had called Joey two hours after driving away from Emma's house. She needed to know what to do. She remembered the last time she heard his voice: "You have to run, Sonia. He can't find out about the baby. You have to go."

She had done everything to save that baby. To help this young girl who she had only just met. To try to have a life together. The three of them. A family.

She thought about Mason growing up without a father. A mother who would have to take on a fake identity just to survive. It had turned her blissful time into a nightmare instantly.

"All I had to do was buy enough time to have the baby—no one knew he even existed as my son." As she thought back to it now, finding Reagan had been a Godsend. If it weren't for her, the plan never would have worked.

Jamie's mouth fell open. "Saul knew."

"What do you mean he knew?" Sonia didn't believe her.

"There was a woman at your house the day after your accident. They must have known about Reagan or Mason or both."

Could it be true? That would mean all of this was for nothing, that Saul had been on the hunt for Reagan for much longer than a few weeks.

"I'm so sorry this happened to you," Jamie finally said. "I don't want you to tell anyone where they are, you hear? Don't trust any of them. Don't even tell me."

"I know."

"Well, there's something else you need to know. My husband accidentally opened the last letter you gave me to send. You need to tell me what the hell is going on."

Sonia felt her brain rushing to find words as she saw Jamie's disappointed look, demanding she explain herself. She took a deep breath. "It was a request for someone I know to look into him. I don't trust him."

As Jamie seemed to contemplate what Sonia had said, her features relaxed a bit. The truth didn't matter at this point because the letter had never made it to the intended target.

"You want Nikki to look into Alex? I'm sure they're already acquainted."

Sonia stumbled over Jamie's statement. "Do you really believe Alex is working for Saul?"

Jamie ignored the question. "What about Nikki—can you trust her?"

Sonia was shaking her head before she realized it. "I loved her. We were never very close, but what happened—it drew a line in the sand for us. We can never be normal again."

"Would she choose Saul over you?"

Sonia took a moment to answer the question, though she knew the answer immediately. "Yes. She loves him like a father. She would do anything for him. Including killing me, if he told her to. Jamie, are you being safe? Are you making sure there is no one following you?" Sonia asked, feeling the dull ache of pain moving in slowly. The stress in her body holding her muscles taut.

Jamie nodded, but her hand went to her stomach and a look of worry crossed her face.

Sonia noticed the action and scowled. "What?"

"I can't imagine what you went through as a mother when you left him—your son—that day." Jamie's voice was laced with sadness.

Guilt seared Sonia. She couldn't do this to Jamie. Jamie had a life and a family of her own.

"You're fired," Sonia said.

Jamie looked at her, a confused expression on her face.

"I'm telling you, you're fired. And so is Alex. I'll get a new lawyer."

Jamie was shaking her head. "I can't abandon you. I won't."

"You don't have to." Sonia felt an unfamiliar emotion slowly entering her. "Because I'm jumping ship."

There were loud voices outside the door now, the guard talking with someone, his tone angry: "I told you, no one goes back."

A man rounded the corner and caught Jamie in his glare. "You need to leave." His hand pointed toward the door, where a defeated-looking guard was waiting.

Jamie grabbed her bag, glanced once more at Sonia and nodded. Sonia wasn't sure what the nod meant, but she reciprocated. Sonia only hoped it was not too late to save Jamie by cutting her out of this whole mess.

42

REAGAN

REAGAN CIRCLED BACK to the campsite until she saw the left-leaning, weather-beaten welcome sign. Her heart sank as low as the gas gauge—she had left their go-bag in the camper, and she only had fifty dollars and no clothes. She had to go back. How could she be so stupid?

They had been driving around for twenty minutes. Mason had stopped crying only a short time ago and was sleeping soundly with tear ridges dried on his face. She cracked the window to let the comforting howl of the wind inside.

Jeremy looked much older than he had since their last face-to-face encounter. The stress of his job or the alcohol abuse she'd witnessed at the farm might have something to do with it. He would go on binges, drinking to the point where he would be unable to climb the stairs to his room, his heavy boots stuttering on the hardwood floor as he mumbled curse words as if it were someone else's useless legs and muddled mind causing his behavior. Sometimes they would find him on the porch passed out in the morning sun with piss running down his leg. She had almost felt bad for him once or twice. But then he would rouse, accusing them of trying to run off—a weak attempt to hide his shame. Most nights he was the only visible guard on the property, but she and the others assumed there were other guards out there somewhere.

She recalled the last time she'd seen him. He had been drunk again. By her count, he slammed his whiskey bottle thirteen times on the porch table; the bottle must be nearly empty by now. Usually, he didn't drink until after dinner, but that day it began early.

The last clients were getting into their trucks and cars to go home to their wives and to kiss their children goodnight. After, these Johns counted out their crisp ATM twenties to their pimp.

Jeremy's loud voice slurred past the screen door. "Make sure you don't dry out the chicken again."

Fong looked distressed as she absently pinched her shirt hem between two tiny fingers. Reagan suspected Jeremy visited Fong sometimes at night, though she didn't ask. The truth was, since Janet had left a week earlier, everyone was on edge. None of them knew where she had gone or what she had done, but they all assumed the worst.

Reagan crept out back to look up at the night sky and breathe in the fresh earthy air. Each night she was tempted to run away, but she was too fearful of the unknown. It was only three of them now, which meant more work for those who remained. Tonight, as she stared up at the stars, she thought about her late period. It was three weeks past due, according to her calculations, and its absence gnawed at her. She didn't take the pills the other girls had insisted she take. It wasn't because she didn't want to; it was because she had forgotten. She barely knew what day it was anymore. She was hanging on by only a thread, and the last thing she could think of was those damned pills. Now she was regretting not taking the situation more seriously.

She watched the sharp shadows cut through the dense woods near the back porch and wondered what her chances of survival would be like, realistically, if she ran now. As it was, she was certain she would be going for that ride with The Spider once Saul found out about the baby.

A breeze scattered the dead leaves off the edge of the concrete stoop. She turned back to the woods as a pale figure separated from the shadows. Reagan jumped up from her seat.

"Shhhh." The small figure waved her over. Reagan looked over her shoulder. Was this some kind of trick? She blinked into the semi-darkness.

"C'mere." It was a woman's voice. Soft and tender, like the breeze on Reagan's cheek. She rose on shaky legs and set off toward the edge of the woods. As she passed through the halo of light from the porch and into the darkness, the woman's face gained character. It was the angry woman from two weeks ago. The one who'd torn off in the silver sports car.

"What's your name?" she asked, reaching a hand to rest on Reagan's shoulder. Reagan flinched away from her touch.

"Jen—na." Her name came out broken, like a child learning to count syllables.

"Are you here because you want to be?"

Reagan evaluated the woman's fancy clothes and perfect makeup. Her skin was like silk and she smelled of warm grapefruit.

Reagan shook her head, feeling tears sting her eyes. She didn't want to cry, but some unguarded emotion swept over her and she was pulled away by its undertow. While this woman continued to ask Reagan questions, she realized she was reacting to the care this woman was displaying toward her, a care Reagan seemed to have forgotten other humans were capable of. An emotion that at one point in her life she would have recognized sooner had she been exposed to it regularly. She wasn't desensitized to the ugliness she endured every day, but one could forget kind words and a tender touch, easily.

"They make me stay here. They make me have sex with—"

Reagan shook in the arms of this stranger for a long while, trying to catch her breath and regain control.

"My name is Emma." The woman looked beyond her, toward the house, her arms anchored on Reagan's shoulders. "How many other girls are in there?"

Before she could answer, the back door banged against the dirty siding and Jeremy emerged, his shadow staggered, his arms out like low-angled airplane wings.

"Reagan?" His angry voice was slurred. "Where the hell are you?"

Emma pulled her farther into the woods until they were both resting behind a large tree trunk. Each moment that passed, Reagan's heart beat harder and faster, and she felt the twitching grow in her muscles, the urge to run while she had a chance. Within the stretched silence she began to hear the sounds of the forest come alive around her. She found herself jerk at the benign sounds: snapping twigs and rustling leaves and the deep, echoing hoot of an owl.

Jeremy's hulking shadow lurched off the porch and moved to the edge of the woods, only twenty feet from them now. Close enough for them to smell the alcohol and sweat pouring off his skin into the humid evening air. She pictured him grabbing at her ankles in the darkness, his nails scratching at her flesh. Would he smell Emma's citrus perfume wafting in the air? Would he hear Reagan's breath dragging into her lungs?

"I'll find you, and when I do, you're dead." He spoke so low she wondered if he didn't know she was right there. As if he found it amusing that she would be tripping and falling through the dark woods and that his words would chase her silently, pushing at her back and shoulders, causing her to stumble.

* * *

Now, as she sped back to her campsite, she knew his words had never left her, and that she had perhaps always expected him to find her again. He was the one on the phone, his heavy breath between them. It was always his face she was searching for in crowds, always his gait and lurching figure she expected would come for her.

As she pulled into Maine Coastal Campground, she drove slowly, taking in everything. The daylight was waning, making her squint as she peered through the bug-plastered windshield. She noticed Max's truck sitting in its usual spot. Next to his, her camper sat silently. She had to assume Jeremy knew she was living here, and that he had possibly already paid the campsite a visit. She recalled the noises she'd heard last night. The wind had whipped around a flag, snapping it against the pole. She used to sleep with a white noise machine but had to give it up for fear she wouldn't be able to hear when someone came for them.

Reagan parked the Honda at Max's site rather than her own. She would have to trust him; she couldn't do this on her own. Leaving Mason sleeping in the car seat, she got out, locked the van, and ran to Max's door. Bang. Bang. Bang. She turned to look over the darkening landscape. Shadows were beginning to creep over the grass, sharp tree limbs reaching across the space, tricking her eyes with their movement. Bang. Bang. Bang.

Why wasn't Charlie barking?

"Max," she said in a loud whisper. She tried the knob, and it turned. She told herself it wasn't a big deal, he never locked it, but her heart was pounding against her temples. Without warning, something soft brushed her fingers hanging down next to her leg. She jerked her head down to see Charlie.

"Where's Max, boy?" she asked nervously.

She tried to push into the space only for the door to push back on her halfway. An arm lay still on the floor, its palm facing up to the ceiling, like a child's cupped hand waiting for candy. Max's hand. Charlie growled a low cackling sound at her side as his nose pushed at the door just enough for him to wiggle inside. She could see the shallow rise and fall of Max's chest. He was alive! She closed the door, trapping both Max and Charlie inside.

But before she could turn and run for the van, she felt two large arms reach around her and a hot breath on her ear. "Move, and I'll kill the boy."

43

JAMIE

JAMIE LEFT the hospital and went right to Ali's office. She needed some answers and she didn't know where else to find them. Kia's fingers clicked over her keyboard as Jamie approached, abruptly stopping when she looked up.

"Any word on Ali?" Jamie asked, noticing that Kia's face was puffy, but not so much as the last time they'd spoken.

"No. Nothing. This can't be good," Kia said. She pulled a tissue up to her eyes, but Jamie saw no tears there. Must be muscle memory. "The police have been here—in and out all week."

"Has Alex been over here?" She glanced across the hall into Alex's suite, where his two young blond assistants usually sat, but they were not in sight.

"Yes. Several times before and after she disappeared."

"Why?"

"Why, what?" Kia's head tilted to the side.

"What was he here to get?"

Kia seemed to think about it. "I'm not sure. He just said she left some things for him regarding a case they were sharing."

"Are they sharing any cases?"

"They help each other."

Jamie considered. "What about Sonia Rossi's case?"

"No way, not that one." Kia leaned toward Jamie. "I was under strict orders not to give anyone information on Sonia's case. Anyone." She raised her brows, giving Jamie the indication that she was on that long list too.

"What happened to the case after Ali disappeared?"

"I think Alex went to Stuart, one of the partners, and asked to take over. It was the same morning Ali disappeared. I guess he didn't want the case to lose any momentum."

"And Stuart said yes?" Jamie glanced back across the hall. She felt...watched.

"Yes. The same day Alex went up to ask, Stuart sent me an email confirming Alex was taking over the case."

Jamie thanked her and crossed the hall into Alex's suite. The outer office was silent as she walked to Alex's open door.

Jamie looked back over her shoulder. What if she just took a peek at his desk—just to see what he was working on? She would hear him coming, and if she did, she would take a seat by his desk as if she was merely waiting to speak to him. No big deal.

She approached the desk slowly and looked over it first, touching nothing but memorizing the layout of his papers and objects, so she could return anything she might end up moving to its original spot. She knew and understood Alex's tendencies. He would know right away if someone had touched or moved his things.

A copy of Sonia's appeal lay in the center of his desk, angry red ink marking up the surface with the tiny initials *SR* next to each. He said he had already filed these. Jamie set the papers back down and noticed a file drawer on the right was open slightly. She bit the inside of her cheek and pulled the drawer open. A picture of her and Alex from their engagement party years ago looked up at her. Both of them smiling into the camera.

She had thought she was the luckiest girl in the world when the picture was taken. It was several months later that she would learn what a weasel she nearly married. How could she not have seen what a nasty, egotistical man he was—the most calculating opportunist she had ever met.

Listening for footsteps but hearing none, she turned back to his desk. Why was Alex keeping this photo around? She hadn't thought to ask if he was seeing anyone; she didn't really care. Suddenly, it was very important to her that he move on and find someone new.

She put the picture back and found more paperwork, a hiss of air pressed from her lips when she found a file labeled "Nina Nelson". Jamie's heart buckled, then tripped to life again. She skimmed the pages quickly, trying to keep some of her attention on the door. Nina was appealing her conviction, and it appeared that Alex was representing her. How could he? Did he want Jamie dead?

Underneath the papers was a clear bag with several cell-phones inside. Jamie thought about the calls at all hours of the night. Nina's crazed confessions, her mindless laughter. No—he wouldn't, would he? Was he providing phones to Nina so she could harass Jamie?

She thrust the folder back in its place and a sick feeling stirred in her. Just what the hell was Alex up to now? He might just be narcissistic enough to help Nina get out of the mental facility solely to get his revenge.

She felt sweat along her hairline as she shut the desk drawer. Had she heard the ding of the elevator stopping on this floor, or was it ringing in her ears? She crept to the doorway. No one.

As much as she didn't want to be here, she still needed to find some information on Sonia's case. She pulled on the drawers at the far side of his desk; they were locked.

This would pay him back for all the times he had gone into her office when she wasn't there. She knew why he had done it.

To take ownership of something that was hers. To let her know nothing was off limits. But he had been wrong. She didn't get that feeling as she went through Alex's things. She felt sick about it. She didn't want to touch his stuff, and worse, she was afraid what she might find hiding in here.

She looked through each of the papers he had filed in the brief for Sonia and a single page slipped out. It was a printout for lab results from the women's clinic Joey and Sonia were referred to. It stated: *Patient has no viable eggs. Will consider an egg donor. Searching bank of candidates.*

According to the forms, a donor with the number tag 5764 was used to produce two fertilized eggs. The date of implant was two months before Sonia fled. Yet another thing Alex had chosen not to share with her.

Voices moved down the hallway and Jamie quickly arranged the papers back again just before Alex walked in to find her seated in front of his desk.

"What are you doing?" He yanked at the knot in his tie.

"Why did you put a block on visitors to Sonia?"

His eyes narrowed at her as he rounded his desk, taking in all the items on it. "I told you in our meeting the other day. I don't want you visiting her without me there. I need to be there. She doesn't trust me for some reason. It's a buffer." Alex seemed to wave off her concern.

"I need to talk to her, and I can't do everything around your schedule. Did you file her appeal?"

Alex's head tilted to the side. "Not yet. Someone messed up on some forms and they all have to be redone."

"It's important that we move quickly on this, Alex." Jamie's voice was bullish. "She needs to get out and get back to her family."

"What family? You mean Reagan and Mason? She can just help herself out and tell us where they are and we can go get them. We can bring them to her."

"We? You know she isn't going to do that." Jamie bit down on her tongue. He was acting like a spoiled child; things aren't always handed to us. "We don't need them to appeal her case."

"I do," Alex said.

Jamie sat back in her chair. "When did you start working for Saul?"

His mouth gaped; his features looked cartoonish. "Take that back! You have no proof for those kinds of accusations. That would be a big ethical violation," Alex said with a hard edge to his voice. He stood and began rounding the desk toward her, grabbing for her wrist, but she was too fast. She cut across the room to the door and stepped out to see Lauren, his assistant, at her desk.

"I just wanted to let you know that Sonia fired all of us today," Jamie said to him with a smirk. "Don't contact her, or me for that matter. Now you only work for Saul."

And she walked off down the hallway, leaving him standing there with his mouth hanging open.

44

SONIA

I⒯ was 10:00 p.m. when Sonia heard the clack of approaching footsteps outside her hospital room. The guard, Jerry, lumbered into the room, grunting and shoving his chair toward the recess of light in the corner. A moment later she heard the crackle of cellophane. She took a deep breath. Last night he had slept four hours, his snores randomly shattering the silence of the room. His partner—first name Mag—spent most of her time at the nurse's station, flirting with the hospital staff. Earlier, Sonia had heard the nurse speak in a low tone to Jerry about Sonia's pain medication knocking her out. "She'll be passed out in a few minutes," the nurse had said. And she had been right.

Tonight, she told a different nurse she didn't want the pain medication. "It's making me sick," she said. "I don't want any." Truth was, the pain was making her sicker. It radiated down her side and into her leg. Moving over her like a slow burn that turned into a roaring fire, making her muscles twitch and sweat gather over her skin. She must look like a junkie in search of her next fix.

"Well, if it isn't my favorite inmate." The Warden's voice caused the lazy guard to jump to his feet; the Warden smirked.

Cool air seemed to follow him into the room and caused Sonia to shudder.

"At ease, man. I'm just checking up on her. I have a few questions to ask. Why don't you take a few minutes outside?" He hiked his head toward the hallway, and the guard moved to the door, his large frame ducking away.

"How are you feeling?" the Warden asked. Sonia opened her mouth to respond, but he continued talking. "I want to ask you some questions, and I have places to be, so instead of drawing this out I'll make it quick."

A mercy. Sonia snapped her mouth shut.

"Who did this to you?"

Sonia shook her head.

"At least you're consistent," the Warden mocked. "We analyzed what appears to be a toothbrush that was found in your back." He seemed to consider what he'd said. She pictured him pulling the shank from the cords of muscles and smooth flesh over and over, the act giving him a sort of perverse joy.

An alarm sounded in the distance, followed by a group of staff running down the hall shouting directions to one another.

"It appears…that the only prints found on the weapon—were yours." His brows rose, making his eyes look way too big while shrinking his liver-spotted forehead. He was waiting for her to speak. "I don't suppose you know how that could be?"

Sonia took a deep, shaky breath. "I have no idea."

"Really?" Another smirk. "I'm charging you with possession of a weapon." He smiled back at her. This man was truly ugly, and it had nothing to do with his ruddy features or beer belly. "You'll be on restrictions when you get back. No library, no groups, no anything." His delivery was cheerful. "I don't have time for this, and because you are unwilling to cooperate, this is all I can do."

She watched as he shook his head slowly and disappeared out the doorway without affording her the opportunity to argue.

The minutes ticked by as she looked at the shadows on the walls. The guard took nearly twenty minutes to make it back to his chair and was now eating a pastry, falling crumbs gathering on his gray polo shirt. Sonia turned away and stared up at the TV, trying to get the image of the Warden out of her mind, but it was like a noxious gas that clung to the air around her.

* * *

THREE HOURS LATER, the light beyond the window had faded to black. The staff in the hallways had quieted. On occasion Sonia could hear chatter from down the hall. The clock read 12:30 p.m., and the guard had been fast asleep for almost an hour, his partner silently creeping down the hall to chat with the nurses. Sonia sat up, slipping her hand out of the cuff she had closed around her wrist two hours ago after she came back from the bathroom. She had been careful not to cinch it all the way down, just enough to appease Jerry. She was counting on his laziness and apathy for his job, and she had been right. Her legs were trembling as the pain grew stronger. Slowly, she lowered her feet to the ground, its coolness penetrating her stocking feet. She shifted her weight to her legs as her unused core muscles protested but held up.

She crept to the doorway and peered out. The nurse's station was to the left, near the elevators set back from the view of her doorway. She heard the faint ring of a phone. Her legs wobbled under her and she grabbed at the wall to regain her balance. She would need to find some clothes.

The rush in her ears was so loud that everything else faded: no more ringing phone or loud snores, just the solid pounding of blood. She stepped into the hallway as naturally as she could manage. At any moment a staff member could duck out of a room and catch her. She wasn't sure if they would recognize her, but her hospital clothes and her ass flapping in the breeze would give her away. After passing two open doors, she ducked into a third. A hissing ventilator sounded in the darkness, a soft stream of light coming from an emergency sign.

Her eyes quickly adjusted to the darkness, and she noticed clothes in a pile by a duffel bag: men's clothes, much too large for her frame, folded together. Skipping the clothes, she took a cell phone that was sitting on the table and crept toward the door. Her shaking hand pressed to her side, trying to ignore the roaring pain of her injury, she entered the hallway and went two doors down. There was a TV on in the room, its occupant, a woman, lying motionless in her bed. Sonia noticed a handbag and clothing on the floor near the bathroom.

Sonia crept to the clothes—they would have to do. She pictured the snoring guard waking any minute and sounding the alarm on her escape. She thought of the Warden's words about her fingerprints being all over the weapon. She thought of just how desperate she was to get out of there.

Now, garbed in a white Nirvana t-shirt and baggy jeans, she realized these clothes must have been left here by a visitor. Surely they were not meant for the aging woman in the bed. No matter. She was able to grab three twenty-dollar bills out of the wallet she found in the purse and stuffed them into the pocket of the jeans. Head low, she walked into the hallway toward the stairwell that was opposite the nurse's station. Still no loud shouting, no alarm, but she anticipated it with every new step. A laugh carried down the hall after her: Mag. Mag was behind her, the squeak of her boots along the polished floor moving in her direction. Sonia kept her eyes forward, pushing through the pain to walk naturally. Any second, she would reach Sonia's room and find the sleeping guard next to the empty bed. Only feet away from the exit, she heard Mag's yell, "Where is she, dumbass!"

And Sonia smiled as she hit the push bar for the door and disappeared down the stairs.

They would be watching most of the exits of the hospital now, so she had to move faster. She followed the signs for the emergency exit, which led to a single door with a fire alarm attached to it. There was no time. She would have to risk using it. She pushed out into the warm night air and the alarm blared behind her. It was dark but for the light of the streetlamps over what appeared to be a parking garage exit.

The pale light of the moon slashed down through the rectangular concrete openings as the stale smell of exhaust fumes filled the air. She weaved in between cars just in case security followed her out the door she had just left. The red glow of a mounted camera caught her attention and she was careful to avoid its eye. The squeal of tires sounded in the distance, but she couldn't gauge which direction the sound was coming from as the sounds bounced off the cement walls. She could be walking right into the oncoming car.

Another sign for a stairwell lit up, and she cautiously followed it. Nudging the door, she listened for noisy footsteps or voices, then went for it, grabbing her side tightly to smother the pain as she descended the stairs quickly. As she neared the last flight, she watched a security car pulling around the door at the bottom. She ducked into the garage again. A voice, distorted from radio, sounded nearby.

"Be on the lookout for a white female, possibly in a hospital gown. Brown hair, five-five."

Sonia felt her heart buck in her chest as she ducked behind a parked car. A spotlight traveled the darkness, searching like a robotic eye.

Searching for her.

The car on which the spotlight was mounted traveled at a slow pace, but it was heading in her direction. She heard footsteps on the stairs behind her. A red pickup truck rested silently next to her and before she could change her mind, she pulled herself into its metal bed. Dog cages abutted the cab, or at least they appeared to be dog cages in the semi-darkness. She felt thick blankets under her knees and quickly pulled them over her body. The door to her left burst open and a man shouted to the approaching car. "See her?"

"No, I've only checked this level," a woman responded in an irritated tone.

"You should have checked on five first. That's where she came out." His footsteps were loud as he approached. It sounded like he was only feet from where she was hunkered down, maybe even at the trucks bumper.

"What the hell do you want me to do, Tom?" the woman's voice retorted.

"Check five down. Hurry the hell up."

The car took off and the man began walking away, muttering under his breath. The pain in Sonia's side was nearly unbearable. A wave of nausea caused her to puke, and a blackness crept into her vision. She couldn't pass out now, she was almost there...

But it was too late.

45

JAMIE

JAMIE PASSED through the wide cement tunnel that opened into a small green space. Dotting the grass were five large spheres, two set atop pools wedged between lanes of traffic. The air was humid, and the sun was hot. Several homeless people were lined up on the sidewalks, gathering their possessions to head out for the day. She'd asked Javi and Ming to meet her here. They were already waiting for her on a park bench. Javi muttered a greeting while Ming watched Jamie cross to them, a hard set to her face.

"Sorry I'm late. Have you been waiting long?"

"No matter," Javi said, keeping his eyes on the screen. "Why are we here?"

Ming tipped a delicate hand open to the sky and looked to Jamie. The breeze floated past, brushing Ming's short black hair against her cheek.

"Yeah, about that," said Jamie. "We've been fired. Sonia wants a new lawyer."

Ming began gathering her things. "Why come down here then?"

"Wait." Jamie put a hand out, touching it to the other

woman's. Javi looked up and watched the exchange. "She needs our help. She has no one she can trust."

"You said she fired us." Ming shouldered her bag.

"I know what I said. But I'm not giving up, and I need your help."

Ming sat back on the bench, cradling her bag in her lap as if ready to spring up at any moment.

Then Javi spoke. "I found something."

Jamie looked at him, almost worried about what he would say. She nodded.

"Emma contacted the FBI only days before her murder." Javi motioned for Jamie to take a look at his computer screen. It was an email to Emma from an FBI agent named Miller. The email discussed a meeting that was supposed to happen the day after Emma was killed.

"How did we only now learn about this?" Jamie wondered aloud. "Where did you find it?"

Javi turned back to the computer, perhaps finding it easier to communicate with the device between them.

"Alex knew." Ming's voice was low. "I heard him tell Ali the night before she went missing. Something about her working with the Feds on a property Saul owned. Something called 'The Farm'. I didn't bring it up before because I just assumed that if it was relevant, Alex would have brought it up with the group."

Or perhaps, Jamie thought, Ming just didn't want anyone to know she'd been eavesdropping.

"It burned down," Jamie said.

"Yes. Just before this email was received," Javi confirmed.

"You think Emma was going to help the government build a case against her own father?" Jamie blurted. She had never met Emma, but it must have been difficult to do such a thing. Turn on your own family. She recalled talking with Sonia about Saul and Emma's relationship. Emma didn't support her father's business dealings. It was one thing to turn a blind eye, but it was a whole other to get the government involved. There were so many questions she had for Sonia. She pulled out a notebook and began jotting them down before she could forget them.

"Alex never mentioned this to me," Jamie said as she scribbled.

"What do we think happened?" Ming asked. "Do we think Emma was killed by her father because she was talking to the FBI?"

Jamie's cheeks pinched. There was no way of knowing with the limited information they had now. She didn't know Saul personally, only Sonia's tainted perspective.

"It's possible," Javi stated.

"The odd thing is, Saul has only appeared a few times in the last few years. His business is essentially run by his stepdaughter, Nikki Angelo, and one other person." Jamie had learned this from Drew after he'd made a call to an old friend from the academy who worked in Arlington P.D.

"And we know what she does." Ming looked knowingly at Jamie.

"Kills people. Sonia had a visit from Saul last week," Jamie added. "Do we have any proof that Nikki was involved in the Montana killings? Or with Joey?"

Javi began typing quickly. "I think she would be too smart to travel under her own name to these places...let me look at something."

The breeze caressed Jamie's face as she watched Javi work.

"Yes. I got it. Nikki took a trip to Texas just before Joey was killed."

"But he was in Arizona. You think she rented a car and drove there?" Jamie asked.

Javi nodded. "That's exactly what she did. She never stayed in Texas. Rented a car, drove there and back, and flew out four days after landing."

"What about Montana?"

"She flew out to a border town in South Dakota a day before the murders," Javi said.

"Nikki's the killer. Seems pretty lazy," Jamie whispered. "Saul's looking for Sonia's son."

Both Ming and Javi were nodding. So maybe Saul had only suspected Sonia was pregnant, and Joey confirmed it? "And Joey was the one who told them she was pregnant." The realization hit her hard. This little boy was going to be killed because of some old man's desire to get even with his daughter's killer. Because Saul couldn't live without making Sonia pay the ultimate price. He must not believe she was innocent, and perhaps never would, not even after her appeal—or he was just too far gone to care.

"Do we know where Saul could be now?" Ming asked.

Jamie considered this for a moment.

"He has a lot of properties around the country and beyond," Javi said.

"Where?" Jamie's pen was poised over her notepad.

"Two in Virginia. One in Maine, Texas and Florida."

"He could be anywhere," Jamie said as she stopped writing. "But I think he would want to be here."

"Why?" Ming asked.

"To be near Sonia. To get his revenge. Where is the other house in Virginia?"

"The mountains. Appalachian Trail. It's a hunting cabin," Javi said.

"What's the address?" Jamie asked, and wrote it down as Javi recited it for her.

"What should we do now?" Javi asked.

"Be careful." Jamie packed up her things. "I'll contact you if I learn anything. You do the same. Remember, Alex is out."

They nodded to her.

As she was walking toward the large tunnel, her phone rang.

Her nerves rattled like the cart of the homeless man in front of her. He pulled up to the grass and looked back at her with dirt-stained skin.

She answered her phone. "Hello."

"Jamie," Butch's voice snapped. "Where the hell are you?"

"Meeting with Ming and Javi," she said, moving quickly past the man, whose eyes stayed on her.

"I take it you haven't heard yet?"

"Heard what?"

"Sonia escaped from the hospital last night. That woman is in the wind."

46

SONIA

HER MIND EBBED and flowed against the dark curtain of her consciousness. As soon as she'd float closer to the surface, she heard the echo of footsteps or the start of a car engine, just long enough to feel the steel ridges in the truck bed digging into her ribs, she'd be pulled back under by her sluggish brain. She muffled a whimper as pain stirred through her.

She wasn't sure how long this pattern had lasted by the time she felt the truck shift from the weight of someone getting inside. The motor roared, sending a low vibration through her body, followed by the motion of shifting momentum as the truck backed out of its parking space.

She could smell exhaust fumes and the harsh scent of dog cages near her head. The glow of daylight ringed the edges of the blanket she had pulled over herself, her body tucked into its hiding place where she'd been blacked out all night.

The truck came to a stop and Sonia felt her heart patter. Were they checking cars? At any moment someone would pull the blanket back and find her broken body resting underneath.

"I heard they didn't find her," came a man's voice from nearby.

"Nope. Got away," another man said. "Thanks, Doc. See you tomorrow?"

"No. I'm off for three days—going to the dog show up in Midland." His voice was deep and bordering on jovial, and she couldn't help but think she was stuck in a dream. Reality took on a thin, animated quality as she listened to the mundane conversation.

"I heard you picked up third place last time."

"Yeah, last year."

Her head rolled into the sharp edge of one of the cages and she smothered a cry with her palm.

"Might make first this year with my Mel, little Scottish Terrier."

A horn sounded nearby.

"Let me know how it goes."

"Will do."

The truck crept forward until she could feel the full glare of the sun on her even through the thick blanket, and only after several moments did she dare to lower the blanket and look around. Excitement planted firmly in her mind: she had gotten out! All she had with her was the money she'd grabbed from the woman's purse at the hospital and the cell phone in her pocket. Both items would be needed when they finally stopped. She dragged in the fresh air swirling around the truck bed.

Each pothole and bump they traveled over sent a scatter of angry nerve endings throughout her body. She was beginning to wish that the conversation that started all of this had never taken place. But she was free—at least for now. And it was all thanks to Tammie.

One week ago, when she'd met Tammie, Sonia had sent a stern and clear warning that you never stab your cellmate while on lockdown—that way they would know who'd done it. It seemed a trivial thing to mention at the time, as Sonia had nearly given up hope of seeing the light of day. But after she told the young girl this, she found herself asking, the next day, "Do you want to get on Ginger's good side?"

The question had caused Tammie to stop twisting a knot of hair around her finger and look over at Sonia, who had her head laid back against the pillow. It was nighttime, the darkness seeping in all around, but Tammie was a night owl. Sitting on the floor, facing the cell door, she was braiding her hair and humming softly until Sonia spoke.

"What d'you mean?" Tammie said.

"I mean I need something from you, and it'll help you around the block. Maybe even get you that fix you been cruising for."

Tammie scooted toward the bed, her face visible in the darkness only by smooth shadows. "I'm listening."

"It's important when you do it that you hit the spot I mark exactly." Sonia sat up. "I'll supply the weapon."

Tammie barked a short laugh and pushed away from her. "You really are one crazy bitch."

Sonia still didn't know how much she could trust this girl, but she sensed Tammie was out for number one, which would work in Sonia's favor. From the start of their awkward relationship, Tammie was constantly trying to manipulate her surroundings. Sonia wasn't even sure if the girl was aware of her own tactics.

"I know Ginger asked you to hurt me."

"What are you talking about?" But Tammie's tone gave it all away.

"Look, I'm not new to how this all works. You're the new kid on the block and she intends to use you to get me." There was a beat of silence. The dim voices from outside could barely be heard. Sonia lowered her voice even more, causing Tammie to scoot closer. "I know she needs your help, and all I'm saying is we can both get what we want."

"What the hell's wrong with you? You want to die, why not kill yourself?"

"Did I ask you to kill me?" Sonia answered sharply. "I asked you to stab me. My reasons are my own."

The silence told Sonia all she needed to know.

"You snitch on Ginger?" Tammie said suspiciously.

"No."

"That's not what the word is. Are you setting me up?"

"I get what I want and you get the credit. You won't get caught if you do exactly what I tell you," Sonia said. She could see the girl nodding. "They'll protect you." There was a short silence and Sonia felt the need to reassure her. "I don't snitch."

"Neither do I."

Sonia didn't buy that; she was sure Tammie would snitch if it was to her own benefit. But she was also counting on Tammie's self-preservation to help Sonia get out of prison for the last time.

"Okay," said Tammie. "Tell me what to do."

* * *

THE TRUCK ROCKED TO A STOP. Sonia jerked the blanket over her head and listened to the door creak open. She heard the muted shuffle of items being moved around and the door slammed. After several minutes of silence, she pulled the blanket away. The air was fresh and dogs barked in the distance. Trees hung in her view. She'd never thought she would be this close to freedom again in her life. The air was sweet, the buzz of bugs nearby, a beautiful sound. She only realized now that there were so many sounds she'd never noticed she was missing. The crack of a stick, the whistle of the wind in the trees. This was what life sounded like. Alive around her, crackling with energy, moving endlessly.

She slowly raised her head over the edge of the truck bed and looked around.

A rambler the color of eggshells rested just before a vast forest. The leaves of the trees danced and swayed. Seeing no other movement, she slowly slunk from the rear of the truck and knelt down. Her muscles protested against her weight and her vision swayed. She searched in her pockets quickly and felt the bulge of the phone still there. Relief washed over her as she slowly stood and headed down the stone-paved driveway, trying to pick up her pace the farther she was from the truck, but her gait slowed her down as much as the pain from her side. The driveway was long and finally ended at the road, and she scanned for any road signs. None.

She pulled the phone from her pocket and noticed she had a signal, opened the map application and zoomed in. According to the image on the screen, she was an hour and a half from Arlington. She opened the phone keypad and typed in the second of two phone numbers she had committed to memory in the last five years.

"Who is this?" came a gruff female voice.

"How about you do your baby sister a favor," Sonia said.

"You might be all out of favors from me." But she didn't hang up. "I'm listening."

47

REAGAN

Reagan screamed, the sound now guttural and hoarse. A wet burn traveled up her dry throat as angry tears coursed down her cheeks. It was dark in here. Wherever here was. And her shoulders burned from her hands being pulled together behind her to meet just above her butt. Panic had taken over some time ago, when she first opened her eyes to a landscape of blackness. During the car ride down, she'd held back tears for Mason's sake. He was clearly stressed from the situation, and if she lost it, it would be worse. But when Jeremy separated them, she had screamed, unable to stop herself.

"Let me outta here!" She wasn't sure why she was surprised that her voice didn't echo off the blackness. Instead, emptiness swallowed her words and returned a static silence. She pulled against the restraints and felt something dig into her tender flesh.

"How have you been, Reagan?" The voice caused her to freeze. The familiar pitch of his voice so close, too close. The darkness disorienting her as she scanned her surroundings, her eyes constantly trying to find some shred of light to focus them.

"I've missed you," Saul said. His voice dripped with possession. And all at once the past that she was so careful to hide away came tumbling back like an overstuffed closet being thrust open.

"Get away from me," she hissed.

Had he found out about Mason? Is that why she was here—because he thought Mason was his son?

"Let me go." Her voice sounded like a whimper. So weak it angered her. She refused to be his victim ever again. "Let me go," she said more firmly.

A light switched on; its glow stung her eyes and she slammed them shut instinctually. Even with her eyes closed, she felt the light move over her like a placebo of warmth.

"Maine, huh? It's beautiful up there. I have a cabin on the northern tip." It seemed like a long while before she could open her eyes to the light, but when she did, she almost didn't recognize the man who sat before her. His once-handsome features were covered by creases and a heavy dusting of hair. His eyes, still blue, were dull and unfocused, his belly a large round mass resting atop his bent legs. She opened her mouth to speak, but no words formed.

"You look—exactly the same." He scooted to the edge of his chair, coming close enough for her to smell the thick, heavy odor of liquor on his breath.

"Where's Mason?"

"He is…perfect," he said, staring back at her with visible reverence. She thought she saw his eyes twinkling, then realized he was crying.

She shook her head. "What do you want with him?"

"Mason—is exactly what I imagined he would be since I found out about him." He shifted in his seat.

Reagan felt a quiver inside of her, like a bony hand reaching inside to shake her belly. He couldn't think…he'd never found out she was pregnant. No one but Emma and Sonia knew.

"I could have changed your life. I would have found a place for us."

"There was never an *us*." The last word caved her mouth into a scowl. "I'm not your property."

He was nodding now. "I never meant for you to feel that way. I loved you." His proclamation sounded like that of a washed-up old man, not unlike the image she saw outwardly. She felt her defiance gathering steam, but she pulled it back when she thought of Mason.

"What do you want from us?"

Her surroundings were coming into focus. She was lying on a single bed in a room enclosed with bare wood walls. Two windows covered in dark red curtains on the wall farthest away from her were just beyond the chair Saul had set up next to the bed. How long had he been sitting in the dark, listening to her scream?

The wind outside howled as the tiny smattering of tree branches clawed the windows.

"He isn't who you think he is," she said finally, when the silence had grown impossible.

"Who is he?"

"He isn't your son. I—" Her voice tripped over her lips. "I lost my child."

"You didn't have to run away. I would have given you anything you needed," Saul mused. Reagan had a sinking feeling that something had cracked in the old man. He hadn't seemed to hear what she'd said. His head tipped to the side, his hand brushing the length of his beard. No sign of emotion entered his features. "I knew who Mason was the moment I laid eyes on him."

She didn't like his statement, nor did she like where this was headed. It wasn't that he hadn't heard her—he knew something she didn't.

"What are you going to do to us? Where is he?"

Saul only shook his head.

Pain blazed a trail across her shoulders as she tried to keep the tension off her joints. They were too tight, but she didn't want Saul to see her struggle. She didn't want to show this man any sign of weakness.

"Were you there when Emma was killed?" he asked, his body as still as a statue. For a fraction of a second she felt sorry for the man who had brutalized her for so long. Just a moment of weakness.

"Yes. I was."

"Was it her? Did Sonia kill her?" He probably didn't mean to sound so desperate. He sat back abruptly, as if noticing his mistake, and took a long pull of a dark amber liquid from a glass clutched in his hand.

She shook her head. "Sonia didn't kill your daughter. She loved her."

He sagged back into the chair, his drink sloshing over the sides of the glass and raining onto the floor. "Why'd she do it?" he muttered with a shake of his head.

"Why'd she do what?"

"Take the fall."

"To protect me and Mason from you."

"As if I'd kill my own flesh and blood."

Reagan felt her heart stutter. "I don't know who killed Emma. I only heard her voice; I didn't see her face."

"Her?"

"Yes. A woman."

"What happened?"

The woman's voice echoed off the walls of her memory.

Emma had let Reagan sleep in her guest bedroom, where she found herself crouched. It was only two days since she'd escaped the farm, and Emma said she was trying to figure out what to do. Reagan was afraid Emma would go to the police and things would worsen. She wasn't legally an adult yet, and she knew that meant they would put her in foster care. Emma had insisted they make an appointment at a clinic in a fake name. But today

Reagan had begun to bleed. She was torn between all the emotions battering her. Until she heard the shouts downstairs.

"He's your father. You can't turn against your own father!" A woman's voice.

Emma fired back. "He's not a good man. He keeps children against their will in a house to have sex with men." By the end of her statement, she was nearly yelling in disgust. Reagan crept toward the door and pushed it open an inch, fearing she might be seen through the open railing down to the first floor.

"He's your *father.*"

"I don't care. Right is right," Emma said. Then the gasping began. A hideous hiss of air pressed from wet lungs. Things being knocked to the ground in a loud blast of banging. There was no screaming, no other sounds for a long time. Then she heard the slow, steady sound of feet coming up the stairs. Reagan quickly crawled under the bed just as the door creaked open. Black boots entered the room, and she was nearly choking on the fear, cold and clinging to her bones, arresting her in place. Slowly, the boots moved to the bedside, then the closet. Finally, after what felt like an eternity, the boots receded. She listened as the woman went downstairs and continued to search the house as the damned phone kept ringing.

What had she done to Emma? Morbid thoughts crept in as she lay there. When she finally moved out from under the bed, a new noise downstairs startled her. More movement and a long scream. Reagan rushed to the closet.

"Who was she?" Saul's voice seethed with anger, pulling her back into the present. "Who killed my daughter?"

"I don't know. All I know is she said 'You can't do this to your own father.' She mentioned going to the federal authorities about what you were doing."

"Who said that?"

"The woman, the one who killed Emma, the one wearing black boots."

Saul abruptly stood up, wide-eyed, pushing the chair back into the wall with a loud bang.

"No. No. This can't be." He landed an open palm against her exposed cheek. The pain cracked through her as her shock caught up to the action. "No. You're lying."

"I'm not lying." She pressed her cheek into the pillow to quell the pain.

And suddenly she understood. Saul knew who killed his daughter. He left the room, slamming the door behind him, and Reagan allowed herself to cry.

48

SONIA

Sonia spotted the dark-colored SUV moving up the road toward her. Nikki always did like to drive fast. It pulled to the side of the road, throwing a cloud of dust into the air, and Sonia limped toward the passenger door that swung open as she reached for the handle.

"You look like hell," Nikki said with a wide smile. "You're bleeding through your t-shirt."

"Nice to see you, sis. Three hours? Really?" She pulled herself into the soft leather seat and winced as she reached for the door to pull it shut, her abs screaming in protest.

"You're lucky I came at all. You're a fugitive, little sister."

"You've done much worse than rescue me, I'm sure of that." Sonia thought of the letters she had given to Jamie. How the second one had never made it. She wondered if Jamie would ever find out what Sonia had asked Nikki to do.

"Where to?" Nikki asked as she slumped into the large driver's seat. Nikki wasn't a big girl. In fact, the size of this Yukon XL would have had Sonia laughing if she wasn't in so much pain.

"Why the hell are you smiling? I'll take you wherever you

want to go. In the state," she clarified sternly. "I'm on call with the boss."

"Why are you doing this?" Sonia asked as she bit down a wave of nausea. The pain was battering her. She didn't fully understand the extent of her injuries. Her cheeks felt hot to the touch, but her body shivered—she might have a fever.

"I don't know what you mean."

She should play nice, but before she could stop her word vomit, she was speaking. "He's not a good man."

Nikki shrugged. Sonia forced down the reaction she had to this juvenile gesture. As if her big sister didn't care that she worked for a monster—no big deal.

"It didn't stop you from asking me to do you a favor." The words were a stinging rebuke.

"So, I can't kill for him, but I can for you, is that it?" She chuckled, like Sonia had said something funny.

"Shhh." Sonia shifted her legs, trying to take the pressure off her lower back. "I did what I had to do to protect what's mine. I went to prison! I have no idea what he would do if he found them."

A fleeting smirk flashed over Nikki's face.

Sonia insisted, "I didn't want to do that. I had no choice."

"Beggars can't be choosers. A sin is a sin, and a murder is a murder, even if it was to hide your little secret."

Sonia wasn't expecting things to escalate this quickly. She had to keep it together. She needed Nikki right now. And the worst part was, she was right. Sonia had chosen who lived and who had to die, despite the righteous cause she kept telling herself about.

Mason and Reagan got to live because of her choices. Or at least that's how she appeased her guilt.

"Who were those people?" Nikki asked, appraising her red nails. She was still pretty in a tender kind of way. Her soft full cheeks made her look just as young as when Sonia had last seen her, in the back of the courtroom on the day she was sentenced. She had a scowl on her face to hide the emotional pain Sonia knew was buried there.

"It doesn't matter anymore." *People who could have told Saul about Mason.*

"Suit yourself." Nikki put the truck in gear and continued in the direction Sonia had come.

"I want to see Saul."

Nikki snorted in response. "That's not gonna happen. He'll kill you. If that's what you want, let's just get it over with right here."

"What did Joey tell you before you killed him?" Sonia watched Nikki's eyes slide over to look at her just for a split second. "You said you would make it painless."

"I didn't kill Joey," Nikki said. Her voice indifferent.

"Don't lie to me."

She held up a hand away from the steering wheel as if to silence Sonia. Not much had changed. "I promised you, before you went away, that I would protect Joey. I meant it."

"What happened?" Sonia recalled the last time she'd spoken with Nikki. Nikki's visit to the jail just before they moved Sonia to Flint Hill. She had made Nikki promise that if she found Joey, she would make his death quick and painless. She knew her sister's loyalty was to Saul, but Nikki would do this for her. She had to. She promised.

"Saul cut me out of the search for him after he found out about some IVF process Emma had."

What? Sonia turned to watch the landscape rush past her window as she tried to disguise her reaction. "Why torture Joey if he already knew about Mason?" Sonia wondered aloud.

"Because he wanted to know where to find the boy." Nikki's tone was near exasperation. "He wouldn't give them up."

"He didn't know!" Sonia yelled. Anger rippled through her,

and she reached out to hit the dashboard with a crack. Pain sliced up her arm, and she winced.

"Hey—don't take it out on the car." Nikki's tone a mix of boredom and annoyance.

Sonia gave up and switched tactics. "I need to talk to Saul. I have to convince him we just want to live our lives. I didn't kill Emma."

"I know you didn't," Nikki said, turning her blinker on.

Sonia let the comment go, and they rode in silence for a long while. Every bump and pothole they drove over sent stabs of pain through her. A hiss sometimes escaped her unguarded lips.

"You need to see a doctor?" Nikki asked.

"That's not going to happen. You got any water?"

"Yeah." She pulled a bottle of water out of a cup holder and handed it to Sonia. "I got a guy, totally off the books. He would see you. Maybe even give you some tits while you're under." Nikki snickered.

"No. I don't need a doctor." She tried to rein in her insolent tone. "I need to heal, that's all."

"How'd you escape?"

"Risked my liver and took my chances."

"What does that mean?" Nikki's smooth brow wrinkled.

"I had someone stab me so I could get a ride to the hospital. The rest is history."

"Man, you really are a crazy bitch." She took a pull on her vape, expelling a thin line of smoke through the cracked window.

"I need to see him, sis." Her plea hung in the air between them. Nikki's fingers restless on the wheel. "Don't make me beg. I need my life back."

She shook her head. "That's the last thing Saul D'Luca is gonna offer you."

49

JAMIE

JAMIE SLAMMED on her brakes and jerked the car to the side of the road, the phone pinched between her shoulder and cheek. "Okay, go ahead."

Javi read off an address in the Appalachian Mountains. A cabin owned by Saul.

"Thanks! I owe you one," Jamie told him, and hung up. He had given her the address earlier but, in her rush, she had misplaced it. After leaving two frantic messages on his phone, he had finally called back.

As she maneuvered out onto the road, her phone rang again. She wasn't going to answer it at first, but curiosity got the best of her. She wanted to see him come apart, if she was being honest.

"Where the hell are you?" Alex hissed.

"I'm in my office," Jamie lied. She pressed on the gas, guiding the Saab into an empty lane. It would take her several hours to get to Saul's cabin, but she would go, even if no one was there.

"I need you here, now."

"Do you hear yourself? We were fired. You are no longer

involved with her case." Jamie felt herself cringe inwardly. The desire to reach across the phone line and slap him was palpable.

"She escaped."

"I know." Jamie wondered if Alex could hear the smile in her tone. As soon as she had gotten the news, she'd gone to her office to get as much information as possible on anywhere Sonia might go.

"Where is she? Did she tell you where this woman and baby are?"

"Alex, I'm not helping you ruin them. I know you're working with Saul. If not *for* him." The silence lingered on the line and she looked down at her phone screen. He hadn't hung up.

"Look. They won't be hurt." Alex's argument was weak. He knew Jamie too well, and she was shocked he had even asked.

"Go to hell." Jamie hung up and tossed the phone onto the passenger seat.

It was already ringing again. She ignored it. Control was an issue Alex had never learned to manage. Well, he didn't control her, and never would.

Her GPS directed her onto the highway. She had no idea what she might find at this cabin, but she had to try.

50

SONIA

I⟶ was 4:00 p.m. by the time Nikki pulled onto a dirt road crowded by trees. The passenger window was cracked, allowing the afternoon's warm air to seep into Sonia's lungs. Slashes of sunlight flashed against her skin through the thick canopy of trees. She tried not to think about what was happening. She could die. Hell, she expected she would. He was not going to be happy to see her.

"I'm warning you. He's not the same as before. He spends most of his time up here."

Did Nikki know about his recent visit to her in prison? "Where's Mom?"

Nikki rolled her eyes. "I don't know. I haven't talked to her."

"Has he killed her?" Sonia's tone tinged with anger.

"What?" Nikki was shaking her head. "You really think I'd let him do that?"

"I really don't know, Nik."

"Whatever. You never liked him, that's fine, but he loves me. He wouldn't do anything to hurt Mom. The last I heard, the government had her somewhere."

The Yukon rolled over potholes in the dirt path, causing the

SUV to buck roughly. Sonia felt a slash of pain across her low back, her head dizzy. How was she going to protect herself in this condition? The thought forced her next words out.

"Are you gonna let me die?"

"Don't do this to me. I told you not to come. I told you." Nikki stuck a finger in the air, her eyes on the dirt road as they passed the last cropping of trees, which broke into an open field. "You wanted this. I won't get involved."

"You know who he is?"

"Who Saul is?"

"No." Sonia looked back out the windshield. "Who Mason is."

Wildflowers seemed to float atop the tall grass, bending and swaying in the breeze. A cabin rested at the end of the driveway, squatting under large oak trees, a collection of raw wood lined the outside that seemed to be a collage of the surrounding trees.

"It doesn't matter to me who he is," Nikki finally answered, pulling the SUV up behind a pickup truck. "I just want this to be over. Then I'll take you where you need to go."

Sonia found comfort in her words: there would be an "after." She had to resolve this with Saul, or she would always be looking over her shoulder.

She pushed open the door and stretched gently.

"Let's go," Nikki said roughly as she walked up beside her.

"Who else is here?"

Nikki looked around, then down at the ground. She only shook her head, not answering.

They walked up to the door and Nikki pushed inside, clearly knowing the door would be open. "Saul!"

The layout of the cabin was simple. A living room and kitchen shared a large space with floor to ceiling windows. The cabin might be old, but Saul had kept it up to date with granite countertops and sparkling new skylights above, allowing the afternoon sunlight to stream down onto the bamboo floor.

In the center of the living room, perched on a deep-red wing-back chair, was Saul.

"What the hell is this?" he asked. His eyes scanned both of them as they stood in the entryway.

"I need to speak with you," Sonia said, holding her side, trying to stifle the pain.

He nodded towards a chair and Nikki walked into the kitchen.

"Make yourself comfortable," Saul said, but his voice wasn't warm or friendly. The fingers of one hand drummed on the table next to him as the other grasped a glass of whiskey. A lump rose in Sonia's throat. She wasn't afraid of this man, but she wasn't stupid either.

"I didn't kill Emma."

Saul nodded at her, lifting the tumbler to his lips and taking a slow, deliberate drink. "I know."

Sonia stumbled mentally as she watched him. Nikki banged a cupboard shut and her footsteps moved toward them. A beer hung from her hand as she took a seat on the sofa.

"Then why this?" Sonia waved toward her body. "Why torture me?"

"I didn't know you didn't kill her until recently. I wish to God I never met that mother of yours."

Sonia saw Nikki flinch. Not dramatically, but a soft sort of registering of Saul's words. That he didn't want any of them in his life.

"All I want to do is live my life. Will you leave me alone?" Sonia asked.

"Sure." His response snapped through the room. "I have no need for you anymore."

Alarm shot threw her. *Anymore.*

"What have you done?" She thought of Reagan and Mason. All alone. There was no way he'd found them…"What about Reagan?"

"That whore. I have no use for her either." Saul snorted. Taking another pull of his drink, some spilling down his chest. He was drunk.

Nikki sat on the edge of her seat, her eyes trained on Saul, sensing something was wrong. His hands shaking slightly.

"What about Mason?" Sonia asked.

"He's mine," Saul snapped. "He's all I have left." His eyes cut to her face, pain and anger smoldering under the surface.

"What are you talking about, old man?" Nikki said, her tone jesting.

"Shut up!" He stood now, his weight wobbly on his thick legs, his drink spilling to the floor with a crash of shattering glass. It happened so quickly, Sonia was unsure if he'd dropped it or cast it aside.

"Emma should have told me what she was doing. But in the end, there, she was always keeping secrets and lying." He hovered above Nikki, but his eyes were on Sonia. "He's all I have left of my daughter," he said, his voice lower now, and Sonia thought she saw his lower lip quiver. "He looks so much like her."

"He's my son," Sonia said.

"There isn't any part of you in him." He sounded grateful.

"What's he talking about?" Nikki asked, looking at Sonia.

"She didn't tell you. I knew she wouldn't. Because she can't trust you." His breath was heavy with exertion. "I won't miss another minute of his life."

It hit Sonia like a thundering charge to her heart: Saul had not asked Sonia where Mason was. Why hadn't he asked? He should be demanding information—

"You're an animal." Sonia stood, causing Nikki to rise from her seat. All three of them traded glances at each other before Sonia began scanning the room. A red backpack with a Spiderman design lay on the table; small shoes rested at the door. Shoes of a child: of a boy.

"He's here!" Sonia felt adrenaline course through her veins, but before she understood what was happening, Nikki doubled over, clutching her stomach, and Saul stood back. It was as subtle as a hug, or a kiss on the cheek, but a knife handle was sticking out of Nikki's gut, and blood, red and bright, spread on her shirt.

"Oh, God!" Sonia cried out and reached for her. "What did you do?"

Nikki's eyes blinked rapidly, and a whimper of pain pressed past her lips. Her head dipped as she looked at the knife's handle as if she didn't understand what it was doing lodged in her stomach.

"You killed my daughter. My only child," Saul said. "It was you all along. I trusted you," he spat.

Nikki staggered back to fall onto the couch. Blood gathered in the corner of her lips. "I tried to protect you," she pleaded.

"I would have died for her!" he yelled. His voice seemed to echo off the beams overhead. Nikki's breath turned wheezy, and she moaned.

"You were the only other person I told about Emma talking to the FBI. I only trusted you—and it got her killed." His face was inches from hers and too close for Sonia to intervene. "I wanted *my* daughter. Not you." His words cut across Nikki's face as tears of pain bubbled over. Sonia watched as Nikki's emotional pain eclipsed her physical pain, a look that reminded her of the last five years.

Nikki closed her eyes as Saul moved back to look at Sonia. "He's my grandson. He stays with me."

Sonia was shaking her head and backing away from him as he slowly advanced. She was looking at each of the exits to the room. Two doors to her left and one to her right. They would be bedrooms, but she might get it wrong. She was no match for him, even if he was drunk and without a weapon.

"He's my son," she repeated. "He won't turn into you. Emma wouldn't want that."

Saul's face flashed red and his jaw flexed. He was moving toward her now, tripping on the coffee table separating them, falling with a thud on his knees. His large hands balled up at his sides as he flailed. He would be content to beat her to death with those hands.

Sonia turned and ran to the far doorway. It led to a hallway with three different doors. She could hear Saul cuss behind her and continue to advance. "I'm going to kill you." His voice was an eerie promise. She pulled on the first door handle. An empty room lay before her.

"Reagan!" she called.

No response. His hulking figure entered the hallway. He was only feet away from her now. She pulled a picture off the wall and hurled it at him. A sickening thump sounded as it hit his head, and he staggered back into the living room.

She quickly moved to the next door. Opening it, she saw a form writhing on the bed. Reagan's wide eyes stared over at her, her teeth pulled over a gag wedged between her lips. Sonia pulled the door shut behind her and locked it. Rushing to the bed, she tugged at the thick plastic zip ties that held Reagan's hands in place. They wouldn't budge. Angry red marks twisting around her wrists, covered in dried blood. Sonia looked over the room to find something she could use to cut the bindings away. A glass rested on the table and Sonia hit it against the edge of the bed. It shattered into pieces, and Sonia snatched up one shard big enough to cut. Pain seared through her hand as the glass cut into her own flesh as she moved it back and forth. At last Reagan's hands pulled free, and she reached up to remove the gag.

"Is it really you?" Reagan asked. "Where's Mason?"

"I don't know. He's got to be here somewhere," Sonia said as she moved toward the door to listen. No approaching footsteps.

No loud shouting. Could she risk unlocking the door if Saul was standing just on the other side?

"We need to get Mason. And kill Saul," Sonia said in a harsh whisper.

Reagan nodded and motioned to the window. "Can we get out there?"

"I'm not leaving this house without Mason." Sonia slowly turned the lock, and it clicked loudly. The door creaked open like a yawn in a silent theater. Her heart froze. Saul was gone. She moved out of the doorway and pulled Reagan with her. The girl's hand was shaking in hers.

"You're bleeding," Reagan whispered.

"Shhh."

Reagan pulled against her. When Sonia turned back, Reagan hitched her chin toward the last door in the hallway. Sonia gave her a nod, and they surrounded the door. Just before opening it, Reagan signaled she was ready. The door swung in to reveal an empty bed, a tall dresser and another doorway into a bathroom. The room was empty.

"The man who brought us here," Reagan said. "His name is Jeremy. He might have Mason."

Sonia thought. "We need to check every space in this house. I saw Mason's shoes at the door. I think he's here."

They both reentered the hallway and crept toward the living room. Nikki's lifeless body was still, bent awkwardly over the arm of the sofa.

Reagan gasped at the sight, but Sonia kept moving, eyes scanning the room for any sign that Saul was hiding around the corner. Creeping into the kitchen, she grabbed a knife. It slid out of the cutting block with a soft hiss of glinting metal. She didn't want to do it. Just like she didn't want to write the names of two innocent people her sister would later kill. But she had to cover her tracks then, and now she had to bury Saul. She needed to be sure he would never come after them again.

A piercing squeal came from somewhere outside. Sonia rushed to the front door in time to see Saul pulling a boy—Mason—toward his truck.

"No!" Sonia bolted out the door. If Saul was able to get Mason into that truck and drive away, she would never see her son again. And even if it wasn't her egg he had come from, he would always be hers. She rammed into Saul with her shoulder, downing them both. The splinter of pain roared through her whole body as she hit the ground hard. She landed on her side, pebbles in the driveway biting into her exposed skin. A cry escaped her lungs as air was forced out. Disoriented, she pulled her hands up to protect herself from the man on the ground. "Get Mason!" Sonia yelled.

Saul rolled toward her, his legs dragging behind him. Blood poured from a fresh gash in his forehead.

Her hands scrabbled in the dirt: the knife! She'd lost it. Pulling her head up, dizziness rippled through her, her vision swimming like heat off the blacktop in summer.

"Come here, baby!" Reagan begged.

"Mommy," Mason whimpered as he ran across the stones.

"Get him out of here," Sonia ordered. "GO! I'll come get—" She cried out in pain as a hand clamped down on her leg. "Go—"

Sonia kicked out, her legs hitting only air, jerking her whole body, as Saul ducked away from her.

"Little bi—" he began to growl, but her kick connected. A garbled moan, and he let go. She was able to raise her head to see the driveway and beyond to the grass cropping up in her slightly wobbly view. The glint of the knife's blade caught the sun, and she pulled herself forward by her elbows. She had to save them this time. Even if it killed her. Stones bit into her arms and scraped along her bare belly as her shirt gathered under her breasts. *Keep going.* Everything was on fire.

She heard the crunch of gravel behind her and rolled to see

Saul nearly on his feet. His hand cupped his nose as blood drooled down his chin. He lurched toward her, unsteady on his feet. She couldn't tell if it was the booze or the head wound that was so affecting his balance. With one last effort, she reached for the knife and pointed it skyward just as Saul came crashing down onto her, his fists slamming into her face and neck.

She felt her wrist torque as his full force landed on the knife and its black handle pushed back into her belly. A sickening gurgle escaped his lips, and she pushed out from under him with all her might, causing him to roll onto his back. The knife's handle pointed skyward, piercing his round belly.

She cried out and scrambled backward. Turning her head, she vomited in the dry grass.

She had done it, but there was no relief in her actions. Instead, emptiness stretched and grew and swallowed her up.

It was a while before she pulled herself to her feet. She scanned the tree line and saw Mason and Reagan making their way back to her. She had to get them away from here, and fast. They needed a car. She limped back into the house, her right leg nearly dragging behind her, grabbing Mason's shoes, his backpack and other items of his she spotted as she headed toward the bedrooms. She had to hurry. Whoever this Jeremy was, he might still be nearby.

As her eyes skipped over her sister's lifeless form, Sonia began to shake, small tremors at first that grew into a trembling of her whole body. She was probably going into shock. She needed Saul's car keys. And some money. Something to help them get out of here. His wallet was on his nightstand, fat with cash and credit cards. But no keys.

She ambled back into the kitchen and found Nikki's keys resting on the counter in a shallow blue glass bowl. She probably always put them there when she visited. She had done it less than an hour ago, never even suspecting it would be the last time.

She staggered to the door and dropped to her knees on the porch.

"Sonia!" Reagan cried as she rushed to her.

Sonia waved her off. "I'm okay. It's just shock hitting me." But when she looked down her shirt was nearly soaked with blood. She didn't know if it was hers or Saul's. "I missed you," Sonia whispered in Reagan's ear as they held each other.

"I love you," Reagan whispered back.

After pausing a moment to catch her breath, Sonia spoke. "You drive." She handed the keys to Reagan. Mason peered at Sonia from around Reagan's hunched body, eyes wide with fear. He did look just like Emma, but he had Joey's dark hair. A blend of the two people Sonia loved the most.

"Let's go, baby," Sonia whispered.

51

SONIA

THE AREA WAS BOGGED down with tourists. Sonia shuffled through the market, where people sold trinkets from all over the world. She breathed in the smoke-filled air, vanilla tinged with clove.

"How's the leg?" Reagan asked, pulling up beside her, a small cloth bag hanging from her fingers.

"It'll do," Sonia said as they continued on together, Mason clutching Reagan's hand as they walked. She never thought her heart would feel full again.

It had been several months since they were smuggled out of the United States into Canada. They were making arrangements to get farther away, but it would take time for the paperwork to come through. In the meantime, they worked and saved their money. Sonia only recently learned her mother was back home, safe and sound. While authorities were still looking for Ali. Sonia knew she was dead, but they may never find the body. Nikki was good like that.

Reagan didn't say it, but Sonia could see she was missing something, or someone. Finally one night she'd broken down and told Sonia about a man named Max. They had met not long after Joey was murdered. Maybe Reagan had loved him.

"What happened to him?" Sonia asked.

"I don't know," Reagan said, her eyes growing wet. Sonia felt it then, the guilt of what she had done to this girl. It wasn't what Sonia wanted, and Reagan had gone along with it, but she needed to have a normal life. Wherever they ended up, Sonia would help her work toward that. She had told Reagan to stay in the States. To get a job and start a life, maybe find this Max guy. She reminded her that Saul wasn't a threat any longer. But Reagan wouldn't leave her and Mason. She kept mentioning Jeremy. How he might come looking for her again, and that it was best to get out while she could.

When their paperwork finally came through, the three of them boarded a flight to Ireland. "I never dreamed I would see Ireland," Reagan said, excited, as they walked onto the plane.

The night before they left, Sonia had placed two packages in the mail.

The first was a letter to Harriet, congratulating her on winning her appeal. Sonia had read the news in Harriet's hometown paper after an internet search. Harriet had made it. It was only the beginning for her.

The other package was a small box she sent to Jamie.

They would land on their feet somehow. They would get jobs and try to live a normal life without fear. Sonia reached out and grasped Mason's small hand in hers. "Ready, baby?"

He nodded.

52

JAMIE

IT WOULD BE seven months after Jamie suspected she'd passed Sonia on that back road when Jamie received the package. A small, hand-crafted wooden box, no return address. She pulled the thin silver latch open and revealed a small bag. Its embroidery dark pink over pale pink, split by golden letters. Jamie smiled. Inside was a postcard from a woman named Paulina, its postmark from Ottawa, Canada. A simple message scrolled in black ink.

Anzan, because we could all use a little luck. Until we meet again. Thank you.

Jamie looked up the meaning of the word on her phone. An omamori for a healthy pregnancy. How had she known Jamie was pregnant?

"Who's that from?" Drew asked, coming up behind her and rubbing her belly. A habit he had formed since finding out she was pregnant. Now that she was nearing nine months, he was barely able to reach around all of her.

"An old friend."

WHAT TO BE NOTIFIED WHEN EVA'S NEXT BOOK DROPS?

Sign up to her e-mail list on her website:
   http://evamackenzie.com/contact

Or, visit her on social media:
   http://instagram.com/evamackenzie_reads
   http://www.facebook.com/eva.mackenzie.3762
   http://goodreads.com/evamackenzie

If you would like to contact Eva Mackenzie personally, please e-mail
   her at Evamackenzie.thrillers@gmail.com

Lastly, if you enjoyed this book, Eva would greatly appreciate if you left a review on Goodreads or Amazon.

ABOUT THE AUTHOR

About the Author

Eva Mackenzie lives on the east coast with her husband and her three littles.

When she isn't writing or spending time with her family, she can be found hiking, training for another marathon or cooking. On top of the aforementioned she writes domestic suspense, psychological thrillers and romantic suspense novels. She enjoys writing about good people who do bad things for complicated reasons.

Please feel free to reach out to her via her social medias or e-mail.